Young Wolf:

THE EARLY ADVENTURE STORIES of JACK LONDON

EDITED BY
Howard Lachtman

Capra Press
SANTA BARBARA
1984

For my three adventurers:
Kimberley, Courtney and Tiffany Anne

COVER DESIGN BY JUDY SUTCLIFFE
TYPOGRAPHY BY JIM COOK/SANTA BARBARA

Printed in the United States of America.

LIBRARY OF CONGRESS CATALOGUING IN PUBLICATION DATA
London, Jack, 1876-1916. Young wolf.
1. Adventure stories, American. I. Lachtman, Howard, 1941- . II. Title.
PS3523.O46Y68 1984 813′.52 83-25185
ISBN 0-88496-210-5 (paperback)

PUBLISHED BY CAPRA PRESS
Post Office Box 2068
Santa Barbara, California 93120

CONTENTS

Introduction

JACK LONDON: THE VEIN OF GOLD

"WRITING'S THE HARDEST WORK in the world," Jack London told a young literary hopeful who had asked his advice on how to enter the tough, competitive arena of professional writing.

London was no stranger to hard work. Or to giving straight-from-the-shoulder opinions to aspiring authors who implored him to read and judge their works.

"The stuff you're producing at present is clumsy, incoherent tripe," he told his astonished admirer, "but every so often there's a streak of fire on your pages. You're only a kid, but everything registers with you, and you've a zest for life. If you're game enough to take all the lickings that will come to you and keep on writing and writing, you'll make out."

London was speaking from his own experience here. He was the "kid" who never lost his taste for adventure and his zest for life. He was the devoted professional who took his lickings, paid his dues, and kept on writing and writing. Above all, he was a sensitive and faithful recorder of the world he knew, an individual on whom everything "registered." Henry James might almost have had him in mind when he remarked: "Be one of those on whom nothing is lost. . . . Live all you can; it's a mistake not to."

London, the tireless rover who never outgrew his need to engage and record life in all its phases, was a true disciple not only of Teddy Roosevelt's "strenuous life," but of the Jamesian philosophy of finely-gathered experience. He lived "all he could," and by so doing, enriched the lives of readers everywhere who discovered new worlds of vicarious participation and emotional consolation in his stories.

Practicing the same authorial virtues he would later preach to those who asked his "secrets of success," young London soon found that his tenacious persistence, methodical discipline, and storytelling talent paid off. Only twenty-three when he began publishing his Klondike stories regularly in 1899, he saw his first book in print at age twenty-four, and struck bestselling paydirt three summers later with *The Call of the Wild*. Popular favorites like *The Sea Wolf* and *White Fang*, plus a steady stream of Klondike short stories, solidified his reputation, and gained the young writer an enormous reading audience whose interest and affection for him soon rivaled that given Mark Twain and O. Henry.

London was a born teller of tales who wrote as he lived—in a hurry. The writer, like the man, was a creature of force and eloquence, pulsing with enthusiasm or indignation. The strength of his characters and the vividness of his perceptions derived largely from the virtues of his own personality.

And what a personality he must have been to encounter in person. Eyewitnesses reported that when London entered a room, the electricity jumped. He had the "voltage" of the truly charismatic individual. "Jack," said one of his friends, "had a mind like a sword, and when he grew eloquent about some subject which was close to his heart, the air crackled."

In his forty brief years of life, this remarkable individual wrote fifty books (forty-three of which saw publication in his own lifetime), brought adventure from the far-flung corners of the world home to millions of readers, and created a legend which endures to this day. Though there have been more polished and pretentious writers, there has never been another literary hero quite like London. The excitement he engendered in his tales led readers to imagine him as a swashbuckling sailor of fortune, dog-sledding pioneer, and adventurer *par excellence* who was only doing what came naturally by "spinning yarns" drawn from his own colorful and dramatic experience.

London is also a fascinating study in contradiction. Famous for his brutal realism and no-holds-barred portrayal of existence, he was also, at times, a romantic, an idealist, and a visionary.

Controversial as an ardent socialist, he glorified individuals rather than systems. Often dismissed by literary critics as a magazine writer of limited importance, he has been the subject of intense critical and scholarly rediscovery in the 1970s and 1980s, culminating in a two-volume representation of his works in the prestigious Library of America series. A major edition of his correspondence is now in preparation at Stanford University Press.

While he exhibits the faults of any professional writer who has written too much too fast, London's best writing remains permanently alive—incisive, invigorating, and appealing. His pages are filled with the battles and the hopes of a younger, more confident America. They preserve wonderful memories of our own younger reading days when, by flickering campfire or by furtive flashlight under the blankets, we first thrilled to this writer's vivid word pictures of a world we had never known. In London's stories, we first heard the howl of wolf dogs raising a cry at the eerie glimmer of the aurora. We stood on wave-washed foredecks with indomitable sailors at war with the capriciousness of the sea and the ruthlessness of all-powerful captains. And we first tried out our imaginative snowshoes in the company of frost-blurred gold-hunters pitting their luck, their matches, and their lives against the numbing power of a cold so intense and pervasive that it seemed to be endowed with an almost cosmic character, an alien power capable of crushing the dreams and dousing the fires of exuberant sourdoughs.

What reader, young or old, can forget those moments of high adventure, or the consummate skill of the writer who made them so intensely real that we, too, seemed to be living them? Action and introspection, suspenseful dramas of heroism put to the test, conquests of nature coupled with unexpected flashes of insight into the innermost heart of pioneers who risk the ultimate stake—these were London's literary trademarks. He wrote compellingly and persuasively, for he himself had witnessed—and survived—many of the events he described. Indeed, no other writer of his day had seen so much of the world, so much of the sheer human variety of life.

London toiled in factories and sweatshops, sailed before the mast across the Pacific and rode the rails both ways across the American continent. His energy, like his curiosity, was boundless, and he wandered everywhere in search of experience.

As a footloose adventurer-reporter, the world was his beat: boxing in Australia, revolution in Mexico, earthquake in California, surfers and lepers in Hawaii, gold and tall tales in the Klondike, slum life in Europe, kings and cannibals in the South Seas, skirmishes in China.

As an ecologically-minded California dreamer, he created a working ranch, complete with stone barns and prize herds, on a spread of over one thousand acres in the high green hills of Sonoma (today it is the site of the Jack London State Historic Park, one of the most popular wilderness refuges and tourist attractions in all of northern California).

As a writer, London has a long list of literary achievements to his credit. He wrote the first inside accounts of a professional writer's private life *(Martin Eden* and *John Barleycorn)*, the best political prophecy before Orwell's *Animal Farm (The Iron Heel)*, a time-travel novel *(The Star Rover)* which would make an excellent television series, two views of life at the bottom of the social-economic ladder *(The Road* and *The People of the Abyss)*, a classic of small-boat sailing *(The Cruise of the Snark)*, a savage yet sublime fantasy of an alien starship lost in the back of beyond *(The Red One)*, and two of the best animal fables in the English language *(White Fang* and *The Call of the Wild)*.

Of all his many achievements as a writer, however, London is probably most admired and most universally recognized as a master craftsman of the short story. He excelled in this briefer form of storytelling, and though it is not quite accurate to say (as one critic has said) that London was a natural sprinter rather than a long-distance runner, it is certainly true that his shorter fictions have a timeless power to capture the interest and stir the emotions of readers.

Vigorous yet lyric, compressed yet dynamic, these tales still have an appreciative and even enthusiastic following who find it impossible to "sample" one story and not wish for more. When, for example, a San Francisco Sunday newspaper recently ran an abridged and illustrated version of a London short story, some readers complained that they had been cheated because the entire story hadn't been published; others wanted to know why it was they had to endure the usual articles on preparing exotic quiches and building better hot tubs when they could be enjoying Jack London stories on a regular basis!

One suspects that these 1983 readers were responding to the sheer storytelling magic their grandparents found similarly irresistible back in 1903. For unlike the many writers of yesterday who have had their brief moment in the sun and then faded into the shadows, London is one of our brightest and most enduring literary constants. In his robust company, we experience what it means to be truly alive, feel what it is like to live on the edge of the world, and know, as London knew, what a precious, precarious thing existence is.

In the most remote outposts of civilization, where so many of his exciting tales of struggle and survival take place, evolutionary progress and social pretensions are stripped away. We are confronted with the chilling specter of the old savage lurking beneath the civilized skin, and yet we are warmed by the opportunity to assert individuality and to realize valiant, even heroic, possibilities. Always, however, London's goldhunters and trailblazers come to know their limitations and shrink from the vanity of thinking themselves godlike. "Civilization [which is part of the circle of his imaginings] has spread a veneer over the surface of the soft-shelled animal known as man," London observed. "It is a very thin veneer; but so wonderfully is man constituted that he squirms on his bit of achievement and believes he is garbed in armor plate." That comforting illusion is one of the first to be shed in the Klondike.

The stories in this volume, all reflections of the young writer's progress toward celebrity status, were some of the earliest indications reading audiences had of a particularly promising American storyteller who brought all the golden glamour and frost-rimmed danger of the Northland home to armchair adventurers. They can be read for pleasure today by a new generation yearning for contact with something solid and elemental and invigorating in fictional entertainment. They can be enjoyed for the magic of their atmospheric realism and suspenseful plotting that can rekindle the primal joys of the storytelling experience (and can make some of our vaunted modern writers seem tepid by comparison). And they can be taken as proof that the promising writer of turn-of-the-century America has become a storyteller for all seasons.

"Wolf" was the nickname given young Jack by his close friend and patient proofreader, George Sterling, in honor of the four-legged wolf dogs of *The Call of the Wild* and "Wolf" Larsen, predatory captain of *The Sea Wolf.* It is important to remember that these back-to-back bestsellers gave the writer his reputation when he was only in his mid-20s. Like Byron, Melville, and Norman Mailer, London awoke to find himself famous. He also suffered the fate of every "overnight success' who has had his later works judged by the standard of his first triumph. Only critics who never read London widely could claim (as some did) that he never lived up to his early promise. In fact, *The Call of the Wild* was a short story which, as London admitted, "ran away"; *The Sea Wolf* slackened considerably after a shipboard romance began to blossom, and much of the writer's best work still lay ahead.

"Wolves," as Jane E. Brody has recently written about the once-feared creatures, "are highly sociable animals with a strong respect for family, status, and territory, and have a rich language that sustains the group and fosters individual survival."

Much of this definition also applies to Jack "Wolf" London. The highly sociable London was never happier than when his home was crowded with guests and his table full of visitors from every walk of life. He was usually very thoughtful of his friends and his family (despite the strain of an unhappy first marriage). He played the status game by acquiring a yacht and valet, constructing a redwood-and-stone mansion (Wolf House, it was called), and amassing over one thousand acres of mountainside territory for his ranch up on the high slopes overlooking the Sonoma Valley. And surely the "rich language" of his tales and novels about individual survival have sustained readers in far, perilous places just as much as they have those who like to go adventuring with a book in the safety and comfort of their easychairs.

London seldom wrote so well as when he wrote of the Klondike, and perhaps that was because the Klondike was not only a real country, but a territory of the mind. When the intrepid author pushed off into the frozen, uncharted wastes (which were the blank pages of his typewriter as well as the recollected wilderness of his youthful prospecting days), he was going home. The Northland so deeply engaged his unconscious literary artistry that he was characteristically unable to recognize his creative powers, let alone share the general opinion of himself as an author who repeatedly touched the richest ore of human character and drama. His inability to perceive his true stature as an American storyteller should not surprise us. "It is in men as in soils," as Swift reminds us, "where sometimes there is a vein of gold which the owner knows not of."

I.

Adventures on the Frost Trail

Love of Life

"This out of all will remain—
They have lived and have tossed:
So much of the game will be gain,
Though the gold of the dice has been lost."

THEY LIMPED painfully down the bank, and once the foremost of the two men staggered among the rough-strewn rocks. They were tired and weak, and their faces had the drawn expression of patience which comes of hardship long endured. They were heavily burdened with blanket packs which were strapped to their shoulders. Head-straps, passing across the forehead, helped support these packs. Each man carried a rifle. They walked in a stooped posture, the shoulders well forward, the head still farther forward, the eyes bent upon the ground.

"I wish we had just about two of them cartridges that's layin' in that cache of ourn," said the second man.

His voice was utterly and drearily expressionless. He spoke without enthusiasm; but the first man, limping into the milky stream that foamed over the rocks, vouchsafed no reply.

The other man followed at his heels. They did not remove their foot-gear, though the water was icy cold—so cold that their ankles ached and their feet went numb. In places the water dashed against their knees, and both men staggered for footing.

The man who followed slipped on a smooth boulder, nearly fell, but recovered himself with a violent effort, at the same time uttering a sharp exclamation of pain. He seemed faint and dizzy, and put out his free hand while he reeled, as though seeking support against the air. When he had steadied himself he stepped forward, but reeled again and nearly fell. Then he stood still and looked at the other man, who had never turned his head.

The man stood still for fully a minute, as though debating with himself. Then he called out:

"I say, Bill, I've sprained my ankle."

Bill staggered on through the milky water. He did not look around. The man watched him go, and though his face was expressionless as ever, his eyes were like the eyes of a wounded deer.

The other man limped up the farther bank and continued straight on without looking back. The man in the stream watched him. His lips trembled a little, so that the rough thatch of brown hair which covered them was visibly agitated. His tongue even strayed out to moisten them.

"Bill!" he cried out.

It was the pleading cry of a strong man in distress, but Bill's head did not turn. The man watched him go, limping grotesquely and lurching forward with stammering gait up the slow slope toward the soft sky-line of the low-lying hill. He watched him go till he passed over the crest and disappeared. Then he turned his gaze and slowly took in the circle of the world that remained to him now that Bill was gone.

Near the horizon the sun was smoldering dimly, almost obscured by formless mists and vapors, which gave an impression of mass and density without outline or tangibility. The man pulled out his watch, the while resting his weight on one leg. It was four o'clock, and as the season was near the last of July or first of August—he did not know the precise date within a week or two—he knew that the sun roughly marked the northwest. He looked to the south and knew that somewhere beyond those bleak hills lay the Great Bear Lake; also, he knew that in that direction the Arctic Circle cut its forbidding way across the Canadian

Barrens. This stream in which he stood was a feeder to the Coppermine River, which in turn flowed north and emptied into Coronation Gulf and the Arctic Ocean. He had never been there, but he had seen it, once, on a Hudson Bay Company chart.

Again his gaze completed the circle of the world about him. It was not a heartening spectacle. Everywhere was soft sky-line. The hills were all low-lying. There were no trees, no shrubs, no grasses—naught but a tremendous and terrible desolation that sent fear swiftly dawning into his eyes.

"Bill!" he whispered, once and twice; "Bill!"

He cowered in the midst of the milky water, as though the vastness were pressing in upon him with overwhelming force, brutally crushing him with its complacent awfulness. He began to shake as with an ague fit, till the gun fell from his hand with a splash. This served to rouse him. He fought with his fear and pulled himself together, groping in the water and recovering the weapon. He hitched his pack farther over on his left shoulder, so as to take a portion of its weight from off the injured ankle. Then he proceeded, slowly and carefully, wincing with pain, to the bank.

He did not stop. With a desperation that was madness, unmindful of the pain, he hurried up the slope to the crest of the hill over which his comrade had disappeared—more grotesque and comical by far than that limping, jerking comrade. But at the crest he saw a shallow valley, empty of life. He fought with his fear again, overcame it, hitched the pack still farther over on his left shoulder, and lurched on down the slope.

The bottom of the valley was soggy with water, which the thick moss held, sponge-like, close to the surface. This water squirted out from under his feet at every step, and each time he lifted a foot the action culminated in a sucking sound as the wet moss reluctantly released its grip. He picked his way from muskeg to muskeg, and followed the other man's footsteps along and across the rocky ledges which thrust like islets through the sea of moss.

Though alone he was not lost. Farther on he knew he would come to where dead spruce and fir, very small and weazened, bordered the shore of a little lake, the *tit-chin-nichilie*—in the tongue of the country, the "land of little sticks." And into that lake flowed a small stream, the water of which was not milky. There was rushgrass on that stream—this he remembered well—but no timber, and he would follow it till its first trickle ceased at a divide. He would cross this divide to the first trickle of another stream, flowing to the west, which he would follow until it emptied into the River Dease, and here he would find a cache under an upturned canoe and piled over with many rocks. And in this cache would be ammunition for his empty gun, fish-hooks and lines, a small net—all the utilities for the killing and snaring of food. Also, he would find flour—not much—a piece of bacon and some beans.

Bill would be waiting for him there, and they would paddle away south down the Dease to the Great Bear Lake. And south across the lake they would go, ever south, till they gained the Mackenzie. And south, still south, they would go, while the winter raced vainly after them, and the ice formed in the eddies, and the days grew chill and crisp, south to some warm Hudson Bay Company post, where timber grew tall and generous and there was grub without end.

These were the thoughts of the man as he strove onward. But hard as he strove with his body, he strove equally hard with his mind, trying to think that Bill had not deserted him, that Bill would surely wait for him at the cache. He was compelled to think this thought, or else there would not be any use to strive, and he would have lain down and died. And as the dim ball of the sun sank slowly into the northwest he covered every inch, and many times, of his and Bill's flight south before the downcoming winter. And he conned the grub of the cache and the grub of the Hudson Bay Company post over and over again. He had not eaten for two days; for a longer time he had not had all he wanted to eat. Often he stooped and picked pale muskeg berries, put them into his mouth and chewed and swallowed them. A muskeg berry is a bit of seed enclosed in a bit of water. In the mouth the water melts away and the seed chews sharp and bitter. The man knew there was no nourishment in the berries, but he chewed them patiently with a hope greater than knowledge and defying experience.

At nine o'clock he stubbed his toe on a rocky ledge, and from sheer weariness and weakness staggered and fell. He lay for some time, without movement, on his side. Then he slipped out of the pack-straps and clumsily dragged himself into a sitting posture. It was not yet dark, and in the lingering twilight he groped about among the rocks for shreds of dry moss. When he had gathered a heap he built a fire—a smoldering, smudgy fire—and put a tin pot of water on to boil.

He unwrapped his pack and the first thing he did was to count his matches. There were sixty-seven. He counted them three times to make sure. He divided them into several portions, wrapping them in oil paper, disposing of one bunch in his empty tobacco pouch, of another bunch in the inside band of his battered hat, of a third bunch under his shirt on the chest. This accomplished, a panic came upon him and he unwrapped them all and counted them again. There were still sixty-seven.

He dried his wet foot-gear by the fire. The moccasins were in soggy shreds. The blanket socks were worn through in places and his feet were raw and bleeding. His ankle was throbbing and he gave it an examination. It had swollen to the size of his knee. He tore a long strip from one of his two blankets and bound the ankle tightly. He tore other strips and bound them about his feet to serve for both moccasins and socks. Then he drank the pot of water, steaming hot, wound his watch, and crawled between his blankets.

He slept like a dead man. The brief darkness around midnight came and went. The sun arose in the northeast—at least the day dawned in that quarter, for the sun was hidden by gray clouds.

At six o'clock he awoke, quietly lying on his back. He gazed straight up into the gray sky and knew that he was hungry. As he rolled over on his elbow he was startled by a loud snort, and saw a bull caribou regarding him with alert curiosity. The animal was not more than fifty feet away, and instantly into the man's mind leaped the vision and the savor of a caribou steak sizzling and frying over a fire. Mechanically he reached for the empty gun, drew a bead, and pulled the trigger. The bull snorted and leaped away, his hoofs rattling and clattering as he fled across the ledges.

The man cursed and flung the empty gun from him. He groaned aloud as he started to drag himself to his feet. It was a slow and arduous task. His joints were like rusty hinges. They worked harshly in their sockets, with much friction, and each bending or unbending was accomplished only through a sheer exertion of will. When he finally gained his feet another minute or so was consumed in straightening up, so that he could stand erect as a man should stand.

He crawled up a small knoll and surveyed the prospect. There were no trees, no bushes, nothing but a gray sea of moss scarcely diversified by gray rocks, gray-colored lakelets, and gray streamlets. The sky was gray. There was no sun or hint of sun. He had no idea of north, and he had forgotten the way he had come to this spot the night before. But he was not lost. He knew that. Soon he would come to the land of the little sticks. He felt that it lay off to the left somewhere, not far—possibly just over the next low hill.

He went back to put his pack into shape for traveling. He assured himself of the existence of his three separate parcels of matches, though he did not stop to count them. But he did linger, debating, over a squat moose-hide sack. It was not large. He could hide it under his two hands. He knew that it weighed fifteen pounds—as much as all the rest of the pack—and it worried him. He finally set it to one side and proceeded to roll the pack. He paused to gaze at the squat moose-hide sack. He picked it up hastily with a defiant glance about him, as though the desolation were trying to rob him of it; and when he rose to his feet to stagger on into the day, it was included in the pack on his back.

He bore away to the left, stopping now and again to eat muskeg berries. His ankle had stiffened, his limp was more pronounced, but the pain of it was as nothing compared with the pain of his stomach. The hunger pangs were sharp. They gnawed and gnawed until he could not keep his mind steady on the course he must pursue to gain the land of little sticks. The muskeg berries did not allay this gnawing, while they made his tongue and the roof of his mouth sore with their irritating bite.

He came upon a valley where rock ptarmigan rose on whirring wings from the ledges and muskegs. Ker—ker—ker was the cry they made. He threw stones at them but could not hit them. He placed his pack on the ground and stalked them as a cat stalks a sparrow. The sharp rocks cut through his pants' legs till his knees left a trail of blood; but the hurt was lost in the hurt of his hunger. He squirmed over the wet moss, saturating his clothes and chilling his body; but he was not aware of it, so great was his fever for food. And always the ptarmigan rose, whirring, before him, till their ker—ker—ker became a mock to him, and he cursed them and cried aloud at them with their own cry.

Once he crawled upon one that must have been asleep. He did not see it till it shot up in his face from its rocky nook. He made a clutch as startled as was the rise of the ptarmigan, and there remained in his hand three tail-feathers. As he watched its flight he hated it, as though it had done him some terrible wrong. Then he returned and shouldered his pack.

As the day wore along he came into valleys or swales where game was more plentiful. A band of caribou passed by, twenty and odd animals, tantalizingly within rifle range. He felt a wild desire to run after them, a certitude that he could run them down. A black fox came toward him, carrying a ptarmigan in his mouth.

The man shouted. It was a fearful cry, but the fox leaping away in fright did not drop the ptarmigan.

Late in the afternoon he followed a stream, milky with lime, which ran through sparse patches of rush-grass. Grasping these rushes firmly near the root, he pulled up what resembled a young onion-sprout no larger than a shingle-nail. It was tender and his teeth sank into it with a crunch that promised deliciously of food. But its fibers were tough. It was composed of stringy filaments saturated with water, like the berries, and devoid of nourishment. But he threw off his pack and went into the rush-grass on hands and knees, crunching and munching, like some bovine creature.

He was very weary and often wished to rest—to lie down and sleep; but he was continually driven on—not so much by his desire to gain the land of little sticks as by his hunger. He searched little ponds for frogs and dug up the earth with his nails for worms, though he knew in spite that neither frogs nor worms existed so far north.

He looked into every pool of water vainly, until, as the long twilight came on, he discovered a solitary fish, the size of a minnow, in such a pool. He plunged his arm in up to the shoulder, but it eluded him. He reached for it with both hands and stirred up the milky mud at the bottom. In his excitement he fell in, wetting himself to the waist. Then the water was too muddy to admit of his seeing the fish and he was compelled to wait until the sediment had settled.

The pursuit was renewed, till the water was again muddied. But he could not wait. He unstrapped the tin bucket and began to bale the pool. He baled wildly at first splashing himself and flinging the water so short a distance that it ran back into the pool. He worked more carefully, striving to be cool, though his heart was pounding against his chest and his hands were trembling. At the end of half an hour the pool was nearly dry. Not a cupful of water remained. And there was no fish. He found a hidden crevice among the stones through which it had escaped to the adjoining and larger pool—a pool which he could not empty in a night and day. Had he known of the crevice, he could have closed it with a rock at the beginning and the fish would have been his.

Thus he thought, and crumpled up and sank down upon the wet earth. At first he cried softly to himself, then he cried loudly to the pitiless desolation that ringed him around; and for a long time after he was shaken by great dry sobs.

He built a fire and warmed himself by drinking quarts of hot water, and made camp on a rocky ledge in the same fashion he had the night before. The last thing he did was to see that his matches were dry and to wind his watch. The blankets were wet and clammy. His ankle pulsed with pain. But he knew only that he was hungry, and through his restless sleep he dreamed of feasts and banquets and of food served and spread in all imaginable ways.

He awoke chilled and sick. There was no sun. The gray of earth and sky had become deeper, more profound. A raw wind was blowing, and the first flurries of snow were whitening the hilltops. The air about him thickened and grew white while he made a fire and boiled more water. It was wet snow, half rain, and the flakes were large and soggy. At first they melted as soon as they came in contact with the earth, but ever more fell, covering the ground, putting out the fire, spoiling his supply of moss-fuel.

This was the signal for him to strap on his pack and stumble onward he knew not where. He was not concerned with the land of little sticks, nor with Bill and the cache under the upturned canoe by the River Dease. He was mastered by the verb "to eat." He was hunger-mad. He took no heed of the course he pursued, so long as that course led him through the swale bottoms. He felt his way through the wet snow to the watery muskeg berries, and went by feel as he pulled up the rush-grass by the roots. But it was tasteless stuff and did not satisfy. He found a weed that tasted sour and he ate all he could find of it, which was not much, for it was creeping growth, easily hidden under the several inches of snow.

He had no fire that night nor hot water, and crawled under his blanket to sleep the broken hunger-sleep. The snow turned into a cold rain. He awakened many times to feel it falling on his upturned face. Day came—a gray day and no sun. It had ceased raining. The keenness of his hunger had departed. Sensibility, so far as concerned the yearning for food, had been exhausted. There was a dull, heavy ache in his stomach, but it did not bother him so much. He was more rational, and once more he was chiefly interested in the land of little sticks and the cache by the River Dease.

He ripped the remnant of one of his blankets into strips and bound his bleeding feet. Also, he recinched the injured ankle and prepared himself for a day of travel. When he came to his pack he paused long over the squat moose-hide sack, but in the end it went with him.

The snow had melted under the rain and only the hilltops showed white. The sun came out and he succeeded in locating the points of the compass, though he knew now that he was lost. Perhaps, in his previous days' wanderings, he had edged away too far to the left. He now bore off to the right to counteract the possible deviation from his true course.

Though the hunger pangs were no longer so exquisite, he realized that he was weak. He was compelled to pause for frequent rests when he attacked the muskeg berries and rush-grass patches. His tongue felt dry and large, as though covered with a fine hairy growth, and it tasted bitter in his mouth. His heart gave him a great deal of trouble. When he had traveled a few minutes it would begin a remorseless thump, thump, thump, and then leap up and away in a painful flutter of beats that choked him and made him go faint and dizzy.

In the middle of the day he found two minnows in a large pool. It was impossible to bale it, but he was calmer now and managed to catch them in his tin bucket. They were no longer than his little finger, but he was not particularly hungry. The dull ache in his stomach had been growing duller and fainter. It seemed almost that his stomach was dozing. He ate the fish raw, masticating with painstaking care for the eating was an act of pure reason. While he had no desire to eat he knew that he must eat to live.

In the evening he caught three more minnows, eating two and saving the third for breakfast. The sun had dried stray shreds of moss, and he was able to warm himself with hot water. He had not covered more than ten miles that day, and the next day, traveling whenever his heart permitted him, he covered no more than five miles. But his stomach did not give him the slightest uneasiness. It had gone to sleep. He was in a strange country, too, and the caribou were growing more plentiful, also the wolves. Often their yelps drifted across the desolation, and once he saw three of them slinking away before his path.

Another night, and in the morning, being more rational, he untied the leather string that fastened the squat moose-hide sack. From its open mouth poured a yellow stream of coarse gold-dust and nuggets. He roughly divided the gold in halves, caching one half on a prominent ledge, wrapped in a piece of blanket, and returning the other half to the sack. He also began to use strips of the one remaining blanket for his feet. He still clung to his gun, for there were cartridges in that cache by the River Dease.

This was a day of fog, and this day hunger awoke in him again. He was very weak and was afflicted with a giddiness which at times blinded him. It was no uncommon thing now for him to stumble and fall; and stumbling once, he fell squarely into a ptarmigan nest. There were four newly hatched chicks a day old—little specks of pulsating life no more than a mouthful; and he ate them ravenously, thrusting them alive into his mouth and crunching them like egg-shells between his teeth. The mother ptarmigan beat about him with great outcry. He used his gun as a club with which to knock her over, but she dodged out of reach. He threw stones at her and with one chance shot broke a wing. Then she fluttered away, running, trailing the broken wing, with him in pursuit.

The little chicks had no more than whetted his appetite. He hopped and bobbed clumsily along on his injured ankle, throwing stones and screaming hoarsely at times; at other times hopping and bobbing silently along, picking himself up grimly and patiently when he fell, or rubbing his eyes with his hand when the giddiness threatened to overpower him.

The chase led him across swampy ground in the bottom of the valley, and he came upon footprints in the soggy moss. They were not his own—he could see that. They must be Bill's. But he could not stop, for the mother ptarmigan was running on. He would catch her first, then he would return and investigate.

He exhausted the mother ptarmigan; but he exhausted himself. She lay panting on her side. He lay panting on his side, a dozen feet away, unable to crawl to her. And as he recovered she recovered, fluttering out of reach as his hungry hand went out to her. The chase was resumed. Night settled down and she escaped. He stumbled from weakness and pitched head-foremost on his face, cutting his cheek, his pack upon his back. He did not move for a long while; then he rolled over on his side, wound his watch, and lay there until morning.

Another day of fog. Half of his last blanket had gone into foot-wrappings. He failed to pick up Bill's trail. It did not matter. His hunger was driving him too compellingly—only—only he wondered if Bill, too, were lost. By midday the irk of his pack became too oppressive. Again he divided the gold, this time merely spilling half of it on the ground. In the afternoon he threw the rest of it away, there remaining to him only the half-blanket, the tin bucket, and the rifle.

An hallucination began to trouble him. He felt confident that one cartridge remained to him. It was in the chamber of the rifle and he had overlooked it. On the other hand, he knew all the time that the chamber was empty. But the hallucination persisted. He fought it off for hours, then threw his rifle open and was confronted with emptiness. The disappointment was as bitter as though he had really expected to find the cartridge.

He plodded on for half an hour, when the hallucination arose again. Again he fought it and still it persisted, till for very relief he opened his rifle to unconvince himself. At times his mind wandered farther afield, and he plodded on, a mere automaton, strange conceits and whimsicalities gnawing at his brain like worms. But these excursions out of the real were of brief duration, for ever the pangs of the hunger-bite called him back. He was jerked back abruptly once from such an excursion by a sight that caused him nearly to faint. He reeled and swayed, doddering like a drunken man to keep from falling. Before him stood a horse. A horse! He could not believe his eyes. A thick mist was in them, intershot with sparkling points of light. He rubbed his eyes savagely to clear his vision, and beheld not a horse but a great brown bear. The animal was studying him with bellicose curiosity.

The man had brought his gun half way to his shoulder before he realized. He lowered it and drew his hunting-knife from its beaded sheath at his hip. Before him was meat and life. He ran his thumb along the edge of his knife. It was sharp. The point was sharp. He would fling himself upon the bear and kill it. But his heart began its warning thump, thump, thump. Then followed the wild upward leap and tattoo of flutters, the pressing as of an iron band about his forehead, the creeping of the dizziness into his brain.

His desperate courage was evicted by a great surge of fear. In his weakness, what if the animal attacked him! He drew himself up to his most imposing stature, gripping the knife and staring hard at the bear. The bear advanced clumsily a couple of steps, reared up and gave vent to a tentative growl. If the man ran he would run after him; but the man did not run. He was animated now with the courage of fear. He, too, growled, savagely, terribly, voicing the fear that is to life germane and that lies twisted about life's deepest roots.

The bear edged away to one side, growling menacingly, himself appalled by this mysterious creature that appeared upright and unafraid. But the man did not move. He stood like a statue till the danger was past, when he yielded to a fit of of trembling and sank down into the wet moss.

He pulled himself together and went on, afraid now in a new way. It was not the fear that he should die passively from lack of food, but that he should be destroyed violently before starvation had exhausted the last particle of the endeavor in him that made toward surviving. There were the wolves. Back and forth across the desolation drifted their howls, weaving the very air into a fabric of menace that was so tangible that he found himself, arms in the air, pressing it back from him as it might be the walls of a wind-blown tent.

Now and again the wolves in packs of two and three crossed his path. But they sheered clear of him. They were not in sufficient numbers, and besides they were hunting the caribou which did not battle, while this strange creature that walked erect might scratch and bite.

In the late afternoon he came upon scattered bones where the wolves had made a kill. The débris had been a caribou calf an hour before, squawking and running and very much alive. He contemplated the bones, clean-picked and polished, pink with the cell-life in them which had not yet died. Could it possibly be that he might be that ere the day was done! Such was life, eh? A vain and fleeting thing. It was only life that pained. There was no hurt in death. To die was to sleep. It meant cessation, rest. Then why was he not content to die?

But he did not moralize long. He was squatting in the moss, a bone in his mouth, sucking at the shreds of life that still dyed it faintly pink. The sweet meaty taste, thin and elusive almost as a memory, maddened him. He closed his jaws on the bones and crunched. Sometimes it was the bone that broke, sometimes his teeth. Then he crushed the bones between rocks, pounded them to a pulp and swallowed them. He pounded his fingers, too, in his haste, and yet found a moment in which to feel surprise at the fact that his fingers did not hurt much when caught under the descending rock.

Came frightful days of snow and rain. He did not know when he made camp, when he broke camp. He traveled in the night as much as in the day. He rested wherever he fell, crawled on whenever the dying life in him flickered up and burned less dimly. He as a man no longer strove. It was the life in him, unwilling to die, that drove him on. He did not suffer. His nerves had become blunted, numb, while his mind was filled with weird visions and delicious dreams.

But ever he sucked and chewed on the crushed bones of the caribou calf, the least remnants of which he had gathered up and carried with him. He crossed no more hills or divides, but automatically followed a large stream which flowed through a wide and shallow valley. He did not see this stream or this valley. He saw nothing save visions. Soul and body walked or crawled side by side, yet apart, so slender was the thread that bound them.

He awoke in his right mind, lying on his back on a rocky ledge. The sun was shining bright and warm. Afar off he heard the squawking of caribou calves. He was aware of vague memories of rain and wind and snow, but whether he had been beaten by the storm for two days or two weeks he did not know.

For some time he lay without movement, the genial sunshine pouring upon him and saturating his miserable body with its warmth. A fine day, he thought. Perhaps he could manage to locate himself. By a painful effort he rolled over on his side. Below him flowed a wide and sluggish river. Its unfamiliarity puzzled him. Slowly he followed it with his eyes, winding in wide sweeps among the bleak bare hills, bleaker and barer and lower-lying than any hills he had yet encountered. Slowly, deliberately, without excitement or more than the most casual interest, he followed the course of the strange stream toward the sky-line and saw it emptying into a bright and shining sea. He was still unexcited. Most unusual, he thought, a vision or a mirage—more likely a vision, a trick of his disordered mind. He was confirmed in this by sight of a ship lying at anchor in the midst of the shining sea. He closed his eyes for a while, then opened them. Strange how the vision persisted! Yet not strange. He knew there were no seas or ships in the heart of the barren lands, just as he had known there was no cartridge in the empty rifle.

He heard a snuffle behind him—a half-choking gasp or cough. Very slowly, because of his exceeding weakness and stiffness, he rolled over on his other side. He could see nothing near at hand, but he waited patiently. Again came the snuffle and cough, and outlined between two jagged rocks not a score of feet away he made out the gray head of a wolf. The sharp ears were not pricked so sharply as he had seen them on other wolves; the eyes were bleared and blood-shot, the head seemed to droop limply and forlornly. The animal blinked continually in the sunshine. It seemed sick. As he looked it snuffled and coughed again.

This, at least, was real, he thought, and turned on the other side so that he might see the reality of the world which had been veiled from him before by the vision. But the sea still shone in the distance and the ship's spars were plainly discernible. Was it reality after all? He closed his eyes for a long while and thought, and then it came to him. He had been making north by east, away from the Dease Divide and into the Coppermine Valley. This wide and sluggish river was the Coppermine. That shining sea was the Arctic Ocean. That ship was a whaler, strayed east, far east, from the mouth of the Mackenzie, and it was lying at anchor in Coronation Gulf. He remembered the Hudson Bay Company chart he had seen long ago, and it was all clear and reasonable to him.

He sat up and turned his attention to immediate affairs. He had worn through the blanket wrappings, and his feet were like shapeless lumps of raw meat. His last blanket was gone. Rifle and knife were both missing. He had lost his hat somewhere, with the bunch of matches in the band, but the matches against his chest were safe and dry inside the tobacco pouch and oil-paper. He looked at his watch. It marked eleven o'clock and was still running. Evidently he had kept it wound.

He was calm and collected. Though extremely weak he had no sensation of pain. He was not hungry. The thought of food was not even pleasant to him, and whatever he did was done by his reason alone. He ripped off his pants' legs to the knees and bound them about his feet. Somehow he had succeeded in retaining the tin bucket. He would have some hot water before he began what he foresaw was to be a terrible journey to the ship.

His movements were slow. He shook as with a palsy. When he started to collect dry moss he found he could not rise to his feet. He tried again and again, then contented himself with crawling about on hands and knees. Once he crawled near to the sick wolf. The animal dragged itself reluctantly out of his way, licking its chops with a tongue which seemed hardly to have the strength to curl. The man noticed that the tongue was not the customary healthful red. It was a yellowish brown and seemed coated with a rough and half-dry mucus.

After he had drunk a quart of hot water the man found he was able to stand, and even to walk as well as a dying man might be supposed to walk. Every minute or so he was compelled to rest. His steps were feeble and uncertain, just as the wolf's that trailed him were feeble and uncertain; and that night, when the shining sea was blotted out by blackness, he knew he was nearer to it by no more than four miles.

Throughout the night he heard the cough of the sick wolf, and now and then the squawking of the caribou calves. There was life all around him, but it was strong life, very much alive and well, and he knew the sick wolf clung to the sick man's trail in the hope that the man would die first. In the morning, on opening his eyes, he beheld it regarding him with a wistful and hungry stare. It stood crouched, with tail between its legs, like a miserable and woebegone dog. It shivered in the chill morning wind, and grinned dispiritedly when the man spoke to it in a voice which achieved no more than a hoarse whisper.

The sun rose brightly, and all morning the man tottered and fell toward the ship on the shining sea. The weather was perfect. It was the brief Indian Summer of the high latitudes. It might last a week. To-morrow or next day it might be gone.

In the afternoon the man came upon a trail. It was of another man, who did not walk, but who dragged himself on all fours. The man thought it might be Bill, but he thought in a dull, uninterested way. He had no curiosity. In fact sensation and emotion had left him. He was no longer susceptible to pain. Stomach and nerves had gone to sleep. Yet the life that was in him drove him on. He was very weary, but it refused to die. It was because it refused to die that he still ate muskeg berries and minnows, drank his hot water, and kept a wary eye on the sick wolf.

He followed the trail of the other man who dragged himself along, and soon came to the end of it—a few fresh-picked bones where the soggy moss was marked by the foot-pads of many wolves. He saw a squat moose-hide sack, mate to his own, which had been torn by sharp teeth. He picked it up, though its weight was almost too much for his feeble fingers. Bill had carried it to the last. Ha! ha! He would have the laugh on Bill. He would survive and carry it to the ship in the shining sea. His mirth was hoarse and ghastly, like a raven's croak, and the sick wolf joined him, howling lugubriously. The man ceased suddenly. How could he have the laugh on Bill if that were Bill; if those bones, so pinky-white and clean, were Bill!

He turned away. Well, Bill had deserted him; but he would not take the gold, nor would he suck Bill's bones. Bill would have, though, had it been the other way around, he mused as he staggered on.

He came to a pool of water. Stooping over in quest of minnows, he jerked his head back as though he had been stung. He had caught sight of his reflected face. So horrible was it that sensibility awoke long enough to be shocked. There were three minnows in the pool, which was too large to drain; and after several ineffectual attempts to catch them in the tin bucket he forbore. He was afraid, because of his great weakness, that he might fall in and drown. It was for this reason that he did not trust himself to the river astride one of the many drift-logs which lined its sandspits.

That day he decreased the distance between him and the ship by three miles; the next day by two—for he was crawling now as Bill had crawled; and the end of the fifth day found the ship still seven miles away and him unable to make even a mile a day. Still the Indian summer held on, and he continued to crawl and faint, turn and turn about; and ever the sick wolf coughed and wheezed at his heels. His knees had become raw meat like his feet, and though he padded them with the shirt from his back it was a red track he left behind him on the moss and stones. Once glancing back he saw the wolf licking hungrily his bleeding tail, and he saw sharply what his own end might be—unless—unless he could get the wolf. Then began as grim a tragedy of existence as was ever played—a sick man that crawled, a sick wolf that limped, two creatures dragging their dying carcasses across the desolation and hunting each other's lives.

Had it been a well wolf, it would not have mattered so much to the man; but the thought of going to feed the maw of that loathsome and all but dead thing was repugnant to him. He was finicky. His mind had begun to wander again, and to be perplexed by hallucinations, while his lucid intervals grew rarer and shorter.

He was awakened once from a faint by a wheeze close in his

ear. The wolf leaped lamely back, losing its footing and falling in its weakness. It was ludicrous, but he was not amused. Nor was he even afraid. He was too far gone for that. But his mind was for the moment clear, and he lay and considered. The ship was no more than four miles away. He could see it quite distinctly when he rubbed the mists out of his eyes, and he could see the white sail of a small boat cutting the water of the shining sea. But he could never crawl those four miles. He knew that, and was very calm in the knowledge. He knew that he could not crawl half a mile. And yet he wanted to live. It was unreasonable that he should die after all he had undergone. Fate asked too much of him. And, dying, he declined to die. It was stark madness, perhaps, but in the very grip of Death he defied Death and refused to die.

He closed his eyes and composed himself with infinite precaution. He steeled himself to keep above the suffocating languor that lapped like a rising tide through all the wells of his being. It was very like a sea, this deadly languor, that rose and rose and drowned his consciousness bit by bit. Sometimes he was all but submerged, swimming through oblivion with a faltering stroke; and again, by some strange alchemy of soul, he would find another shred of will and strike out more strongly.

Without movement he lay on his back, and he could hear slowly drawing near and nearer the wheezing intake and output of the sick wolf's breath. It drew closer, ever closer, through an infinitude of time, and he did not move. It was at his ear. The harsh dry tongue grated like sandpaper against his cheek. His hands shot out—or at least he willed them to shoot out. The fingers were curved like talons, but they closed on empty air. Swiftness and certitude require strength, and the man had not this strength.

The patience of the wolf was terrible. The man's patience was no less terrible. For half a day he lay motionless, fighting off unconsciousness and waiting for the thing that was to feed upon him and upon which he wished to feed. Sometimes the languid sea rose over him and he dreamed long dreams; but ever through it all, waking and dreaming, he waited for the wheezing breath and the harsh caress of the tongue.

He did not hear the breath, and he slipped slowly from some dream to the feel of the tongue along his hand. He waited. The fangs pressed softly; the pressure increased; the wolf was exerting its last strength in an effort to sink teeth in the food for which it had waited so long. But the man had waited long, and the lacerated hand closed on the jaw. Slowly, while the wolf struggled feebly and the hand clutched feebly, the other hand crept across to a grip. Five minutes later the whole weight of the man's body was on top of the wolf. The hands had not sufficient strength to choke the animal, but the face of the man was pressed close to the throat of the wolf and the mouth was full of hair. At the end of half an hour the man was aware of a warm trickle in his throat. It was not pleasant. It was like molten lead being forced into his stomach, but it was forced by his will alone. Later the man rolled over on his back and slept.

THERE WERE SOME MEMBERS of a scientific expedition on the whaleship *Bedford.* From the deck they remarked a strange object on the shore. It was moving down the beach toward the water. They were unable to classify it, and, being scientific men, they climbed into the whaleboat alongside and went ashore to see. And they saw something that was alive but that could hardly be called a man. It was blind, unconscious. It squirmed along the ground like some monstrous worm. Most of its efforts were ineffectual, but it was persistent, and it writhed and twisted and went ahead perhaps a score of feet an hour.

THREE WEEKS AFTERWARD the man lay in a bunk on the whaleship *Bedford*, and with tears streaming down his wasted cheeks told who he was and what he had undergone. He also babbled incoherently of his mother, of sunny Southern California, and a home among the orange groves and flowers.

The days were not many after that when he sat at table with the scientific men and ship's officers. He gloated over the spectacle of so much food, watching it anxiously as it went into the mouths of others. With the disappearance of each mouthful an expression of deep regret came into his eyes. He was quite sane, yet he hated those men at meal-time because they ate so much food. He was haunted by a fear that it would not last. He inquired of the cook, the cabin-boy, the captain, concerning the food stores. They reassured him countless times; but he could not believe them, and pried cunningly about the lazarette to see with his own eyes.

It was noticed that the man was getting fat. He grew stouter with each day. The scientific men shook their heads and theorized. They limited the man at his meals, but still his girth increased and his body swelled prodigiously under his shirt.

The sailors grinned. They knew. And when the scientific men set a watch on the man, they knew too. They saw him slouch for'ard after breakfast, and like a mendicant, with outstretched palm, accost a sailor. The sailor grinned and passed him a fragment of sea biscuit. He clutched it avariciously, looked at it as a miser looks at gold, and thrust it into his shirt bosom. Similar were the donations from other grinning sailors.

The scientific men were discreet. They left him alone. But they privily examined his bunk. It was lined with hardtack; the mattress was stuffed with hardtack; every nook and cranny was filled with hardtack. Yet he was sane. He was taking precautions against another possible famine—that was all. He would recover from it, the scientific men said; and he did, ere the *Bedford*'s anchor rumbled down in San Francisco Bay.

To the Man on the Trail

A KLONDIKE CHRISTMAS

DUMP IT IN."

"But I say, Kid, isn't that going it a little too strong? Whisky and alcohol's bad enough; but when it comes to brandy and pepper-sauce and—"

"Dump it in. Who's making this punch, anyway?" And Malemute Kid smiled benignly through the clouds of steam. "By the time you've been in this country as long as I have, my son, and lived on rabbit-tracks and salmon-belly, you'll learn that Christmas comes only once per annum. And a Christmas without punch is sinking a hole to bedrock with nary a pay-streak."

"Stack up on that fer a high cyard," approved big Jim Belden, who had come down from his claim on Mazy May to spend Christmas, and who, as every one knew, had been living the two months past on straight moose-meat. "Hain't fergot the *hooch* we uns made on the Tanana, hev yeh?"

"Well, I guess yes. Boys, it would have done your hearts good to see that whole tribe fighting drunk—and all because of a glorious ferment of sugar and sour dough. That was before your time," Malemute Kid said as he turned to Stanley Prince, a young mining expert who had been in two years. "No white women in the country then, and Mason wanted to get married. Ruth's father was chief of the Tananas, and objected, like the rest of the tribe. Stiff? Why, I used my last pound of sugar; finest work in that line I ever did in my life. You should have seen the chase, down the river and across the portage."

"But the squaw?" asked Louis Savoy, the tall French-Canadian, becoming interested; for he had heard of this wild deed when at Forty Mile the preceding winter.

Then Malemute Kid, who was a born raconteur, told the unvarnished tale of the Northland Lochinvar. More than one high adventurer of the North felt his heart-strings draw closer, and experienced vague yearnings for the sunnier pastures of the Southland, where life promised something more than a barren struggle with cold and death.

"We struck the Yukon just behind the first ice-run," he concluded, "and the tribe only a quarter of an hour behind. But that saved us; for the second run broke the jam above and shut them out. When they finally got into Nuklukyeto, the whole post was ready for them. And as to the foregathering, ask Father Roubeau here: he performed the ceremony."

The Jesuit took the pipe from his lips, but could only express his gratification with patriarchal smiles, while Protestant and Catholic vigorously applauded.

"By gar!" ejaculated Louis Savoy, who seemed overcome by the romance of it. "La petite squaw; mon Mason brav; by gar!"

Then, as the first tin cups of punch went round, Bettles the Unquenchable sprang to his feet and struck up his favorite drinking song:—

"There's Henry Ward Beecher
And Sunday-school teachers,
    All drink of the sassafras root;
But you bet all the same,
If it had its right name,
    It's the juice of the forbidden fruit."

"O the juice of the forbidden fruit," roared out the Bacchanalian chorus,—

"O the juice of the forbidden fruit;
But you bet all the same,
If it had its right name,
It's the juice of the forbidden fruit."

Malemute Kid's frightful concoction did its work; the men of the camps and trails unbent in its genial glow, and jest and song and tales of past adventure went round the board. Aliens from a dozen lands, they toasted each and all. It was the Englishman, Prince, who pledged "Uncle Sam, the precocious infant of the New World"; the Yankee, Bettles, who drank to "The Queen, God bless her"; and together, Savoy and Meyers, the German trader, clanged their cups to Alsace and Lorraine.

Then Malemute Kid arose, cup in hand, and glanced at the greased-paper window, where the frost stood full three inches thick. "A health to the man on trail this night; may his grub hold out; may his dogs keep their legs; may his matches never miss fire."

CRACK! CRACK!—they heard the familiar music of the dog-whip, the whining howl of the Malemutes, and the crunch of a sled as it drew up to the cabin. Conversation languished, while they waited the issue expectantly.

"An old-timer; cares for his dogs and then himself," whispered Malemute Kid to Prince, as they listened to the snapping jaws and the wolfish snarls and yelps of pain which proclaimed to their practiced ears that the stranger was beating back their dogs while he fed his own.

Then came the expected knock, sharp and confident, and the stranger entered. Dazzled by the light, he hesitated a moment at the door, giving to all a chance for scrutiny. He was a striking personage, and a most picturesque one, in his Arctic dress of wool and fur. Standing six foot two or three, with proportionate breadth of shoulders and depth of chest, his smooth-shaven face nipped by the cold to a gleaming pink, his long lashes and eyebrows white with ice, and the ear and neck flaps of his great wolfskin cap loosely raised, he seemed, of a verity, the Frost King, just stepped in out of the night. Clasped outside his Mackinaw jacket, a beaded belt held two large Colt's revolvers and a hunting-knife, while he carried, in addition to the inevitable dog-whip, a smokeless rifle of the largest bore and latest pattern. As he came forward, for all his step was firm and elastic, they could see that fatigue bore heavily upon him.

An awkward silence had fallen, but his hearty "What cheer, my lads?" put them quickly at ease, and the next instant Malemute Kid and he had gripped hands. Though they had never met, each had heard of the other, and the recognition was mutual. A sweeping introduction and a mug of punch were forced upon him before he could explain his errand.

"How long since that basket-sled, with three men and eight dogs, passed?" he asked.

"An even two days ahead. Are you after them?"

"Yes; my team. Run them off under my very nose, the cusses. I've gained two days on them already,—pick them up on the next run."

"Reckon they'll show spunk?" asked Belden, in order to keep up the conversation, for Malemute Kid already had the coffee-pot on and was busily frying bacon and moose-meat.

The stranger significantly tapped his revolvers.

"When 'd yeh leave Dawson?"

"Twelve o'clock."

"Last night?"—as a matter of course.

"To-day."

A murmur of surprise passed round the circle. And well it might; for it was just midnight and seventy-five miles of rough river trail was not to be sneered at for a twelve hours' run.

The talk soon became impersonal, however, harking back to

the trials of childhood. As the young stranger ate of the rude fare, Malemute Kid attentively studied his face. Nor was he long in deciding that it was fair, honest, and open, and that he liked it. Still youthful, the lines had been firmly traced by toil and hardship. Though genial in conversation, and mild when at rest, the blue eyes gave promise of the hard steel-glitter which comes when called into action, especially against odds. The heavy jaw and square-cut chin demonstrated rugged pertinacity and indomitability of purpose. Nor, though the attributes of the lion were there, was there wanting the certain softness, the hint of womanliness, which bespoke an emotional nature—one which could feel, and feel deeply.

"So that's how me an' the ol' woman got spliced," said Belden, concluding the exciting tale of his courtship. "'Here we be, dad,' sez she. 'An' may yeh be damned,' sez he to her, an' then to me, 'Jim, yeh—yeh git outen them good duds o' yourn; I want a right peart slice o' thet forty acre ploughed 'fore dinner.' An' then he turns on her an' sez, 'An' yeh, Sal; yeh sail inter them dishes.' An' then he sort o' sniffed an' kissed her. An' I was thet happy,—but he seen me an' roars out, 'Yeh, Jim!' An' yeh bet I dusted fer the barn."

"Any kids waiting for you back in the States?" asked the stranger.

"Nope; Sal died 'fore any come. Thet's why I'm here." Belden abstractedly began to light his pipe, which had failed to go out, and then brightened up with, "How 'bout yerself, stranger,—married man?"

For reply, he opened his watch, slipped it from the thong which served for a chain, and passed it over. Belden pricked up the slush-lamp, surveyed the inside of the case critically, and swearing admiringly to himself, handed it over to Louis Savoy. With numerous "By gars!" he finally surrendered it to Prince, and they noticed that his hands trembled and his eyes took on a peculiar softness. And so it passed from horny hand to horny hand—the pasted photograph of a woman, the clinging kind that such men fancy, with a babe at the breast. Those who had not yet seen the wonder were keen with curiosity; those who had, became silent and retrospective. They could face the pinch of famine, the grip of scurvy, or the quick death by field or flood; but the pictured semblance of a stranger woman and child made women and children of them all.

"Never have seen the youngster yet,—he's a boy, she says, and two years old," said the stranger as he received the treasure back. A lingering moment he gazed upon it, then snapped the case and turned away, but not quick enough to hide the restrained rush of tears.

Malemute Kid led him to a bunk and bade him turn in.

"Call me at four, sharp. Don't fail me," were his last words, and a moment later he was breathing in the heaviness of exhausted sleep.

"By Jove, he's a plucky chap," commented Prince. "Three hours' sleep after seventy-five miles with the dogs, and then the trail again. Who is he, Kid?"

"Jack Westondale. Been in going on three years, with nothing but the name of working like a horse, and any amount of bad luck to his credit. I never knew him, but Sitka Charley told me about him."

"It seems hard that a man with a sweet young wife like his should be putting in his years in this God-forsaken hole, where every year counts two on the outside."

"The trouble with him is clean grit and stubbornness. He's cleaned up twice with a stake, but lost it both times."

Here the conversation was broken off by an uproar from Bettles, for the effect had begun to wear away. And soon the bleak years of monotonous grub and deadening toil were being forgotten in rough merriment. Malemute Kid alone seemed unable to lose himself, and cast many an anxious look at his watch. Once he put on his mittens and beaver-skin cap, and leaving the cabin, fell to rummaging about in the cache.

Nor could he wait the hour designated; for he was fifteen minutes ahead of time in rousing his guest. The young giant had stiffened badly, and brisk rubbing was necessary to bring him to his feet. He tottered painfully out of the cabin, to find his dogs harnessed and everything ready for the start. The company wished him good luck and a short chase, while Father Roubeau, hurriedly blessing him, led the stampede for the cabin; and small wonder, for it is not good to face seventy-four degrees below zero with naked ears and hands.

Malemute Kid saw him to the main trail, and there, gripping his hand heartily, gave him advice.

"You'll find a hundred pounds of salmon-eggs on the sled," he said. "The dogs will go as far on that as with one hundred and fifty of fish, and you can't get dog-food at Pelly, as you probably expected." The stranger started, and his eyes flashed, but he did not interrupt. "You can't get an ounce of food for dog or man till you reach Five Fingers, and that's a stiff two hundred miles. Watch out for open water on the Thirty Mile River, and be sure you take the big cut-off above Le Barge."

"How did you know it? Surely the news can't be ahead of me already?"

"I don't know it; and what's more, I don't want to know it. But you never owned that team you're chasing. Sitka Charley sold it to them last spring. But he sized you up to me as square once, and I believe him. I've seen your face; I like it. And I've seen—why, damn you, hit the high places for salt water and that wife of yours, and—" Here the Kid unmittened and jerked out his sack.

"No, I don't need it," and the tears froze on his cheeks as he convulsively gripped Malemute Kid's hand.

"Then don't spare the dogs; cut them out of the traces as fast as they drop; buy them, and think they're cheap at ten dollars a pound. You can get them at Five Fingers, Little Salmon, and the Hootalinqua."

"And watch out for wet feet," was his parting advice. "Keep a-traveling up to twenty-five, but if it gets below that, build a fire and change your socks."

FIFTEEN MINUTES had barely elapsed, when the jingle of bells announced new arrivals. The door opened, and a mounted policeman of the Northwest Territory entered, followed by two half-breed dog-drivers. Like Westondale, they were heavily armed and showed signs of fatigue. The half-breeds had been born to the trail, and bore it easily; but the young policeman was badly exhausted. Still the dogged obstinacy of his race held him to the pace he had set, and would hold him till he dropped in his tracks.

"When did Westondale pull out?" he asked. "He stopped here, didn't he?" This was supererogatory, for the tracks told their own tale too well.

Malemute Kid had caught Belden's eye, and he, scenting the wind, replied evasively, "A right peart while back."

"Come, my man; speak up," he admonished.

"Yeh seem to want him right smart. Hez he ben gittin' cantankerous down Dawson way?"

"Held up Harry McFarland's for forty thousand; exchanged it at the A.C. store for a check on Seattle; and who's to stop the cashing of it if we don't overtake him? When did he pull out?"

Every eye suppressed its excitement, for Malemute Kid had given the cue, and the young officer encountered wooden faces on every hand.

Striding over to Prince, he put the question to him. Though it hurt him, gazing into the frank, earnest face of his fellow countryman, he replied inconsequentially on the state of the trail.

Then he espied Father Roubeau, who could not lie. "A quarter of an hour ago," he answered; "but he had four hours' rest for himself and dogs."

"Fifteen minutes' start, and he's fresh! My God!" The poor fellow staggered back, half-fainting from exhaustion and disappointment, murmuring something about the run from Dawson in ten hours and the dogs being played out.

Malemute Kid forced a mug of punch upon him; then he turned for the door, ordering the dog-drivers to follow. But the warmth and promise of rest was too tempting, and they objected strenuously. The Kid was conversant with their French patois, and followed it anxiously.

They swore that the dogs were gone up; that Siwash and Babette would have to be shot before the first mile was covered; that the rest were almost as bad; and that it would be better for all hands to rest up.

"Lend me five dogs," he asked, turning to Malemute Kid.

But the Kid shook his head.

"I'll sign a check on Captain Constantine for five thousand,—here's my papers,—I'm authorized to draw at my own discretion."

Again the silent refusal.

"Then I'll requisition them in the name of the Queen."

Smiling incredulously, the Kid glanced at his well-stocked arsenal, and the Englishman, realizing his impotency, turned for the door. But the dog-drivers still objecting, he whirled upon them fiercely, calling them women and curs. The swart face of the older half-breed flushed angrily, as he drew himself up and promised in good, round terms that he would then be delighted to plant him in the snow.

The young officer, and it required his whole will, walked steadily to the door, exhibiting a freshness he did not possess. But they all knew and appreciated his proud effort; nor could he veil the twinges of agony that shot across his face. Covered with frost, the dogs were curled up in the snow, and it was almost impossible to get them to their feet. The poor brutes whined under the stinging lash, for the dog-drivers were angry and cruel; nor till Babette, the leader, was cut from the traces, could they break out the sled and get under way.

"A dirty scoundrel and a liar!" "By gar! him no good!" "A thief!" "Worse than an Indian!" It was evident that they were angry—first, at the way they had been deceived; and second, at the outraged ethics of the Northland, where honesty, above all, was man's prime jewel. "An' we gave the cuss a hand; after knowin' what he'd did." All eyes were turned accusingly upon Malemute Kid, who rose from the corner where he had been making Babette comfortable, and silently emptied the bowl for a final round of punch.

"It's a cold night, boys,—a bitter cold night," was the irrelevant commencement of his defense. "You've all traveled trail, and know what that stands for. Don't jump a dog when he's down. You've only heard one side. A whiter man than Jack Westondale never ate from the same pot nor stretched blanket with you or me. Last fall he gave his whole clean-up, forty thousand, to Joe Castrell, to buy in on Dominion. To-day he'd be a millionaire. But while he stayed behind at Circle City, taking care of his partner with the scurvy, what does Castrell do? Goes into McFarland's, jumps the limit, and drops the whole sack. Found him dead in the snow the next day. And poor Jack laying his plans to go out this winter to his wife and the boy he's never seen. Well, he's gone out; and what are you going to do about it?"

The Kid glanced round the circle of his judges, noted the softening of their faces, then raised his mug aloft. "So a health to the man on trail this night; may his grub hold out; may his dogs keep their legs; may his matches never miss fire. God prosper him; good luck go with him; and—"

"Confusion to the Mounted Police!" interpolated Bettles, to the crash of the empty cups.

The Sun-Dog Trail

SITKA CHARLEY smoked his pipe and gazed thoughtfully at the *Police Gazette* illustration on the wall. For half an hour he had been steadily regarding it, and for half an hour I had been slyly watching him. Something was going on in that mind of his, and, whatever it was, I knew it was well worth knowing. He had lived life, and seen things, and performed that prodigy of prodigies, namely, the turning of his back upon his own people, and, in so far as it was possible for an Indian, becoming a white man even in his mental processes. As he phrased it himself, he had come into the warm, sat among us, by our fires, and become one of us. He had never learned to read nor write, but his vocabulary was remarkable, and more remarkable still was the completeness with which he had assumed the white man's point of view, the white man's attitude toward things.

We had struck this deserted cabin after a hard day on trail. The dogs had been fed, the supper dishes washed, the beds made, and we were now enjoying that most delicious hour that comes each day, and but once each day, on the Alaskan trail, the hour when nothing intervenes between the tired body and bed save the smoking of the evening pipe. Some former denizen of the cabin had decorated its walls with illustrations torn from magazines and newspapers, and it was these illustrations that had held Sitka Charley's attention from the moment of our arrival two hours before. He had studied them intently, ranging from one to another and back again, and I could see that there was uncertainty in his mind, and bepuzzlement.

"Well?" I finally broke the silence.

He took the pipe from his mouth and said simply, "I do not understand."

He smoked on again, and again removed the pipe, using it to point at the *Police Gazette* illustration.

"That picture—what does it mean? I do not understand."

I looked at the picture. A man, with a preposterously wicked face, his right hand pressed dramatically to his heart, was falling backward to the floor. Confronting him, with a face that was a composite of destroying angel and Adonis, was a man holding a smoking revolver.

"One man is killing the other man," I said, aware of a distinct bepuzzlement of my own and of failure to explain.

"Why?" asked Sitka Charley.

"That picture is all end," he said. "It has no beginning."

"It is life," I said.

"Life has beginning," he objected.

I was silenced for the moment, while his eyes wandered on to an adjoining decoration, a photographic reproduction of somebody's "Leda and the Swan."

"That picture," he said, "has no beginning. It has no end. I do not understand pictures."

"Look at that picture," I commented, pointing to a third decoration. "It means something. Tell me what it means to you."

He studied it for several minutes.

"The little girl is sick," he said finally. "That is the doctor looking at her. They have been up all night—see, the oil is low in the lamp, the first morning light is coming in at the window. It is a great sickness; maybe she will die, that is why the doctor looks so hard. That is the mother. It is a great sickness, because the mother's head is on the table and she is crying."

"How do you know she is crying?" I interrupted. "You cannot see her face. Perhaps she is asleep."

Sitka Charley looked at me in swift surprise, then back at the picture. It was evident that he had not reasoned the impression.

"Perhaps she is asleep," he repeated. He studied it closely. "No, she is not asleep. The shoulders show that she is not asleep. I have seen the shoulders of a woman who cried. The mother is crying. It is a very great sickness."

"And now you understand the picture," I cried.

He shook his head, and asked, "The little girl—does it die?"

It was my turn for silence.

"Does it die?" he reiterated. "You are a painter-man. Maybe you know."

"No, I do not know," I confessed.

"It is not life," he delivered himself dogmatically. "In life little girl die or get well. Something happen in life. In picture nothing happen. No, I do not understand pictures."

His disappointment was patent. It was his desire to understand all things that white men understand, and here, in this matter, he failed. I felt, also, that there was challenge in his attitude. He was bent upon compelling me to show him the wisdom of pictures. Besides, he had remarkable powers of visualization. I had long since learned this. He visualized everything. He saw life in pictures, felt life in pictures, generalized life in pictures; and yet he did not understand pictures when seen through other men's eyes and expressed by those men with color and line upon canvas.

"Pictures are bits of life," I said. "We paint life as we see it. For instance, Charley, you are coming along the trail. It is night. You see a cabin. The window is lighted. You look through the window for one second, or for two seconds, you see something, and you go on your way. You saw maybe a man writing a letter. You saw something without beginning or end. Nothing happened. Yet it was a bit of life you saw. You remember it afterward. It is like a picture in your memory. The window is the frame of the picture."

I could see that he was interested, and I knew that as I spoke he had looked through the window and seen the man writing the letter.

"There is a picture you have painted that I understand," he said. "It is a true picture. It has much meaning. It is in your cabin at Dawson. It is a faro table. There are men playing. It is a large game. The limit is off."

"How do you know the limit is off?" I broke in excitedly, for here was where my work could be tried out on an unbiassed judge who knew life only, and not art, and who was a sheer master of reality. Also, I was very proud of that particular piece of work. I had named it "The Last Turn," and I believed it to be one of the best things I had ever done.

"There are no chips on the table," Sitka Charley explained. "The men are playing with markers. That means the roof is the limit. One man play yellow markers—maybe one yellow marker worth one thousand dollars, maybe two thousand dollars. One man play red markers. Maybe they are worth five hundred dollars, maybe one thousand dollars. It is a very big game. Everybody play very high, up to the roof. How do I know? You make the dealer with blood little bit warm in face." (I was delighted.) "The lookout, you make him lean forward in his chair. Why he lean forward? Why his face very much quiet? Why his eyes very much bright? Why dealer warm with blood a little bit in the face? Why all men very quiet?—the man with yellow markers? the man with white markers? the man with red markers? Why nobody talk? Because very much money. Because last turn."

"How do you know it is the last turn?" I asked.

"The king is coppered, the seven is played open," he answered. "Nobody bet on other cards. Other cards all gone. Everybody one mind. Everybody play king to lose, seven to win. Maybe bank lose twenty thousand dollars, maybe bank win. Yes, that picture I understand."

"Yet you do not know the end!" I cried triumphantly. "It is the last turn, but the cards are not yet turned. In the picture they will never be turned. Nobody will ever know who wins nor who loses."

"And the men will sit there and never talk," he said, wonder and awe growing in his face. "And the lookout will lean forward, and the blood will be warm in the face of the dealer. It is a strange thing. Always will they sit there, always; and the cards will never be turned."

"It is a picture," I said. "It is life. You have seen things like it yourself."

He looked at me and pondered, then said, very slowly: "No, as you say, there is no end to it. Nobody will ever know the end. Yet it is a true thing. I have seen it. It is life."

For a long time he smoked on in silence, weighing the pictorial wisdom of the white man and verifying it by the facts of life. He nodded his head several times, and grunted once or twice. Then he knocked the ashes from his pipe, carefully refilled it, and, after a thoughtful pause, lighted it again.

"Then have I, too, seen many pictures of life," he began; "pictures not painted, but seen with the eyes. I have looked at them like through the window at the man writing the letter. I have seen many pieces of life, without beginning, without end, without understanding."

With a sudden change of position he turned his eyes full upon me and regarded me thoughtfully.

"Look you," he said; "You are a painter-man. How would you paint this which I saw, a picture without beginning, the ending of which I do not understand, a piece of life with the northern lights for a candle and Alaska for a frame."

"It is a large canvas," I murmured.

But he ignored me, for the picture he had in mind was before his eyes and he was seeing it.

"There are many names for this picture," he said. "But in the picture there are many sun-dogs, and it comes into my mind to call it 'The Sun-Dog Trail.' It was a long time ago, seven years ago, the fall of '97, when I saw the woman first time. At Lake Linderman I had one canoe, very good Peterborough canoe. I came over Chilcoot Pass with two thousand letters for Dawson. I was letter carrier. Everybody rush to Klondike at that time. Many people on trail. Last water, snow in the air, snow on the ground, ice on the lake, on the river ice in the eddies. Every day more snow, more ice. Maybe one day, maybe three days, maybe six days, any day maybe freeze-up come, then no more water, all ice, everybody walk, Dawson six hundred miles, long time walk. Boat go very quick. Everybody want to go boat. Everybody say, 'Charley, two hundred dollars you take me in canoe,' 'Charley, three hundred dollars,' 'Charley, four hundred dollars.' I say no, all the time I say no. I am letter carrier.

"In morning I get to Lake Linderman. I walk all night and am much tired. I cook breakfast, I eat, then I sleep on the beach three hours. I wake up. It is ten o'clock. Snow is falling. There is wind, much wind that blows fair. Also, there is a woman who sits in the snow alongside. She is white woman, she is young, very pretty, maybe she is twenty years old, maybe twenty-five years old. She look at me. I look at her. She is very tired. She is no dance-woman. I see that right away. She is good woman, and she is very tired.

"'You are Sitka Charley,' she says. I get up quick and roll blankets so snow does not get inside. 'I go to Dawson,' she says. 'I go in your canoe—how much?'

"I do not want anybody in my canoe. I do not like to say no. So I say, 'One thousand dollars.' Just for fun I say it, so woman cannot come with me, much better than say no. She look at me very hard, then she says, 'When you start?' I say right away. Then she says all right, she will give me one thousand dollars.

"What can I say? I do not want the woman, yet have I given my word that for one thousand dollars she can come. I am surprised. Maybe she make fun, too, so I say, 'Let me see thousand dollars.' And that woman, that young woman, all alone on the trail, there in the snow, she take out one thousand dollars, in greenbacks, and she put them in my hand. I look at money, I look at her. What can I say? I say, 'No, my canoe very small. There is no room for outfit.'

She laugh. She says, 'I am great traveler. This is my outfit.' She kick one small pack in the snow. It is two fur robes, canvas outside, some woman's clothes inside. I pick it up. Maybe thirty-five pounds. I am surprised. She take it away from me. She says. 'Come, let us start.' She carries pack into canoe. What can I say? I put my blankets into canoe. We start.

"And that is the way I saw the woman first time. The wind was fair. I put up small sail. The canoe went very fast, it flew like a bird over the high waves. The woman was much afraid. 'What for you come Klondike much afraid?' I ask. She laugh at me, a hard laugh, but she is still much afraid. Also is she very tired. I run canoe through rapids to Lake Bennett. Water very bad, and woman cry out because she is afraid. We go down Lake Bennett, snow, ice, wind like a gale, but woman is very tired and go to sleep.

"That night we make camp at Windy Arm. Woman sit by fire and eat supper. I look at her. She is pretty. She fix hair. There is much hair, and it is brown, also sometimes it is like gold in the firelight, when she turn her head, so, and flashes come from it like golden fire. The eyes are large and brown, sometimes warm like a candle behind a curtain, sometimes very hard and bright like broken ice when sun shines upon it. When she smile—how can I say?—when she smile I know white man like to kiss her, just like that, when she smile. She never do hard work. Her hands are soft, like baby's hand. She is soft all over, like baby. She is not thin, but round like baby; her arm, her leg, her muscles, all soft and round like baby. Her waist is small, and when she stand up, when she walk, or move her head or arm, it is—I do not know the word—but it nice to look at, like—maybe I say she is built on lines like the lines of a good canoe, just like that, and when she move she is like the movement of the good canoe sliding through still water or leaping through water when it is white and fast and angry. It is very good to see.

"Why does she come into Klondike, all alone, with plenty of

money? I do not know. Next day I ask her. She laugh and says: 'Sitka Charley, that is none of your business. I give you one thousand dollars take me to Dawson. That only is your business.' Next day after that I ask her what is her name. She laugh, then she says, 'Mary Jones, that is my name.' I do not know her name, but I know all the time that Mary Jones is not her name.

"It is very cold in canoe, and because of cold sometimes she not feel good. Sometimes she feel good and she sing. Her voice is like a silver bell, and I feel good all over like when I go into church at Holy Cross Mission, and when she sing I feel strong and paddle like hell. Then she laugh and says, 'You think we get to Dawson before freeze-up, Charley?' Sometimes she sit in canoe and is thinking far away, her eyes like that, all empty. She does not see Sitka Charley, nor the ice, nor the snow. She is far away. Very often she is like that, thinking far away. Sometimes, when she is thinking far away, her face is not good to see. It looks like a face that is angry, like the face of one man when he want to kill another man.

"Last day to Dawson very bad. Shore-ice in all the eddies, mush-ice in the stream. I cannot paddle. The canoe freeze to ice. I cannot get to shore. There is much danger. All the time we go down Yukon in the ice. That night there is much noise of ice. Then ice stop, canoe stop, everything stop. 'Let us go to shore,' the woman says. I say no, better wait. By and by, everything start down-stream again. There is much snow. I cannot see. At eleven o'clock at night, everything stop. At one o'clock everything start again. At three o'clock everything stop. Canoe is smashed like eggshell, but is on top of ice and cannot sink. I hear dogs howling. We wait. We sleep. By and by morning come. There is no more snow. It is the freeze-up, and there is Dawson. Canoe smash and stop right at Dawson. Sitka Charley has come in with two thousand letters on very last water.

"The woman rent a cabin on the hill, and for one week I see her no more. Then, one day, she come to me. 'Charley,' she says, 'how do you like to work for me? You drive dogs, make camp, travel with me.' I say that I make too much money carrying letters. She says, 'Charley, I will pay you more money.' I tell her that pick-and-shovel man get fifteen dollars a day in the mines. She says, 'That is four hundred and fifty dollars a month.' And I say, 'Sitka Charley is no pick-and-shovel man.' Then she says, 'I understand, Charley. I will give you seven hundred and fifty dollars each month.' It is a good price, and I go to work for her. I buy for her dogs and sled. We travel up Klondike, up Bonanza and Eldorado, over to Indian River, to Sulphur Creek, to Dominion, back across divide to Gold Bottom and to Too Much Gold, and back to Dawson. All the time she look for something, I do not know what. I am puzzled. 'What thing you look for?' I ask. She laugh. 'You look for gold?' I ask. She laugh. Then she says, 'That is none of your business, Charley.' And after that I never ask any more.

"She has a small revolver which she carries in her belt. Sometimes, on trail, she makes practice with revolver. I laugh. 'What for you laugh, Charley?' she ask. 'What for you play with that?' I say. 'It is no good. It is too small. It is for a child, a little plaything.' When we get back to Dawson she ask me to buy good revolver for her. I buy a Colt's 44. It is very heavy, but she carry it in her belt all the time.

"At Dawson comes the man. Which way he come I do not know. Only do I know he is *che-cha-quo*—what you call tenderfoot. His hands are soft, just like hers. He never do hard work. He is soft all over. At first I think maybe he is her husband. But he is too young. Also, they make two beds at night. He is maybe twenty years old. His eyes blue, his hair yellow, he has a little mustache which is yellow. His name is John Jones. Maybe he is her brother. I do not know. I ask questions no more. Only I think his name is not John Jones. Other people call him Mr. Girvan. I do not think that is his name. I do not think her name is Miss Girvan, which other people call her. I think nobody know their names.

"One night I am asleep at Dawson. He wake me up. He says, 'Get the dogs ready; we start.' No more do I ask questions, so I get the dogs ready and we start. We go down the Yukon. It is night-time, it is November, and it is very cold—sixty-five below. She is soft. He is soft. The cold bites. They get tired. They cry under their breaths to themselves. By and by I say better we stop and make camp. But they say that they will go on. Three times I say better to make camp and rest, but each time they say they will go on. After that I say nothing. All the time, day after day, is it that way. They are very soft. They get stiff and sore. They do not understand moccasins, and their feet hurt very much. They limp, they stagger like drunken people, they cry under their breaths; and all the time they say, 'On! on! We will go on!'

"They are like crazy people. All the time do they go on, and on. Why do they go on? I do not know. Only do they go on. What are they after? I do not know. They are not after gold. There is no stampede. Besides, they spend plenty of money. But I ask questions no more. I, too, go on and on, because I am strong on the trail and because I am greatly paid.

"We make Circle City. That for which they look is not there. I think now that we will rest, and rest the dogs. But we do not rest, not for one day do we rest. 'Come,' says the woman to the man, 'let us go on.' And we go on. We leave the Yukon. We cross the divide to the west and swing down into the Tanana Country. There are new diggings there. But that for which they look is not there, and we take the back trail to Circle City.

"It is a hard journey. December is most gone. The days are short. It is very cold. One morning it is seventy below zero. 'Better that we do not travel to-day,' I say, 'else will the frost be unwarmed in the breathing and bite all the edges of our lungs. After that we will have bad cough, and maybe next spring will come pneumonia.' But they are *che-cha-quo*. They do not understand the trail. They are like dead people they are so tired, but they say, 'Let us go on.' We go on. The frost bites their lungs, and they get the dry cough. They cough till the tears run down their cheeks. When bacon is frying they must run away from the fire and cough half an hour in the snow. They freeze their cheeks a little bit, so that the skin turns black and is very sore. Also, the man freezes his thumb till the end is like to come off, and he must wear a large thumb on his mitten to keep it warm. And sometimes, when the frost bites hard and the thumb is very cold, he must take off the mitten and put the hand between his legs next to the skin, so that the thumb may get warm again.

"We limp into Circle City, and even I, Sitka Charley, am tired. It is Christmas Eve. I dance, drink, make a good time, for to-morrow is Christmas Day and we will rest. But no. It is five o'clock in the morning—Christmas morning. I am two hours asleep. The man stand by my bed. 'Come, Charley,' he says, 'harness the dogs. We start.'

"Have I not said that I ask questions no more? They pay me seven hundred and fifty dollars each month. They are my masters. I am their man. If they say, 'Charley, come, let us start for hell,' I will harness the dogs, and snap the whip, and start for hell. So I harness the dogs, and we start down the Yukon. Where do we go? They do not say. Only do they say, 'On! on! We will go on!'

"They are very weary. They have traveled many hundreds of miles, and they do not understand the way of the trail. Besides, their cough is very bad—the dry cough that makes strong men swear and weak men cry. But they go on. Every day they go on. Never do they rest the dogs. Always do they buy new dogs. At every camp, at every post, at every Indian village, do they cut out the tired dogs and put in fresh dogs. They have much money, money without end, and like water they spend it. They are crazy? Sometimes I think so, for there is a devil in them that drives them on and on, always on. What is it that they try to find? It is not gold. Never do they dig in the ground. I think a long time. Then I think it is a man they try to find. But what man? Never do we see the man. Yet are they like wolves on the trail of the kill. But they are funny wolves, soft wolves, baby wolves who do not understand the way of the trail. They cry aloud in their sleep at night. In their sleep they moan and groan with the pain of their weariness. And in the day, as they stagger along the trail, they cry under their breaths. They are funny wolves.

"We pass Fort Yukon. We pass Fort Hamilton. We pass Minook. January has come and nearly gone. The days are very short. At nine o'clock comes daylight. At three o'clock comes night. And it is cold. And even I, Sitka Charley, am tired. Will we go on forever this way without end? I do not know. But always do I look along the trail for that which they try to find. There are few people on the trail. Sometimes we travel one hundred miles and never see a sign of life. It is very quiet. There is no sound. Sometimes it snows, and we are like wandering ghosts. Sometimes it is clear, and at midday the sun looks at us for a moment over the hills to the south. The northern lights flame in the sky, and the sun-dogs dance, and the air is filled with frost-dust.

"I am Sitka Charley, a strong man. I was born on the trail, and all my days have I lived on the trail. And yet have these two baby wolves made me very tired. I am lean, like a starved cat, and I am glad of my bed at night, and in the morning and I greatly weary. Yet ever are we hitting the trail in the dark before daylight, and still on the trail does the dark after nightfall find us. These two baby wolves! If I am lean like a starved cat, they are lean like cats that have never eaten and have died. Their eyes are sunk deep in their heads, bright sometimes as with fever, dim and cloudy sometimes like the eyes of the dead. Their cheeks are hollow like caves in a cliff. Also are their cheeks black and raw from many freezings. Sometimes it is the woman in the morning who says, 'I cannot get up. I cannot move. Let me die.' And it is the man who stands beside her and says, 'Come, let us go on.' And they go on. And sometimes it is the man who cannot get up, and the woman says, 'Come, let us go on.' But the one thing they do, and always do, is to go on. Always do they go on.

"Sometimes, at the trading posts, the man and woman get letters. I do not know what is in the letters. But it is the scent that they follow, these letters themselves are the scent. One time an Indian gives them a letter. I talk with him privately. He says it is a man with one eye who gives him the letter, a man who travels fast down the Yukon. That is all. But I know that the baby wolves are after the man with the one eye.

"It is February, and we have traveled fifteen hundred miles. We are getting near Bering Sea, and there are storms and blizzards. The going is hard. We come to Anvig. I do not know, but I think sure they get a letter at Anvig, for they are much excited, and they say, 'Come, hurry, let us go on.' But I say we must buy grub, and they say we must travel light and fast. Also, they say that we can get grub at Charley McKeon's cabin. Then do I know that they take the big cut-off, for it is there that Charley McKeon lives where the Black Rock stands by the trail.

"Before we start, I talk maybe two minutes with the priest at Anvig. Yes, there is a man with one eye who has gone by and who travels fast." And I know that for which they look is the man with the one eye. We leave Anvig with little grub, and travel light and fast. There are three fresh dogs bought in Anvig, and we travel very fast. The man and woman are like mad. We start earlier in the morning, we travel later at night. I look sometimes to see them die. They go on and on. When the dry cough take hold of them hard, they hold their hands against their stomach and double up in the snow, and cough, and cough, and cough. They cannot walk, they cannot talk. Maybe for ten minutes they cough, maybe for half an hour, and they they straighten up, the tears from the coughing frozen on their faces, and the words they say are, 'Come, let us go on.'

"Even I, Sitka Charley, am greatly weary, and I think seven hundred fifty dollars is a cheap price for the labor I do. We take the big cut-off, and the trail is fresh. The baby wolves have their noses down to the trail, and they say, 'Hurry!' All the time do they say, 'Hurry! Faster! Faster!' It is hard on the dogs. We have not much food and we cannot give them enough to eat, and they grow weak. Also, they must work hard. The woman has true sorrow for them, and often, because of them, the tears are in her eyes. But the devil in her that drives her on will not let her stop and rest the dogs.

"And then we come upon the man with the one eye. He is in the snow by the trail, and his leg is broken. Because of the leg he has made a poor camp, and has been lying on his blankets for three days and keeping a fire going. When we find him he is swearing. He swears like hell. Never have I heard a man swear like that man. I am glad. Now that they have found that for which they look, we will have rest. But the woman says, 'Let us start. Hurry!'

"I am surprised. But the man with the one eye says, 'Never mind me. Give me your grub. You will get more grub at McKeon's cabin to-morrow. Send McKeon back for me. But do you go on.' Here is another wolf, an old wolf, and he, too, thinks but the one thought, to go on. So we give him our grub, which is not much, and we chop wood for his fire, and we take his strongest dogs and go on. We left the man with one eye there in the snow, and he died there in the snow, for McKeon never went back for him. And who that man was, and why he came to be there, I do not know. But I think he was greatly paid by the man and the woman, like me, to do their work for them.

"That day and that night we had nothing to eat, and all next day we traveled fast, and we were weak with hunger. Then we came to the Black Rock, which rose five hundred feet above the trail. It was at the end of the day. Darkness was coming, and we could not find the cabin of McKeon. We slept hungry, and in the morning looked for the cabin. It was not there, which was a strange thing, for everybody knew that McKeon lived in a cabin at Black Rock. We were near to the coast, where the wind blows hard and there is much snow. Everywhere there were small hills of snow where the wind had piled it up. I have a thought, and I dig in one and another of the hills of snow. Soon I find the walls of the cabin, and I dig down to the door. I go inside. McKeon is dead. Maybe two or three weeks he is dead. A sickness had come upon him so that he could not leave the cabin. The wind and the snow had covered the cabin. He had eaten his grub and died. I looked for his cache, but there was no grub in it.

"'Let us go on,' said the woman. Her eyes were hungry, and her hand was upon her heart, as with the hurt of something inside. She bent back and forth like a tree in the wind as she stood there. 'Yes, let us go on,' said the man. His voice was hollow, like the *klonk* of an old raven, and he was hunger-mad. His eyes were like live coals of fire, and as his body rocked to and fro, so rocked his soul inside. And I, too, said, 'Let us go on.' For that one thought, laid upon me like a lash for every mile of fifteen hundred miles, had burned itself into my soul, and I think that I, too, was mad. Besides, we could only go on, for there was no grub. And we went on, giving no thought to the man with the one eye in the snow.

"There is little travel on the big cut-off. Sometimes two or three months and nobody goes by. The snow had covered the trail, and there was no sign that men had ever come or gone that way. All day the wind blew and the snow fell, and all day we traveled, while our stomachs gnawed their desire and our bodies grew weaker with every stop they took. Then the woman began to fall. Then the man. I did not fall, but my feet were heavy and I caught my toes and stumbled many times.

"That night is the end of February. I kill three ptarmigan with the woman's revolver, and we are made somewhat strong again. But the dogs have nothing to eat. They try to eat their harness, which is of leather and walrus-hide, and I must fight them off with a club and hang all the harness in a tree. And all night they howl and fight around that tree. But we do not mind. We sleep like dead people, and in the morning get up like dead people out of their graves and go on along the trail.

"That morning is the first of March, and on that morning I see the first sign of that after which the baby wolves are in search. It is clear weather, and cold. The sun stay longer in the sky, and there are sun-dogs flashing on either side, and the air is bright with frost-dust. The snow falls no more upon the trail, and I see the fresh sign of dogs and sled. There is one man with that outfit, and I see in the snow that he is not strong. He, too, has not enough to eat. The young wolves see the fresh sign, too, and they are much excited. 'Hurry!' they say. All the time they say, 'Hurry! Faster, Charley, faster!'

"We make hurry very slow. All the time the man and the woman fall down. When they try to ride on sled the dogs are too weak, and the dogs fall down. Besides, it is so cold that if they ride on the sled they will freeze. It is very easy for a hungry man to freeze. When the woman fall down, the man help her up. Sometimes the woman help the man up. By and by both fall down and cannot get up, and I must help them up all the time, else they will not get up and will die there in the snow. This is very hard work, for I am greatly weary, and as well I must drive the dogs, and the man and woman are very heavy with no strength in their bodies. So, by and by, I, too, fall down in the snow, and there is no one to help me up. I must get up by myself. And always do I get up by myself, and help them up, and make the dogs go on.

"That night I get one ptarmigan, and we are very hungry. And that night the man says to me, 'What time start to-morrow, Charley?' It is like the voice of a ghost. I say, 'All the time you make start at five o'clock.' 'To-morrow,' he says, 'we will start at three o'clock.' I laugh in great bitterness, and I say, 'You are dead man.' And he says, 'To-morrow we will start at three o'clock.'

"And we start at three o'clock, for I am their man, and that which they say is to be done, I do. It is clear and cold, and there is no wind. When daylight comes we can see a long way off. And it is very quiet. We can hear no sound but the beat of our hearts, and in the silence that is a very loud sound. We are like sleep-walkers, and we walk in dreams until we fall down; and then we know we must get up, and we see the trail once more and hear the beating of our hearts. Sometimes, when I am walking in dreams this way, I have strange thoughts. Why does Sitka Charley live? I ask myself. Why does Sitka Charley work hard, and go hungry, and have all this pain? For seven hundred and fifty dollars a month, I make the answer, and I know it is a foolish answer. Also is it a true answer. And after that never again do I care for money. For that day a large wisdom came to me. There was a great light, and I saw clear, and I knew that it was not for money that a man must live, but for a happiness that no man can give, or buy, or sell, and that is beyond all value of all money in the world.

"In the morning we come upon the last-night camp of the man who is before us. It is a poor camp, the kind a man makes who is hungry and without strength. On the snow there are pieces of blanket and of canvas, and I know what has happened. His dogs have eaten their harness, and he has made new harness out of his blankets. The man and woman stare hard at what is to be seen, and as I look at them my back feels the chill as of a cold wind against the skin. Their eyes are toil-mad and hunger-mad, and burn like fire deep in their heads. Their faces are like the faces of people who have died of hunger, and their cheeks are black with the dead flesh of many freezings. 'Let us go on,' says the man. But the woman coughs and falls in the snow. It is the dry cough where the frost has bitten the lungs. For a long time she coughs, then like a woman crawling out of her grave she crawls to her feet. The tears are ice upon her cheeks, and her breath makes a noise as it comes and goes, and she says, 'Let us go on.'

"We go on. And we walk in dreams through the silence. And every time we walk is a dream and we are without pain; and every time we fall down is an awakening, and we see the snow and the mountains and the fresh trail of the man who is before us, and we know all our pain again. We come to where we can see a long way over the snow, and that for which they look is before them. A mile away there are black spots upon the snow. The black spots move. My eyes are dim, and I must stiffen my soul to see. And I see one man with dogs and a sled. The baby wolves see, too. They can no longer talk, but they whisper, 'On, on. Let us hurry!'

"And they fall down, but they go on. The man who is before us, his blanket harness breaks often, and he must stop and mend it. Our harness is good, for I have hung it in trees each night. At eleven o'clock the man is half a mile away. At one o'clock he is a quarter of a mile away. He is very weak. We see him fall down many times in the snow. One of his dogs can no longer travel, and he cuts it out of the harness. But he does not kill it. I kill it with the axe as I go by, as I kill one of my dogs which loses its legs and can travel no more.

"Now we are three hundred yards away. We go very slow. Maybe in two, three hours we go one mile. We do not walk. All the time we fall down. We stand up and stagger two steps, maybe three steps, then we fall down again. And all the time I must help up the man and woman. Sometimes they rise to their knees and fall forward, maybe four or five times before they can get to their feet again and stagger two or three steps and fall. But always do they fall forward. Standing or kneeling, always do they fall forward, gaining on the trail each time by the length of their bodies.

"Sometimes they crawl on hands and knees like animals that live in the forest. We go like snails, like snails that are dying we go slow. And yet we go faster than the man who is before us. For he, too, falls all the time, and there is no Sitka Charley to lift him up. Now he is two hundred yards away. After a long time he is one hundred yards away.

"It is a funny sight. I want to laugh out loud, ha! ha! just like that, it is so funny. It is a race of dead men and dead dogs. It is like in a dream when you have a nightmare and run away very fast for your life and go very slow. The man who is with me is mad. The woman is mad. I am mad. All the world is mad, and I want to laugh, it is so funny.

"The stranger-man who is before us leaves his dogs behind and goes on alone across the snow. After a long time we come to the dogs. They lie helpless in the snow, their harness of blanket and canvas on them, the sled behind them, and as we pass them they whine to us and cry like babies that are hungry.

"Then we, too, leave our dogs and go on alone across the snow. The man and the woman are nearly gone, and they moan and groan and sob, but they go on. I, too, go on. I have but one thought. It is to come up to the stranger-man. Then it is that I shall rest, and not until then shall I rest, and it seems that I must lie down and sleep for a thousand years, I am so tired.

"The stranger-man is fifty yards away, all alone in the white snow. He falls and crawls, staggers, and falls and crawls again. He is like an animal that is sore wounded and trying to run from the hunter. By and by he crawls on hands and knees. He no longer stands up. And the man and woman no longer stand up. They, too, crawl after him on hands and knees. But I stand up. Sometimes I fall, but always do I stand up again.

"It is a strange thing to see. All about is the snow and the silence, and through it crawl the man and the woman, and the stranger-man who goes before. On either side the sun are sun-dogs, so that there are three suns in the sky. The frost-dust is like the dust of diamonds, and all the air is filled with it. Now the woman coughs, and lies still in the snow until the fit has passed, when she crawls on again. Now the man looks ahead, and he is blear-eyed as with old age and must rub his eyes so that he can see the stranger-man. And now the stranger-man looks back over his shoulder. And Sitka Charley, standing upright, maybe falls down and stands upright again.

"After a long time the stranger-man crawls no more. He stands slowly upon his feet and rocks back and forth. Also does he take off one mitten and wait with revolver in his hand, rocking back and forth as he waits. His face is skin and bones and frozen black. It is a hungry face. The eyes are deep-sunk in his head, and the lips are snarling. The man and woman, too, get upon their feet and they go toward him very slowly. And all about is the snow and the silence. And in the sky are three suns, and all the air is flashing with the dust of diamonds.

"And thus it was that I, Sitka Charley, saw the baby wolves make their kill. No word is spoken. Only does the stranger-man snarl with his hungry face. Also does he rock to and fro, his shoulders drooping, his knees bent, and his legs wide apart so that he does not fall down. The man and the woman stop maybe fifty feet away. Their legs, too, are wide apart so that they do not fall down, and their bodies rock to and fro. The stranger-man is very weak. His arm shakes, so that when he shoots at the man his bullet strikes in the snow. The man cannot take off his mitten. The stranger-man shoots at him again, and this time the bullet goes by in the air. Then the man takes the mitten in his teeth and pulls it off. But his hand is frozen and he cannot hold the revolver, and it falls in the snow. I look at the woman. Her mitten is off, and the big Colt's revolver is in her hand. Three times she shoot, quick, just like that. The hungry face of the stranger-man is still snarling as he falls forward into the snow.

"They do not look at the dead man. 'Let us go on,' they say. And we go on. But now that they have found that for which they look, they are like dead. The last strength has gone out of them. They can stand no more upon their feet. They will not crawl, but desire only to close their eyes and sleep. I see not far away a place for camp. I kick them. I have my dog-whip, and I give them the lash of it. They cry aloud, but they must crawl. And they do crawl to the place for camp. I build fire so that they will not freeze. Then I go back for sled. Also, I kill the dogs of the stranger-man so that we may have food and not die. I put the man and woman in blankets and they sleep. Sometimes I wake them and give them little bit of food. They are not awake, but they take the food. The woman sleep one day and a half. Then she wake up and go to sleep again. The man sleep two days and wake up and go to sleep again. After that we go down to the coast at St. Michaels. And when the ice goes out of Bering Sea, the man and woman go away on a steamship. But first they pay me my seven hundred and fifty dollars a month. Also, they make me a present of one thousand dollars. And that was the year that Sitka Charley gave much money to the Mission at Holy Cross."

"But why did they kill the man?" I asked.

Sitka Charley delayed reply until he had lighted his pipe. He glanced at the *Police Gazette* illustration and nodded his head at it familiarly. Then he said, speaking slowly and ponderingly:

"I have thought much. I do not know. It is something that happened. It is a picture I remember. It is like looking in at the window and seeing the man writing a letter. They came into my life and they went out of my life, and the picture is as I have said, without beginning, the end without understanding."

"You have painted many pictures in the telling," I said.

"Ay," he nodded his head. "But they were without beginning and without end."

"The last picture of all had an end," I said.

"Ay," he answered. "But what end?"

"It was a piece of life," I said.

"Ay," he answered. "It was a piece of life."

The White Silence

"CARMEN WON'T LAST more than a couple of days." Mason spat out a chunk of ice and surveyed the poor animal ruefully, then put her foot in his mouth and proceeded to bite out the ice which clustered cruelly between the toes.

"I never saw a dog with a highfalutin' name that ever was worth a rap," he said, as he concluded his task and shoved her aside. "They just fade away and die under the responsibility. Did ye ever see one go wrong with a sensible name like Cassiar, Siwash, or Husky? No, sir! Take a look at Shookum here, he's—"

Snap! The lean brute flashed up, the white teeth just missing Mason's throat.

"Ye will, will ye?" A shrewd clout behind the ear with the butt of the dog whip stretched the animal in the snow, quivering softly, a yellow slaver dripping from its fangs.

"As I was saying, just look at Shookum here—he's got the spirit. Bet ye he eats Carmen before the week's out."

"I'll bank another proposition against that," replied Malemute Kid, reversing the frozen bread placed before the fire to thaw. "We'll eat Shookum before the trip is over. What d'ye say, Ruth?"

The Indian woman settled the coffee with a piece of ice, glanced from Malemute Kid to her husband, then at the dogs, but vouchsafed no reply. It was such a palpable truism that none was necessary. Two hundred miles of unbroken trail in prospect, with a scant six days' grub for themselves and none for the dogs, could admit no other alternative. The two men and the woman grouped about the fire and began their meager meal. The dogs lay in their harnesses, for it was a midday halt, and watched each mouthful enviously.

"No more lunches after today," said Malemute Kid. "And we've got to keep a close eye on the dogs—they're getting vicious. They'd just as soon pull a fellow down as not, if they get a chance."

"And I was president of an Epworth once, and taught in the Sunday school." Having irrelevantly delivered himself of this, Mason fell into a dreamy contemplation of his steaming moccasins, but was aroused by Ruth filling his cup. "Thank God, we've got slathers of tea! I've seen it growing, down in Tennessee. What wouldn't I give for a hot corn pone just now! Never mind, Ruth; you won't starve much longer, nor wear moccasins either."

The woman threw off her gloom at this, and in her eyes welled up a great love for her white lord—the first white man she had ever seen—the first man whom she had known to treat a woman as something better than a mere animal or beast of burden.

"Yes, Ruth," continued her husband, having recourse to the macaronic jargon in which it was alone possible for them to understand each other; "wait till we clean up and pull for the Outside. We'll take the White Man's canoe and go to the Salt Water. Yes, bad water, rough water—great mountains dance up and down all the time. And so big, so far, so far away—you travel ten sleep, twenty sleep, forty sleep"—he graphically enumerated the days on his fingers—"all the time water, bad water. Then you come to great village, plenty people, just the same mosquitoes next summer. Wigwams oh, so high—ten, twenty pines. *Hiyu skookum!*"

He paused impotently, cast an appealing glance at Malemute Kid, then laboriously placed the twenty pines, end on end, by sign language. Malemute Kid smiled with cheery cynicism; but Ruth's eyes were wide with wonder, and with pleasure; for she half believed he was joking, and such condescension pleased her poor woman's heart.

"And then you step into a—a box, and pouf! up you go." He tossed his empty cup in the air by way of illustration and, as he deftly caught it, cried: "And biff! down you come. Oh, great medicine men! You go Fort Yukon, I go Arctic City—twenty-five sleep—big string, all the time—I catch him string—I say, 'Hello, Ruth! How are ye?'—and you say, 'Is that my good husband?'—and I say, 'Yes'—and you say, 'No can bake good bread, no more soda'—then I say, 'Look in cache, under flour; good-by.' You look and catch plenty soda. All the time you Fort Yukon, me Arctic City. *Hi-yu* medicine man!"

Ruth smiled so ingenuously at the fairy story that both men burst into laughter. A row among the dogs cut short the wonders of the Outside, and by the time the snarling combatants were separated, she had lashed the sleds and all was ready for the trail.

"MUSH! BALDY! Hi! Mush on!" Mason worked his whip smartly and, as the dogs whined low in the traces, broke out the sled with the gee pole. Ruth followed with the second team, leaving Malemute Kid, who had helped her start, to bring up the rear. Strong man, brute that he was, capable of felling an ox at a blow, he could not bear to beat the poor animals, but humored them as a dog driver rarely does—nay, almost wept with them in their misery.

"Come, mush on there, you poor sore-footed brutes!" he murmured, after several ineffectual attempts to start the load. But his patience was at last rewarded, and though whimpering with pain, they hastened to join their fellows.

No more conversation; the toil of the trail will not permit such extravagance. And of all deadening labors, that of the Northland trail is the worst. Happy is the man who can weather a day's travel at the price of silence, and that on a beaten track.

And of all heartbreaking labors, that of breaking trail is the worst. At every step the great webbed shoe sinks till the snow is level with the knee. Then up, straight up, the deviation of a fraction of an inch being a certain precursor of disaster, the snowshoe must be lifted till the surface is cleared; then forward, down, and the other foot is raised perpendicularly for the matter of half a yard. He who tries this for the first time, if haply he avoids bringing his shoes in dangerous propinquity and measures not his length on the treacherous footing, will give up exhausted at the end of a hundred yards; he who can keep out of the way of the dogs for a whole day may well crawl into his sleeping bag with a clear conscience and a pride which passeth all understanding; and he who travels twenty sleeps on the Long Trail is a man whom the gods may envy.

The afternoon wore on, and with the awe, born of the White Silence, the voiceless travelers bent to their work. Nature has many tricks wherewith she convinces man of his finity—the ceaseless flow of the tides, the fury of the storm, the shock of the earthquake, the long roll of heaven's artillery—but the most tremendous, the most stupefying of all, is the passive phase of the White Silence. All movement ceases, the sky clears, the heavens are as brass; the slightest whisper seems sacrilege, and man becomes timid, affrighted at the sound of his own voice. Sole speck of life journeying across the ghostly wastes of a dead world, he trembles at his audacity, realizes that his is a maggot's life, nothing more. Strange thoughts arise unsummoned, and the mystery of all things strives for utterance. And the fear of death, of God, of the universe, comes over him—the hope of the Resurrection and the Life, the yearning for immortality, the vain striving of the imprisoned essence—it is then, if ever, man walks alone with God.

So wore the day away. The river took a great bend, and Mason headed his team for the cutoff across the narrow neck of land. But the dogs balked at the high bank. Again and again, though Ruth and Malemute Kid were shoving on the sled, they slipped back. Then came the concerted effort. The miserable creatures, weak from hunger, exerted their last strength. Up—up—the sled poised on the top of the bank; but the leader swung the string of dogs behind him to the right, fouling Mason's snowshoes. The result was grievous. Mason was whipped off his feet; one of the dogs fell in the traces; and the sled toppled back, dragging everything to the bottom again.

Slash! the whip fell among the dogs savagely, especially upon the one which had fallen.

"Don't, Mason," entreated Malemute Kid; "the poor devil's on its last legs. Wait and we'll put my team on."

Mason deliberately withheld the whip till the last word had fallen, then out flashed the long lash, completely curling about the offending creature's body. Carmen—for it was Carmen—cowered in the snow, cried piteously, then rolled over on her side.

It was a tragic moment, a pitiful incident of the trail—a dying dog, two comrades in anger. Ruth glanced solicitously from man to man. But Malemute Kid restrained himself, though there was a world of reproach in his eyes, and, bending over the dog, cut the traces. No word was spoken. The teams were double-spanned and the difficulty overcome; the sleds were under way again, the dying dog dragging herself along in the rear. As long as an animal can travel, it is not shot, and this last chance is accorded it—the crawling into camp, if it can, in the hope of a moose being killed.

Already penitent for his angry action, but too stubborn to make amends, Mason toiled on at the head of the cavalcade, little dreaming that danger hovered in the air. The timber clustered thick in the sheltered bottom, and through this they threaded their way. Fifty feet or more from the trail towered a lofty pine. For generations it stood there, and for generations destiny had had this one end in view—perhaps the same had been decreed of Mason.

He stooped to fasten the loosened thong of his moccasin. The sleds came to a halt, and the dogs lay down in the snow without a whimper. The stillness was weird; not a breath rustled the frost-encrusted forest; the cold and silence of outer space had chilled the heart and smote the trembling lips of nature. A sigh pulsed through the air—they did not seem to actually hear it, but rather felt it, like the premonition of movement in a motionless void. Then the great tree, burdened with its weight of years and snow, played its last part in the tragedy of life. He heard the warning crash and attempted to spring up but, almost erect, caught the blow squarely on the shoulder.

The sudden danger, the quick death—how often had Malemute Kid faced it! The pine needles were still quivering as he gave his commands and sprang into action. Nor did the Indian girl faint or raise her voice in idle wailing, as might many of her white sisters. At his order, she threw her weight on the end of a quickly extemporized handspike, easing the pressure and listening to her husband's groans, while Malemute Kid attacked the tree with his axe. The steel rang merrily as it bit into the frozen trunk, each stroke being accompanied by a forced, audible respiration, the "Huh!" "Huh!" of the woodsman.

At last the Kid laid the pitiable thing that was once a man in the snow. But worse than his comrade's pain was the dumb anguish in the woman's face, the blended look of hopeful, hopeless query. Little was said; those of the Northland are early taught the futility of words and the inestimable value of deeds. With the temperature at sixty-five below zero, a man cannot lie many minutes in the snow and live. So the sled lashings were cut, and the sufferer, rolled in furs, laid on a couch of boughs. Before him roared a fire, built of the very wood which wrought the mishap. Behind and partially over him was stretched the primitive fly—a piece of canvas, which caught the radiating heat and threw it back and down upon him—a trick which men may know who study physics at the fount.

And men who have shared their bed with death know when the call is sounded. Mason was terribly crushed. The most cursory examination revealed it. His right arm, leg, and back were broken; his limbs were paralyzed from the hips; and the likelihood of internal injuries was large. An occasional moan was his only sign of life.

No hope; nothing to be done. The pitiless night crept slowly by—Ruth's portion, the despairing stoicism of her race, and Malemute Kid adding new lines to his face of bronze. In fact, Mason suffered least of all, for he spent his time in eastern Tennessee, in the Great Smoky Mountains, living over the scenes of his childhood. And most pathetic was the melody of his long-forgotten Southern vernacular, as he raved of swimming holes and coon hunts and watermelon raids. It was as Greek to Ruth, but the Kid understood and felt—felt as only one can feel who has been shut out for years from all that civilization means.

Morning brought consciousness to the stricken man, and Malemute Kid bent closer to catch his whispers.

"You remember when we foregathered on the Tanana, four years come next ice run? I didn't care so much for her then. It was more like she was pretty, and there was a smack of excitement about it, I think. But d'ye know, I've come to think a heap of her. She's been a good wife to me, always at my shoulder in the pinch. And when it comes to trading, you know there isn't her equal. D'ye recollect the time she shot the Moosehorn Rapids to pull you and me off that rock, the bullets whipping the water like hailstones?—and the time of the famine at Nuklukyeto?—or when she raced the ice run to bring the news? Yes, she's been a good wife to me, Well, I tried it once, down in the States. That's why I'm here. Been raised together, too. I came away to give her a chance for divorce. She got it.

"But that's got nothing to do with Ruth. I had thought of cleaning up and pulling for the Outside next year—her and I—but it's too late. Don't send her back to her people, Kid. It's beastly hard for a woman to go back. Think of it!—nearly four years on our bacon and beans and flour and dried fruit, and then to go back to her fish and caribou. It's not good for her to have tried our ways, to come to know they're better'n her people's, and then return to them. Take care of her, Kid—why don't you—but no, you always fought shy of them—and you never told me why you came to this country. Be kind to her, and send her back to the States as soon as you can. But fix it so she can come back—liable to get homesick, you know.

"And the youngster—it's drawn us closer, Kid. I only hope it is a boy. Think of it!—flesh of my flesh, Kid. He mustn't stop in this country. And if it's a girl, why, she can't. Sell my furs; they'll fetch at least five thousand, and I've got as much more with the company. And handle my interests with yours. I think that bench claim will show up. See that he gets good schooling; and, Kid, above all, don't let him come back. This country was not made for white men.

"I'm a gone man, Kid. Three or four sleeps at the best. You've got to go on. You must go on! Remember, it's my wife, it's my boy—O God! I hope it's a boy! You can't stay by me—and I charge you, a dying man, to pull on."

"Give me three days," pleaded Malemute Kid. "You may change for the better; something may turn up."

"No."

"Just three days."

"You must pull on."

"Two days."

"It's my wife and my boy, Kid. You would not ask it."

"One day."

"No, no! I charge—"

"Only one day. We can shave it through on the grub, and I might knock over a moose."

"No—all right; one day, but not a minute more. And, Kid, don't—don't leave me to face it alone. Just a shot, one pull on the trigger. You understand. Think of it! Think of it! Flesh of my flesh, and I'll never live to see him!

"Send Ruth here. I want to say good-by and tell her that she must think of the boy and not wait till I'm dead. She might refuse to go with you if I didn't. Good-by, old man; good-by.

"Kid! I say—a—sink a hole above the pup, next to the slide. I panned out forty cents on my shovel there.

"And, Kid!" He stooped lower to catch the last faint words, the dying man's surrender of his pride. "I'm sorry—for—you know—Carmen."

Leaving the girl crying softly over her man, Malemute Kid slipped into his parka and snowshoes, tucked his rifle under his arm, and crept away into the forest. He was no tyro in the stern sorrows of the Northland, but never had he faced so stiff a problem as this. In the abstract, it was a plain, mathematical proposition—three possible lives as against one doomed one. But now he hesitated. For five years, shoulder to shoulder, on the rivers and trails, in the camps and mines, facing death by field and flood and famine, had they knitted the bonds of their comradeship. So close was the tie that he had often been conscious of a vague jealousy of Ruth, from the first time she had come between. And now it must be severed by his own hand.

Though he prayed for a moose, just one moose, all game seemed to have deserted the land, and nightfall found the exhausted man crawling into camp, lighthanded, heavyhearted. An uproar from the dogs and shrill cries from Ruth hastened him.

Bursting into the camp, he saw the girl in the midst of the snarling pack, laying about her with an axe. The dogs had broken the iron rule of their masters and were rushing the grub. He joined the issue with his rifle reversed, and the hoary game of natural selection was played out with all the ruthlessness of its primeval environment. Rifle and axe went up and down, hit or missed with monotonous regularity; lithe bodies flashed, with wild eyes and dripping fangs; and man and beast fought for supremacy to the bitterest conclusion. Then the beaten brutes crept to the edge of the firelight, licking their wounds, voicing their misery to the stars.

The whole stock of dried salmon had been devoured, and perhaps five pounds of flour remained to tide them over two hundred miles of wilderness. Ruth returned to her husband, while Malemute Kid cut up the warm body of one of the dogs, the skull of which had been crushed by the axe. Every portion was carefully put away, save the hide and offal, which were cast to his fellows of the moment before.

MORNING BROUGHT fresh trouble. The animals were turning on each other. Carmen, who still clung to her slender thread of life, was downed by the pack. The lash fell among them unheeded. They cringed and cried under the blows, but refused to scatter till the last wretched bit had disappeared—bones, hide, hair, everything.

Malemute Kid went about his work, listening to Mason, who was back in Tennessee, delivering tangled discourses and wild exhortations to his brethren of other days.

Taking advantage of neighboring pines, he worked rapidly, and Ruth watched him make a cache similar to those sometimes used by hunters to preserve their meat from the wolverines and dogs. One after the other, he bent the tops of two small pines toward each other and nearly to the ground, making them fast with thongs of moosehide. Then he beat the dogs into submission and harnessed them to two of the sleds, loading the same with everything but the furs which enveloped Mason. These he wrapped and lashed tightly about him, fastening either end of the robes to the bent pines. A single stroke of his hunting knife would release them and send the body high in the air.

Ruth had received her husband's last wishes and made no struggle. Poor girl, she had learned the lesson of obedience well. From a child, she had bowed, and seen all women bow, to the lords of creation, and it did not seem in the nature of things for woman to resist. The Kid permitted her one outburst of grief, as she kissed her husband—her own people had no such custom—

then led her to the foremost sled and helped her into her snowshoes. Blindly, instinctively, she took the gee pole and whip, and "mushed" the dogs out on the trail. Then he returned to Mason, who had fallen into a coma, and long after she was out of sight crouched by the fire, waiting, hoping, praying for his comrade to die.

It is not pleasant to be alone with painful thoughts in the White Silence. The silence of gloom is merciful, shrouding one as with protection and breathing a thousand intangible sympathies; but the bright White Silence, clear and cold, under steely skies, is pitiless.

An hour passed—two hours—but the man would not die. At high noon the sun, without raising its rim above the southern horizon, threw a suggestion of fire athwart the heavens, then quickly drew it back. Malemute Kid roused and dragged himself to his comrade's side. He cast one glance about him. The White Silence seemed to sneer, and a great fear came upon him. There was a sharp report; Mason swung into his aerial sepulcher, and Malemute Kid lashed the dogs into a wild gallop as he fled across the snow.

II.

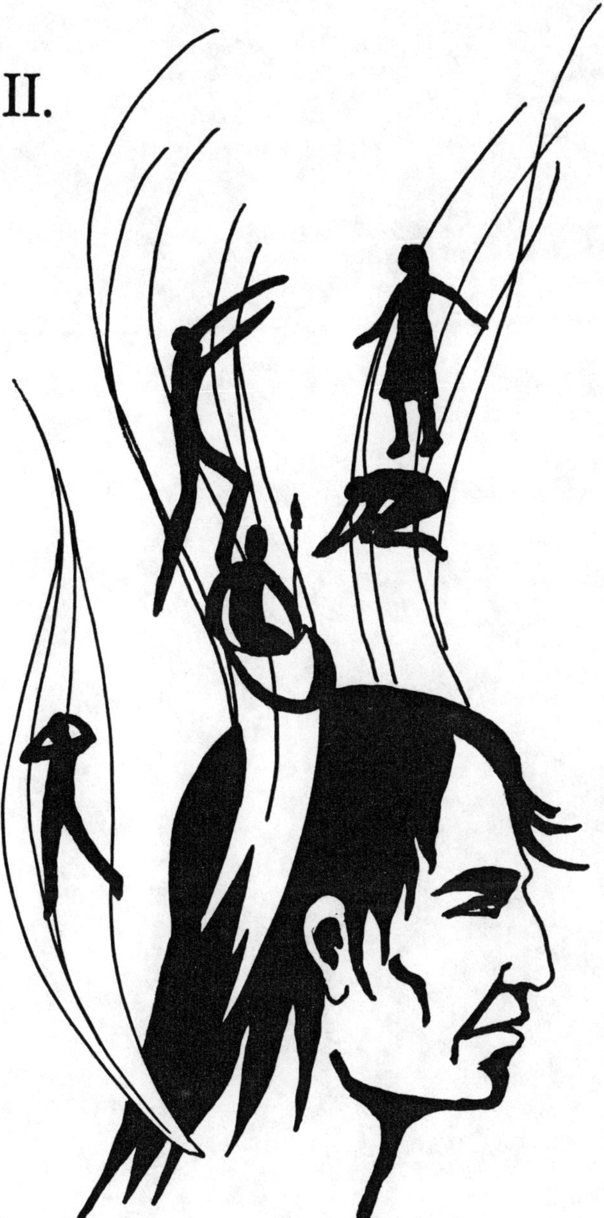

Tales of Indian Life

The Law of Life

OLD KOSKOOSH listened greedily. Though his sight had long since faded, his hearing was still acute, and the slightest sound penetrated to the glimmering intelligence which yet abode behind the withered forehead, but which no longer gazed forth upon the things of the world. Ah! That was Sit-cum-to-ha shrilly anathematizing the dogs as she cuffed and beat them into the harnesses. Sit-cum-to-ha was his daughter's daughter, but she was too busy to waste a thought upon her broken grandfather, sitting alone there in the snow, forlorn and helpless. Camp must be broken. The long trail waited while the short day refused to linger. Life called her, and the duties of life, not death. And he was very close to death now.

The thought made the old man panicky for the moment, and he stretched forth a palsied hand which wandered tremblingly over the small heap of dry wood beside him. Reassured that it was indeed there, his hand returned to the shelter of his mangy furs, and he again fell to listening. The sulky crackling of half-frozen hides to that the chief's moose-skin lodge had been struck, and even then was being rammed and jammed into portable compass. The chief was his son, stalwart and strong, headman of the tribesmen, and a mighty hunter. As the women toiled with the camp luggage, his voice rose, chiding them for their slowness. Old Koskoosh strained his ears. It was the last time he would hear that voice. There went Geehow's lodge! And Tusken's! Seven, eight, nine; only the shaman's could still be standing. There! They were at work upon it now. He could hear the shaman grunt as he piled it on the sled. A child whimpered, and a woman soothed it with soft, crooning gutturals. Little Koo-tec, the old man thought, a fretful child, and not overstrong. It would die soon, perhaps, and they would burn a hole through the frozen tundra and pile rocks above to keep the wolverines away. Well, what did it matter? A few years at best, and as many an empty belly as a full one. And in the end, Death waited, ever-hungry and hungriest of them all.

What was that? Oh, the men lashing the sleds and drawing tight the thongs. He listened, who would listen no more. The whiplashes snarled and bit among the dogs. Hear them whine! How they hated the work and the trail! They were off! Sled after sled churned slowly away into the silence. They were gone. They had passed out of his life, and he faced the last bitter hour alone. No. The snow crunched beneath a moccasin; a man stood beside him; upon his head a hand rested gently. His son was good to do this thing. He remembered other old men whose sons had not waited after the tribe. But his son had. He wandered away into the past, till the young man's voice brought him back.

"It is well with you?" he asked.

And the old man answered, "It is well."

"There be wood beside you," the younger man continued, "and the fire burns bright. The morning is gray, and the cold has broken. It will snow presently. Even now it is snowing."

"Aye, even now it is snowing."

"The tribesmen hurry. Their bales are heavy and their bellies flat with lack of feasting. The trail is long and they travel fast. I go now. It is well?"

"It is well. I am as a last year's leaf, clinging lightly to the stem. The first breath that blows, and I fall. My voice is become like an old woman's. My eyes no longer show me the way of my feet, and my feet are heavy, and I am tired. It is well."

He bowed his head in content till the last noise of the complaining snow had died away, and he knew his son was beyond recall. Then his hand crept out in haste to the wood. It alone stood between him and the eternity that yawned in upon him. At last the measure of his life was a handful of faggots. One by one they would go to feed the fire, and just so, step by step, death would creep upon him. When the last stick had surrendered up its heat, the frost would begin to gather strength. First his feet would yield, then his hands; and the numbness would travel, slowly, from the extremities to the body. His head would fall forward upon his knees, and he would rest. It was easy. All men must die.

He did not complain. It was the way of life, and it was just. He had been born close to the earth, close to the earth he had lived, and the law thereof was not new to him. It was the law of all flesh. Nature was not kindly to the flesh. She had no concern for that concrete thing called the individual. Her interest lay in the species, the race. This was the deepest abstraction old Koskoosh's barbaric mind was capable of, but he grasped it firmly. He saw it exemplified in all life. The rise of the sap, the bursting greenness of the willow bud, the fall of the yellow leaf—in this alone was told the whole history. But one task did Nature set the individual. Did he not perform it, he died. Did he perform it, it was all the same, he died. Nature did not care; there were plenty who were obedient, and it was only the obedience in this matter, not the obedient, which lived and lived always. The tribe of Koskoosh was very old. The old men he had known when a boy had known old men before them. Therefore it was true that the tribe lived, that it stood for the obedience of all its members, way down into the forgotten past, whose very resting places were unremembered. They did not count; they were episodes. They had passed away like clouds from a summer sky. He also was an episode and would pass away. Nature did not care. To life she set one task, gave one law. To perpetuate was the task of life, its law was death. A maiden was a good creature to look upon, full-breasted and strong, with spring to her step and light in her eyes. But her task was yet before her. The light in her eyes brightened, her step quickened, she was now bold with the young men, now timid, and she gave them of her own unrest. And ever she grew fairer and yet fairer to look upon, till some hunter, able no longer to withhold himself, took her to his lodge to cook and toil for him and to become the mother of his children. And with the coming of her offspring her looks left her. Her limbs dragged and shuffled, her eyes dimmed and bleared, and only the little children found joy against the withered cheek of the old squaw by the fire. Her task was done. But a little while, on the first pinch of famine or the first long trail, and she would be left, even as he had been left, in the snow, with a little pile of wood. Such was the law.

He placed a stick carefully upon the fire and resumed his meditations. It was the same everywhere, with all things. The mosquitoes vanished with the first frost. The little tree squirrel crawled away to die. When age settled upon the rabbit it became slow and heavy and could no longer outfoot its enemies. Even the big bald-face grew clumsy and blind and quarrelsome, in the end to be dragged down by a handful of yelping huskies. He remembered how he had abandoned his own father on an upper reach of the Klondike one winter, the winter before the missionary came with his talk books and his box of medicines. Many a time had Koskoosh smacked his lips over the recollection of that box, though now his mouth refused to moisten. The "painkiller" had been especially good. But the missionary was a bother after all, for he brought no meat into the camp, and he ate heartily, and the hunters grumbled. But he chilled his lungs on the divide by the Mayo, and the dogs afterward nosed the stones away and fought over his bones.

Koskoosh placed another stick on the fire and harked back deeper into the past. There was the time of the great famine, when the old men crouched empty-bellied to the fire and let fall from their lips dim traditions of the ancient day when the Yukon ran wide open for three winters, and then lay frozen for three summers. He had lost his mother in that famine. In the summer the salmon run had failed, and the tribe looked forward to the winter and the coming of the caribou. Then the winter came, but with it there were no caribou. Never had the like been known, not even in the lives of the old men. But the caribou did not come, and it was the seventh year, and the rabbits had not replenished, and the dogs were naught but bundles of bones. And through the long darkness the children wailed and died, and the women, and the old men; and not one in ten of the tribe lived to meet the sun when it came back in the spring. That *was* a famine!

But he had seen times of plenty, too, when the meat spoiled on their hands, and the dogs were fat and worthless with over-eating—times when they let the game go unkilled, and the women were fertile, and the lodges were cluttered with sprawling men-children and women-children. Then it was the men became high-stomached, and revived ancient quarrels, and crossed the divides to the south to kill the Pellys, and to the west that they might sit by the dead fires of the Tananas. He remembered, when a boy, during a time of plenty, when he saw a moose pulled down by the wolves. Zing-ha lay with him in the snow and watched—Zing-ha, who later became the craftiest of hunters, and who, in the end, fell through an air hole in the Yukon. They found him, a month afterward, just as he had crawled halfway out and frozen stiff to the ice.

But the moose. Zing-ha and he had gone out that day to play at hunting after the manner of their fathers. On the bed of the creek they struck the fresh track of a moose, and with it the tracks of many wolves. "An old one," Zing-ha, who was quicker at reading the sign, said, "an old one who cannot keep up with the herd. The wolves have cut him from his brothers, and they will never leave him." And it was so. It was their way. By day and night, never resting, snarling on his heels, snapping at his nose, they would stay by him to the end. How Zing-ha and he felt the blood lust quicken! The finish would be a sight to see!

Eager-footed, they took the trail, and even he, Koskoosh, slow of sight and an unversed tracker, could have followed it blind, it was so wide. Hot were they on the heels of the chase, reading the grim tragedy, fresh-written, at every step. Now they came to where the moose had made a stand. Thrice the length of a grown man's body, in every direction, had the snow been stamped about and uptossed. In the midst were the deep impressions of the splay-hoofed game, and all about, everywhere, were the lighter footmarks of the wolves. Some, while their brothers harried the kill, had lain to one side and rested. The full-stretched impress of their bodies in the snow was as perfect as though made the moment before. One wolf had been caught in a wild lunge of the maddened victim and trampled to death. A few bones, well picked, bore witness.

Again, they ceased the uplift of their snowshoes at a second stand. Here the great animal had fought desperately. Twice had he been dragged down, as the snow attested, and twice had he shaken his assailants clear and gained footing once more. He had done his task long since, but nonetheless was life dear to him. Zing-ha said it was a strange thing, a moose once down to get free again; but this one certainly had. The shaman would see signs and wonders in this when they told him.

And yet again, they came to where the moose had made to mount the bank and gain the timber. But his foes had laid on from behind, till he reared and fell back upon them, crushing two deep into the snow. It was plain the kill was at hand, for their brothers had left them untouched. Two more stands were hurried past, brief in time length and very close together. The trail was red now, and the clean stride of the great beast had grown short and slovenly. Then they heard the first sounds of the battle—not the full-throated chorus of the chase, but the short, snappy bark which spoke of close quarters and teeth to flesh. Crawling up the wind, Zing-ha bellied it through the snow, and with him crept he, Koskoosh, who was to be chief of the tribesmen in the years to come. Together they shoved aside the underbranches of a young spruce and peered forth. It was the end they saw.

The picture, like all of youth's impressions, was still strong with him, and his dim eyes watched the end played out as vividly as in that far-off time. Koskoosh marveled at this, for in the days which followed, when he was a leader of men and a head of councilors, he had done great deeds and made his name a curse in the mouths of the Pellys, to say naught of the strange white man he had killed, knife to knife, in open fight.

For long he pondered on the days of his youth, till the fire died down and the frost bit deeper. He replenished it with two sticks this time, and gauged his grip on life by what remained. If Sit-cum-to-ha had only remembered her grandfather, and gathered a larger armful, his hours would have been longer. It would have been easy. But she was ever a careless child, and honored not her ancestors from the time the Beaver, son of the son of Zing-ha, first cast eyes upon her. Well, what mattered it? Had he not done likewise in his own quick youth? For a while he listened to the silence. Perhaps the heart of his son might soften, and he would come back with the dogs to take his old father on with the tribe to where the caribou ran thick and the fat hung heavy upon them.

He strained his ears, his restless brain for the moment stilled. Not a stir, nothing. He alone took breath in the midst of the great silence. It was very lonely. Hark! What was that? A chill passed over his body. The familiar, long-drawn howl broke the void, and it was close at hand. Then on his darkened eyes was projected the vision of the moose—the old bull moose—the torn flanks and bloody sides, the riddled mane, and the great branching horns, down low and tossing to the last. He saw the flashing forms of gray, the gleaming eyes, the lolling tongues, the slavered fangs. And he saw the inexorable circle close in till it became a dark point in the midst of the stamped snow.

A cold muzzle thrust against his cheek, and at its touch his soul leaped back to the present. His hand shot into the fire and dragged out a burning faggot. Overcome for the nonce by his hereditary fear of man, the brute retreated, raising a prolonged call to his brothers; and greedily they answered, till a ring of crouching, jaw-slobbered gray was stretched around about. The old man listened to the drawing in of this circle. He waved his brand wildly, and sniffs turned to snarls; but the panting brutes refused to scatter. Now one wormed his chest forward, dragging his haunches after, now a second, now a third; but never a one drew back. Why should he cling to life? he asked, and dropped the blazing stick into the snow. It sizzled and went out. The circle grunted uneasily but held its own. Again he saw the last stand of the old bull moose, and Koskoosh dropped his head wearily upon his knees. What did it matter after all? Was it not the law of life?

Nam-Bok, The Unveracious

"A BIDARKA, IS IT NOT SO? Look! A bidarka, and one man who drives clumsily with a paddle!"

Old Bask-Wah-Wan rose to her knees, trembling with weakness and eagerness, and gazed out over the sea.

"Nam-Bok was ever clumsy at the paddle," she maundered reminiscently, shading the sun from her eyes and staring across the silver-spilled water. "Nam-Bok was ever clumsy. I remember..."

But the women and children laughed loudly, and there was a gentle mockery in their laughter, and her voice dwindled till her lips moved without sound.

Koogah lifted his grizzled head from his bone-carving and followed the path of her eyes. Except when wide yaws took it off its course, a bidarka was heading in for the beach. Its occupant was paddling with more strength than dexterity, and made his approach along the zigzag line of most resistance. Koogah's head dropped to his work again, and on the ivory dorsal fin of a fish the like of which never swam in the sea.

"It is doubtless the man from the next village," he said finally, "come to consult with me about the marking of things on bone. And the man is a clumsy man. He will never know how."

"It is Nam-Bok," old Bask-Wah-Wan repeated. "Should I not know my son?" she demanded shrilly. "I say, and I say again, it is Nam-Bok."

"And so thou hast said these many summers," one of the women chided softly. "Ever when the ice passed out of the sea hast thou sat and watched through the long day, saying at each chance canoe, 'This is Nam Bok.' Nam-Bok is dead, O Bask-Wah-

Wan, and the dead do not come back. It cannot be that the dead come back."

"Nam-Bok!" the old woman cried, so loud and clear that the whole village was startled and looked at her.

She struggled to her feet and tottered down the sand. She stumbled over a baby lying in the sun, and the mother hushed its crying and hurled harsh words after the old woman, who took no notice. The children ran down the beach in advance of her, and as the man in the bidarka drew closer, nearly capsizing with one of his ill-directed strokes, the women followed. Koogah dropped his walrus tusk and went also, leaning heavily upon his staff, and after him loitered the men in twos and threes.

The bidarka turned broadside and the ripple of surf threatened to swamp it; only a naked boy ran into the water and pulled the bow high up on the sand. The man stood up and sent a questing glance along the line of villagers. A rainbow sweater, dirty and the worse for wear, clung loosely to this broad shoulders, and a red cotton handkerchief was knotted in sailor fashion about his throat. A fisherman's tam-o'-shanter on his close-clipped head, and dungaree trousers and heavy brogans, completed his outfit.

But he was nonetheless a striking personage to these simple fisherfolk of the great Yukon Delta, who, all their lives, had stared out on Bering Sea and in that time seen but two white men—the census enumerator and a lost Jesuit priest. They were a poor people, with neither gold in the ground nor valuable furs in hand, so the whites had passed from afar. Also, the Yukon, through the thousands of years, had shoaled that portion of the sea with the detritus of Alaska till vessels grounded out of sight of land. So the sodden coast, with its long inside reaches and huge mud-land archipelagoes, was avoided by the ships of men, and the fisherfolk new not that such things were.

Koogah, the Bone-Scratcher, retreated backward in sudden haste, tripping over his staff and falling to the ground. "Nam-

Bok!" he cried, as he scrambled wildly for footing. "Nam-Bok, who was blown off to sea, come back!"

The men and women shrank away, and the children scuttled off between their legs. Only Opee-Kwan was brave, as befitted the head man of the village. He strode forward and gazed long and earnestly at the newcomer.

"It *is* Nam-Bok," he said at last, and at the conviction in his voice the women wailed apprehensively and drew farther away.

The lips of the stranger moved indecisively, and his brown throat writhed and wrestled with unspoken words.

"La la, it is Nam-Bok," Bask-Wah-Wan croaked, peering up into his face. "Ever did I say Nam-Bok would come back."

"Ay, it is Nam-Bok come back." This time it was Nam-Bok himself who spoke, putting a leg over the side of the bidarka and standing with one foot afloat and one ashore. Again his throat writhed and wrestled as he grappled after forgotten words. And when the words came forth they were strange of sound and a spluttering of the lips accompanied the gutturals. "Greeting, O brothers," he said, "brothers of old time before I went away with the off-shore wind."

He stepped out with both feet on the sand, and Opee-Kwan waved him back.

"Thou art dead, Nam-Bok," he said.

Nam-Bok laughed. "I am fat."

"Dead men are not fat," Opee-Kwan confessed. "Thou hast fared well, but it is strange. No man may mate with the off-shore wind and come back on the heels of the years."

"I have come back," Nam-Bok answered simply.

"Mayhap thou art a shadow, then, a passing shadow of the Nam-Bok that was. Shadows come back."

"I am hungry. Shadows do not eat."

But Opee-Kwan doubted, and brushed his hand across his brow in sore puzzlement. Nam-Bok was likewise puzzled, and as he looked up and down the line found no welcome in the eyes of the fisherfolk. The men and women whispered together. The children stole timidly back among their elders, and bristling dogs fawned up to him and sniffed suspiciously.

"I bore thee, Nam-Bok, and I gave thee suck when thou wast little," Bask-Wah-Wan whimpered, drawing closer; "and shadow though thou be, or no shadow, I will give thee to eat now."

Nam-Bok made to come to her, but a growl of fear and menace warned him back. He said something in a strange tongue which sounded like "Goddamn," and added, "No shadow am I, but a man."

"Who may know concerning the things of mystery?" Opee-Kwan demanded, half of himself and half of his tribespeople. "We are, and in a breath we are not. If the man may become shadow, may not the shadow become man? Nam-Bok was, but is not. This we know, but we do not know if this be Nam-Bok or the shadow of Nam-Bok."

Nam-Bok cleared his throat and made answer. "In the old time long ago, thy father's father, Opee-Kwan, went away and came back on the heels of the years. Nor was a place by the fire denied him. It is said..." He paused significantly, and they hung on his utterance. "It is said," he repeated, driving his point home with deliberation, "that Sipsip, his *klooch*, bore him two sons after he came back."

"But he had no doings with the off-shore wind," Opee-Kwan retorted. "He went away into the heart of the land, and it is in the nature of things that a man may go on and on into the land."

"And likewise the sea. But that is neither here nor there. It is said...that thy father's father told strange tales of the things he saw."

"Ay, strange tales he told."

"I, too, have strange tales to tell," Nam-Bok stated insidiously. And, as they wavered, "And presents likewise."

He pulled from the bidarka a shawl, marvellous of texture and color, and flung it about his mother's shoulders. The women voiced a collective sigh of admiration, and old Bask-Wah-Wan ruffled the gay material and patted it and crooned in childish joy.

"He has tales to tell," Koogah muttered. "And presents," a woman seconded.

And Opee-Kwan knew that his people were eager, and further, he was aware himself of an itching curiosity concerning those untold tales. "The fishing has been good," he said judiciously, "and we have oil in plenty. So come, Nam-Bok, let us feast."

Two of the men hoisted the bidarka on their shoulders and carried it up to the fire. Nam-Bok walked by the side of Opee-Kwan, and the villagers followed after, save those of the women who lingered a moment to lay caressing fingers on the shawl.

There was little talk while the feast went on, though many and curious were the glances stolen at the son of Bask-Wah-Wan. This embarrassed him—not because he was modest of spirit, however, but for the fact that the stench of the seal-oil had robbed him of his appetite, and that he keenly desired to conceal his feelings on the subject.

"Eat; thou art hungry," Opee-Kwan commanded, and Nam-Bok shut both his eyes and shoved his fist into the big pot of putrid fish.

"La la, be not ashamed. The seal were many this year, and strong men are ever hungry." And Bask-Wah-Wan sopped a particularly offensive chunk of salmon into the oil and passed it fondly and dripping to her son.

In despair, when premonitory symptoms warned him that his stomach was not so strong as of old, he filled his pipe and struck up a smoke. The people fed on noisily and watched. Few of them could boast of intimate acquaintance with the precious weed, though now and again small quantities and abominable qualities were obtained in trade from the Eskimos to the northward. Koogah, sitting next to him, indicated that he was not averse to taking a draw, and between two mouthfuls, with the oil thick on his lips, sucked away at the amber stem. And thereupon Nam-

Bok held his stomach with a shaky hand and declined the proffered return. Koogah could keep the pipe, he said, for he had intended so to honor him from the first. And the people licked their fingers and approved of his liberality.

Opee-Kwan rose to his feet. "And now, O Nam-Bok, the feast is ended, and we would listen concerning the strange things you have seen."

The fisherfolk applauded with their hands, and gathering about them their work, prepared to listen. The men were busy fashioning spears and carving on ivory, while the women scraped the fat from the hides of the hair seal and made them pliable or sewed *muclucs* with threads of sinew. Nam-Bok's eyes roved over the scene, but there was not the charm about it that his recollection had warranted him to expect. During the years of his wandering he had looked forward to just this scene, and now that it had come he was disappointed. It was a bare and meagre life, he deemed, and not to be compared to the one to which he had become used. Still, he would open their eyes a bit, and his own eyes sparkled at the thought.

"Brothers," he began, with the smug complacency of a man about to relate the big things he has done, "it was late summer of many summers back, with much such weather as this promises to be, when I went away. You all remember the day, when the gulls flew low, and the wind blew strong from the land, and I could not hold my bidarka against it. I tied the covering of the bidarka about me so that no water could get in, and all of the night I fought with the storm. And in the morning there was no land—only the sea—and the off-shore wind held me close in its arms and bore me along. Three such nights whitened into dawn and showed me no land, and the off-shore wind would not let me go.

"And when the fourth day came, I was as a madman. I could not dip my paddle for want of food; and my head went round and round, what of the thirst that was upon me. But the sea was no longer angry, and the soft south wind was blowing, and as I looked about me I saw a sight that made me think I was indeed mad."

Nam-Bok paused to pick away a sliver of salmon lodged between his teeth, and the men and women, with idle hands and heads craned forward, waited.

"It was a canoe, a big canoe. If all the canoes I have ever seen were made into one canoe, it would not be so large."

There were exclamations of doubt, and Koogah, whose years were many, shook his head.

"If each bidarka were as a grain of sand," Nam-Bok defiantly continued, "and if there were as many bidarkas as there be grains of sand in this beach, still would they not make so big a canoe as this I saw on the morning of the fourth day. It was a very big canoe, and it was called a *schooner.* I saw this thing of wonder, this great schooner, coming after me, and on it I saw men—"

"Hold, O Nam-Bok!" Opee-Kwan broke in. "What manner of men were they?—big men?"

"Nay, mere men like you and me."

"Did the big canoe come fast?"

"Ay."

"The sides were tall, the men short." Opee-Kwan stated the premises with conviction. "And did these men dip with long paddles?"

Nam-Bok grinned. "There were no paddles," he said.

Mouths remained open, and a long silence dropped down. Opee-Kwan borrowed Koogah's pipe for a couple of contemplative sucks. One of the younger women giggled nervously and drew upon herself angry eyes.

"There were no paddles?" Opee-Kwan asked softly, returning the pipe.

"The south wind was behind," Nam-Bok explained.

"But the wind-drift is slow."

"The schooner had wings—thus." He sketched a diagram of masts and sails in the sand, and the men crowded around and studied it. The wind was blowing briskly, and for more graphic elucidation he seized the corners of his mother's shawl and spread them out till it bellied like a sail. Bask-Wah-Wan scolded and struggled, but was blown down the beach for a score of feet and left breathless and stranded in a heap of driftwood. The men uttered sage grunts of comprehension, but Koogah suddenly tossed back his hoary head.

"Ho! Ho!" he laughed. "A foolish thing, this big canoe! A most foolish thing! The plaything of the wind! Wheresoever the wind goes, it goes too. No man who journeys therein may name the landing beach, for always he goes with the wind, and the wind goes everywhere, but no man knows where."

"It is so," Opee-Kwan supplemented gravely. "With the wind the going is easy, but against the wind a man striveth hard; and for that they had no paddles these men on the big canoe did not strive at all."

"Small need to strive," Nam-Bok cried angrily. "The schooner went likewise against the wind."

"And what said you made the sch—sch—schooner go?" Koogah asked, tripping craftily over the strange word.

"The wind," was the impatient response.

"Then the wind made the sch—sch—schooner go against the wind." Old Koogah dropped an open leer to Opee-Kwan, and, the laughter growing around him, continued: "The wind blows from the south and blows the schooner south. The wind blows against the wind. The wind blows one way and the other at the same time. It is very simple. We understand, Nam-Bok. We clearly understand."

"Thou art a fool!"

"Truth falls from thy lips," Koogah answered meekly. "I was over-long in understanding, and the thing was simple."

But Nam-Bok's face was dark, and he said rapid words which they had never heard before. Bone-scratching and skin-scraping were resumed, but he shut his lips tightly on the tongue that could not be believed.

"This sch—sch—schooner," Koogah imperturbably asked; "it was made of a big tree?"

"It was made of many trees," Nam-Bok snapped shortly. "It was very big."

He lapsed into sullen silence again, and Opee-Kwan nudged Koogah, who shook his head with slow amazement and murmured, "It is very strange."

Nam-Bok took the bait. "That is nothing," he said airily; "you should see the *steamer*. As the grain of sand is to the bidarka, as the bidarka is to the schooner, so the schooner is to the steamer. Further, the steamer is made of iron. It is all iron."

"Nay, nay, Nam-Bok," cried the head man; "how can that be? Always iron goes to the bottom. For behold, I received an iron knife in trade from the head man of the next village, and yesterday the iron knife slipped from my fingers and went down, down, into the sea. To all things there be law. Never was there one thing outside the law. This we know. And, moreover, we know that things of a kind have the one law, and that all iron has the one law. So unsay thy words, Nam-Bok, that we may yet honor thee."

"It is so," Nam-Bok persisted. "The steamer is all iron and does not sink."

"Nay, nay; this cannot be."

"With my own eyes I saw it."

"It is not in the nature of things."

"But tell me, Nam-Bok," Koogah interrupted, for fear the tale would go no farther, "tell me the manner of these men in finding their way across the sea when there is no land by which to steer."

"The sun points out the path."

"But how?"

"At midday the head man of the schooner takes a thing through which his eye looks at the sun, and then he makes the sun climb down out of the sky to the edge of the earth."

"Now this be evil medicine!" cried Opee-Kwan, aghast at the

sacrilege. The men held up their hands in horror, and the women moaned. "This be evil medicine. It is not good to misdirect the great sun which drives away the night and gives us the seal, the salmon, and warm weather."

"What if it be evil medicine?" Nam-Bok demanded truculently. "I, too, have looked through the thing at the sun and made the sun climb down out of the sky."

Those who were nearest drew away from him hurriedly, and a woman covered the face of a child at her breast so that his eye might not fall upon it.

"But on the morning of the fourth day, O Nam-Bok," Koogah suggested; "On the morning of the fourth day when the sch—sch—schooner came after thee?"

"I had little strength left in me and could not run away. So I was taken on board and water was poured down my throat and good food given me. Twice, my brothers, you have seen a white man. These men were all white and as many as have I fingers and toes. And when I saw they were full of kindness, I took heart, and I resolved to bring away with me report of all that I saw. And they taught me the work they did, and gave me good food and a place to sleep.

"And day after day we went over the sea, and each day the head man drew the sun down out of the sky and made it tell where we were. And when the waves were kind, we hunted the fur seal and I marvelled much, for always did they fling the meat and the fat away and save only the skin."

Opee-Kwan's mouth was twitching violently, and he was about to make denunciation of such waste when Koogah kicked him to be still.

"After a weary time, when the sun was gone and the bite of the frost come into the air, the head man pointed the nose of the schooner south. South and east we traveled for days upon days, with never the land in sight, and we were near to the village from which hailed the men—"

"How did they know they were near?" Opee-Kwan, unable to contain himself longer, demanded. "There was no land to see."

Nam-Bok glowered on him wrathfully. "Did I not say the head man brought the sun down out of the sky?"

Koogah interposed, and Nam-Bok went on.

"As I say, when we were near to that village a great storm blew up, and in the night we were helpless and knew not where we were—"

"Thou hast just said the head man knew—"

"Oh, peace, Opee-Kwan! Thou art a fool and cannot understand. As I say, we were helpless in the night, when I heard, above the roar of the storm, the sound of the sea on the beach. And next we struck with a mighty crash and I was in the water, swimming. It was a rock-bound coast, with one patch of beach in many miles, and the law was that I should dig my hands into the sand and draw myself clear of the surf. The other men must have pounded against the rocks, for none of them came ashore but the head man, and him I knew only by the ring on his finger.

"When day came, there being nothing of the schooner, I turned my face to the land and journeyed into it that I might get food and look upon the faces of the people. And when I came to a house I was taken in and given to eat, for I had learned their speech, and the white men are ever kindly. And it was a house bigger than all the houses built by us and our fathers before us."

"It was a mighty house," Koogah said, masking his unbelief with wonder.

"And many trees went into the making of such a house," Opee-Kwan added, taking the cue.

"That is nothing," Nam-Bok shrugged his shoulders in belittling fashion. "As our houses are to that house, so that house was to the houses I was yet to see."

"And they are not big men?"

"Nay; mere men like you and me," Nam-Bok answered. "I had cut a stick that I might walk in comfort, and remembering that I was to bring report to you, my brothers, I cut a notch in the stick for each person who lived in that house. And I stayed there many days, and worked, for which they gave me *money*—a thing of which you know nothing, but which is very good.

"And one day I departed from that place to go farther into the land. And as I walked I met many people, and I cut smaller notches in the stick, that there might be room for all. Then I came upon a strange thing. On the ground before me was a bar of iron, as big in thickness as my arm, and a long step away was another bar of iron—"

"Then wert thou a rich man," Opee-Kwan asserted; "for iron be worth more than anything else in the world. It would have made many knives."

"Nay, it was not mine."

"It was a find, and a find be lawful."

"Not so; the white men had placed it there. And further, these bars were so long that no man could carry them away—so long that as far as I could see there was no end to them."

"Nam-Bok, that is very much iron. Opee-Kwan cautioned.

"Ay, it was hard to believe with my own eyes upon it; but I could not gainsay my eyes. And as I looked I heard. . ." He turned abruptly upon the head man. "Opee-Kwan, thou hast heard the sea-lion bellow in his anger. Make it plain in thy mind of as many sea-lions as they be waves to the sea, and make it plain that all these sea-lions be made into one sea-lion, and as that one sea-lion would bellow so bellowed the thing I heard."

The fisherfolk cried aloud in astonishment, and Opee-Kwan's jaw lowered and remained lowered.

"And in the distance I saw a monster like unto a thousand whales. It was one-eyed, and vomited smoke, and it snorted with exceeding loudness. I was afraid and ran with shaking legs along the path between the bars. But it came with the speed of the wind, this monster, and I leaped the iron bars with its breath hot on my face. . ."

Opee-Kwan gained control of his jaw again. "And—and then, O Nam-Bok?"

"Then it came by on the bars, and harmed me not; and when my legs could hold me up again it was gone from sight. And it is a very common thing in that country. Even the women and children are not afraid. Men make them to do work, these monsters."

"As we make our dogs do work?" Koogah asked, with sceptic twinkle in his eye.

"Ay, as we make our dogs do work."

"And how do they breed these—these things?" Opee-Kwan questioned.

"They breed not at all. Men fashion them cunningly of iron, and feed them with stone, and give them water to drink. The stone becomes fire, and the water becomes steam, and the steam of the water is the breath of their nostrils, and—"

"There, there, O Nam-Bok," Opee-Kwan interrupted. "Tell us of other wonders. We grow tired of this which we may not understand."

"You do not understand?" Nam-Bok asked despairingly.

"Nay, we do not understand," the men and women wailed back. "We cannot understand."

Nam-Bok thought of a combined harvester, and of the machines wherein visions of living men were to be seen, and of the machines from which came the voices of men, and he knew his people could never understand.

"Dare I say I rode this iron monster through the land?" he asked bitterly.

Opee-Kwan threw up his hands, palms outward, in open incredulity. "Say on; say anything. We listen."

"Then did I ride the iron monster, for which I gave money—"

"Thou saidst it was fed with stone."

"And likewise, thou fool, I said money was a thing of which you know nothing. As I say, I rode the monster through the land, and through many villages, until I came to a big village on a salt arm of the sea. And the houses shoved their roofs among the stars in the sky, and the clouds drifted by them, and everywhere was much smoke. And the roar of that village was like the roar of the sea in storm, and the people were so many that I flung away my stick and no longer remembered the notches upon it."

"Hadst thou made small notches," Koogah reproved, "thou mightst have brought report."

Nam-Bok whirled upon him in anger. "Had I made small notches! Listen, Koogah, thou scratcher of bone! If I had made small notches, neither the stick, nor twenty sticks, could have borne them—nay, not all the driftwood of all the beaches between this village and the next. And if all of you, the women and children as well, were twenty times as many, and if you had twenty hands each, and in each hand a stick and a knife, still the notches could not be cut for the people I saw, so many were they and so fast did they come and go."

"There cannot be so many people in all the world," Opee-Kwan objected, for he was stunned and his mind could not grasp such magnitude of numbers.

"What dost thou know of all the world and how large it is?" Nam-Bok demanded.

"But there cannot be so many people in one place."

"Who art thou to say what can be and what cannot be?"

"It stands to reason there cannot be so many people in one place. Their canoes would clutter the sea till there was no room. And they could empty the sea each day of its fish, and they would not all be fed."

"So it would seem," Nam-Bok made final answer; "yet it was so. With my own eyes I saw, and flung my stick away." He yawned heavily and rose to his feet. "I have paddled far. The day has been long, and I am tired. Now I will sleep, and to-morrow we will have further talk upon the things I have seen."

Bask-Wah-Wan, hobbling fearfully in advance, proud indeed,

yet awed by her wonderful son, led him to her igloo and stowed him away among the greasy, ill-smelling furs. But the men lingered by the fire, and a council was held wherein was there much whispering and low-voiced discussion.

An hour passed, and a second, and Nam-Bok slept, and the talk went on. The evening sun dipped toward the northwest, and at eleven at night was nearly due north. Then it was that the head man and the bone-scratcher separated themselves from the council and aroused Nam-Bok. He blinked up into their faces and turned on his side to sleep again. Opee-Kwan gripped him by the arm and kindly but firmly shook his senses back into him.

"Come, Nam-Bok, arise!" he commanded. "It is time."

"Another feast?" Nam-Bok cried. "Nay, I am not hungry. Go on with the eating and let me sleep."

"Time to be gone!" Koogah thundered.

But Opee-Kwan spoke more softly. "Thou wast bidarka-mate with me when we were boys," he said. "Together we first chased the seal and drew the salmon from the traps. And thou didst drag me back to life, Nam-Bok, when the sea closed over me and I was sucked down to the black rocks. Together we hungered and bore the chill of the frost, and together we crawled beneath the one fur and lay close to each other. And because of these things, and the kindness in which I stood to thee, it grieves me sore that thou shouldst return such a remarkable liar. We cannot understand, and our heads be dizzy with the things thou hast spoken. It is not good, and there has been much talk in the council. Wherefore we send thee away, that our heads may remain clear and strong and be not troubled by the unaccountable things."

"These things thou speakest of be shadows," Koogah took up the strain. "From the shadow-world thou hast brought them, and to the shadow-world thou must return them. Thy bidarka be ready, and the tribespeople wait. They may not sleep until thou art gone."

Nam-Bok was perplexed, but hearkened to the voice of the head man.

"If thou art Nam-Bok," Opee-Kwan was saying, "thou art a fearful and most wonderful liar; if thou art the shadow of Nam-Bok, then thou speakest of shadows, concerning which it is not good that living men have knowledge. This great village thou hast spoken of we deem the village of shadows. Therein flutter the souls of the dead; for the dead do not come back. Never have the dead come back—save thou with thy wonder-tales. It is not meet that the dead come back, and should we permit it, great trouble may be our portion."

Nam-Bok knew his people well and was aware that the voice of the council was supreme. So he allowed himself to be led down to the water's edge, where he was put aboard his bidarka and a paddle thrust into his hand. A stray wild-fowl honked somewhere to seaward, and the surf broke limply and hollowly on the sand. A dim twilight brooded over land and water, and in the north the sun smouldered, vague and troubled, and draped about with blood-red mists. The gulls were flying low. The off-shore wind blew keen and chill, and the black-massed clouds behind it gave promise of bitter weather.

"Out of the sea thou camest," Opee-Kwan chanted oracularly, "and back into the sea thou goest. Thus is balance achieved and all things brought to law."

Bask-Wah-Wan limped to the froth-mark and cried, "I bless thee, Nam-Bok, for that thou remembered me."

But Koogah, shoving Nam-Bok clear of the beach, tore the shawl from her shoulders and flung it into the bidarka.

"It is cold in the long nights," she wailed; "and the frost is prone to nip old bones."

"The thing is a shadow," the bone-scratcher answered, "and shadows cannot keep thee warm."

Nam-Bok stood up that his voice might carry. "O Bask-Wah-Wan, mother that bore me!" he called. "Listen to the words of Nam-Bok, thy son. There be room in his bidarka for two, and he would that thou camest with him. For his journey is to where there are fish and oil in plenty. There the frost comes not, and life is easy, and the things of iron do the work of men. Wilt thou come, O Bask-Wah-Wan?"

She debated a moment, while the bidarka drifted swiftly from her, then raised her voice to a quavering treble. "I am old, Nam-Bok, and soon I shall pass down among the shadows. But I have no wish to go before my time. I am old, Nam-Bok, and I am afraid."

A shaft of light shot across the dim-lit sea and wrapped boat and man in a splendor of red and gold. Then a hush fell upon the fisherfolk, and only was heard the moan of the off-shore wind and the cries of the gulls flying low in the air.

Negore, The Coward

HE HAD FOLLOWED the trail of his fleeing people for eleven days, and his pursuit had been in itself a flight; for behind him he knew full well were the dreaded Russians, toiling through the swampy lowlands and over the steep divides, bent on no less than the extermination of all his people. He was traveling light. A rabbit-skin sleeping-robe, a muzzle-loading rifle, and a few pounds of sun-dried salmon constituted his outfit. He would have marveled that a whole people—women and children and aged—could travel so swiftly, had he not known the terror that drove them on.

It was in the old days of the Russian occupancy of Alaska, when the nineteenth century had run but half its course, that Negore fled after his fleeing tribe and came upon it this summer night by the head waters of the Pee-lat. Though near the midnight hour, it was bright day as he passed through the weary camp. Many saw him, all knew him, but few and cold were the greetings he received.

"Negore, the Coward," he heard Illiha, a young woman, laugh, and Sun-ne, his sister's daughter, laughed with her.

Black anger ate at his heart; but he gave no sign, threading his way among the camp-fires until he came to one where sat an old man. A young woman was kneading with skillful fingers the tired muscles of his legs. He raised a sightless face and listened intently as Negore's foot crackled a dead twig.

"Who comes?" he queried in a thin, tremulous voice.

"Negore," said the young woman, scarcely looking up from her task.

Negore's face was expressionless. For many minutes he stood and waited. The old man's head had sunk upon his chest. The young woman pressed and prodded the wasted muscles, resting her body on her knees, her bowed head hidden as in a cloud by her black wealth of hair. Negore watched the supple body, pliant as a young willow stalk, and, withal, strong as only youth is strong. He looked, and was aware of a great yearning, akin in sensation to physical hunger. At last he spoke, saying:

"Is there no greeting for Negore, who has been long gone and has but now come back?"

She looked up at him with cold eyes. The old man chuckled to himself after the manner of the old.

"Thou art my woman, Oona," Negore said, his tones dominant and conveying a hint of menace.

She arose with catlike ease and suddenness to her full height, her eyes flashing, her nostrils quivering like a deer's.

"I was thy woman to be, Negore, but thou art a coward; the daughter of Old Kinoos mates not with a coward!"

She silenced him with an imperious gesture as he strove to speak.

"Old Kinoos and I came among you from a strange land. Thy people took us in by their fires and made us warm, nor asked whence or why we wandered. It was their thought that Old Kinoos had lost the sight of his eyes from age; nor did Old Kinoos say otherwise, nor did I, his daughter. Old Kinoos is a brave man, but Old Kinoos was never a boaster. And now, when I tell thee of how his blindness came to be, thou wilt know, beyond question, that the daughter of Kinoos cannot mother the children of a coward such as thou art, Negore."

Again she silenced the speech that rushed up to his tongue.

"Know, Negore, if journey be added unto journey of all thy journeyings through this land, thou wouldst not come to the unknown Sitka on the Great Salt Sea. In that place there be many Russian folk, and their rule is harsh. And from Sitka, Old Kinoos, who was Young Kinoos in those days, fled away with me, a babe in his arms, along the islands in the midst of the sea. My mother dead tells the tale of his wrong; a Russian, dead with a spear through breast and back, tells the tale of the vengeance of Kinoos.

"But wherever we fled, and however far we fled, always did we find the hated Russian folk. Kinoos was unafraid, but the sight of them was a hurt to his eyes; so we fled on and on, through the seas and years, till we came to the Great Fog Sea, Negore, of which thou hast heard, but which thou hast never seen. We lived among many peoples, and I grew to be a woman; but Kinoos, growing old, took to him no other woman, nor did I take a man.

"At last we came to Pastolik, which is where the Yukon drowns itself in the Great Fog Sea. Here we lived long, on the rim of the sea, among a people by whom the Russians were well hated. But sometimes they came, these Russians, in great ships, and made the people of Pastolik show them the way through the islands uncountable of the many-mouthed Yukon. And sometimes the men they took to show them the way never came back, till the people became angry and planned a great plan.

"So, when there came a ship, Old Kinoos stepped forward and said he would show the way. He was an old man then, and his hair was white; but he was unafraid. And he was cunning, for he took the ship to where the sea sucks in to the land and the waves beat white on the mountain called Romanoff. The sea sucked the ship in to where the waves beat white, and it ground upon the rocks and broke open its sides. Then came all the people of Pastolik, (for this was the plan), with their warspears, and arrows, and some few guns. But first the Russians put out the eyes of Old Kinoos that he might never show the way again, and then they fought, where the waves beat white, with the people of Pastolik.

"Now the head-man of these Russians was Ivan. He it was, with his two thumbs, who drove out the eyes of Kinoos. He it was who fought his way through the white water, with two men left of all his men, and went away along the rim of the Great Fog Sea into the north. Kinoos was wise. He could see no more and was helpless as a child. So he fled away from the sea, up the great, strange Yukon, even to Nulato, and I fled with him.

"With my own eyes I saw, at Nulato, before the gates of the great fort, and but few days gone. I saw the Russian, Ivan, who thrust out my father's eyes, lay the lash of his dog-whip upon thee and beat thee like a dog. This I saw, and knew thee for a coward. But I saw thee not, that night, when all thy people—yea, even the boys not yet hunters—fell upon the Russians and slew them all."

"Not Ivan," said Negore, quietly. "Even now is he on our heels, and with him many Russians fresh up from the sea."

Oona made no effort to hide her surprise and chagrin that Ivan was not dead, but went on:

"In the day I saw thee a coward; in the night, when all men fought, even the boys not yet hunters, I saw thee not and knew thee doubly a coward."

"Thou art done? All done?" Negore asked.

She nodded her head and looked at him askance, as though astonished that he should have aught to say.

"Know then that Negore is no coward," he said; and his speech was very low and quiet. "Know that when I was yet a boy I journeyed alone down to the place where the Yukon drowns itself in the Great Fog Sea. Even to Pastolik I journeyed, and even beyond, into the north, along the rim of the sea. This I did when I was a boy, and I was no coward. Nor was I coward when I journeyed, a young man and alone, up the Yukon farther than man had ever been, so far that I came to another folk, with white faces, who live in a great fort and talk speech other than that the Russians talk. Also have I killed the great bear of the Tanana country, where no one of my people hath ever been. And I have fought with the Nuklukyets, and the Kaltags, and the Sticks in far regions, even I, and alone. These deeds, whereof no man knows, I speak for myself. Let my people speak for me of things I have done which they know. They will not say Negore is a coward."

He finished proudly, and proudly waited.

"These be things which happened before I came into the land," she said, "and I know not of them. Only do I know what I know, and I know I saw thee lashed like a dog in the day; and in the night, when the great fort flamed red and the men killed and were killed, I saw thee not. Also, thy people do call thee Negore, the Coward. It is thy name now, Negore, the Coward."

"It is not a good name," Old Kinoos chuckled.

"Thou dost not understand, Kinoos," Negore said gently. "But I shall make thee understand. Know that I was away on the hunt of the bear, with Kamo-tah, my mother's son. And Kamo-tah fought with a great bear. We had no meat for three days, and Kamo-tah was not strong of arm nor swift of foot. And the great bear crushed him, so, till his bones cracked like dry sticks. Thus I found him, very sick and groaning upon the ground. And there was no meat, nor could I kill aught that the sick man might eat.

"So I said, 'I will go to Nulato and bring thee food, also strong men to carry thee to camp,' And Kamo-tah said, 'Go thou to Nulato and get food, but say no word of what has befallen me. And when I have eaten, and am grown well and strong, I will kill this bear. Then will I return in honor to Nulato, and no man may laugh and say Kamo-tah was undone by a bear.'

"So I gave heed to my brother's words; and when I was come to Nulato, and the Russian, Ivan, laid the lash of his dog-whip upon me, I knew I must not fight. For no man knew of Kamo-tah, sick and groaning and hungry; and did I fight with Ivan, and die, then would my brother die, too. So it was, Oona, that thou sawest me beaten like a dog.

"Then I heard the talk of the shamans and chiefs that the Russians had brought strange sickness upon the people, and killed our men, and stolen our women, and that the land must be made clean. As I say, I heard the talk, and I knew it for good talk, and I knew that in the night the Russians were to be killed. But there was my brother, Kamo-tah, sick and groaning and with no meat; so I could not stay and fight with the men and the boys not yet hunters.

"And I took with me meat and fish, and the lash marks of Ivan, and I found Kamo-tah no longer groaning, but dead. Then I went back to Nulato, and, behold, there was no Nulato—only ashes where the great fort had stood, and the bodies of many men. And I saw the Russians come up the Yukon in boats, fresh from the sea, many Russians; and I saw Ivan creep forth from where he lay hid and make talk with them. And the next day I saw Ivan lead them upon the trail of the tribe. Even now are they upon the trail, and I am here, Negore, but no coward."

"This is a tale I hear," said Oona, though her voice was gentler than before. "Kamo-tah is dead and cannot speak for thee, and I know only what I know, and I must know thee of my own eyes for no coward."

Negore made an impatient gesture.

"There be ways and ways," she added. "Art thou willing to do no less than what Old Kinoos hath done?"

He nodded his head, and waited.

"As thou hast said, they seek for us even now, these Russians. Show them the way, Negore, even as Old Kinoos showed them the way, so that they come, unprepared, to where we wait for them, in a passage up the rocks. Thou knowest the place, where the wall is broken and high. Then will we destroy them, even Ivan. When they cling like flies to the wall, and top is no less near than bottom, our men shall fall upon them from above and either side, with spears, and arrows, and guns. And the women and children, from above, shall loosen the great rocks and hurl them down upon them. It will be a great day, for the Russians will be killed, the land will be made clean, and Ivan, even Ivan who thrust out my father's eyes and laid the lash of his dog-whip upon thee, will be killed. Like a dog gone mad will he die, his breath crushed out of him beneath the rocks. And when the fighting begins, it is for thee, Negore, to crawl secretly away so that thou be not slain."

"Even so," he answered. "Negore will show them the way. And then?"

"And then I shall be thy woman, Negore's woman, the brave man's woman. And thou shalt hunt meat for me and Old Kinoos, and I shall cook thy food, and sew thee warm parkas and strong, and make thee moccasins after the way of my people, which is a better way than thy people's way. And as I say, I shall be thy woman, Negore, always thy woman. And I shall make thy life glad for thee, so that all thy days will be a song and laughter, and thou wilt know the woman Oona as unlike all other women, for she has journeyed far, and lived in strange places, and is wise in the ways of men and in the ways they may be made glad. And in thine old age will she still make thee glad, and thy memory of her in the days of thy strength will be sweet, for thou wilt know always that she was ease to thee, and peace, and rest, and that beyond all women to other men has she been woman to thee."

"Even so," said Negore, and the hunger for her ate at his heart, and his arms went out for her as a hungry man's arms might go out for food.

"When thou hast shown the way, Negore," she chided him; but her eyes were soft and warm, and he knew she looked upon him as woman had never looked before.

"It is well," he said, turning resolutely on his heel. "I go now to make talk with the chiefs, so that they may know I am gone to show the Russians the way."

"Oh, Negore, my man! my man!" she said to herself, as she watched him go, but she said it so softly that even Old Kinoos did not hear, and his ears were over keen, what of his blindness.

THREE DAYS LATER, having with craft ill-concealed his hiding place, Negore was dragged forth like a rat and brought before

Ivan—"Ivan the Terrible" he was known by the men who marched at his back. Negore was armed with a miserable bone-barbed spear, and he kept his rabbit-skin robe wrapped closely about him, and though the day was warm he shivered as with an ague. He shook his head that he did not understand the speech Ivan put at him, and made that he was very weary and sick, and wished only to sit down and rest, pointing the while to his stomach in sign of his sickness, and shivering fiercely. But Ivan had with him a man from Pastolik who talked the speech of Negore, and many and vain were the questions they asked him concerning his tribe, till the man from Pastolik, who was called Karduk, said:

"It is the word of Ivan that thou shalt be lashed till thou diest if thou dost not speak. And know, strange brother, when I tell thee the word of Ivan is the law, that I am thy friend and no friend of Ivan. For I come not willingly from my country by the sea, and I desire greatly to live; wherefore I obey the will of my master—as thou wilt obey, strange brother, if thou art wise, and wouldst live."

"Nay, strange brother," Negore answered, "I know not the way my people are gone, for I was sick, and they fled so fast my legs gave out from under me, and I fell behind."

Negore waited until Karduk talked with Ivan. Then Negore saw the Russian's face go dark, and he saw the men step to either side of him, snapping the lashes of their whips. Whereupon he betrayed a great fright, and cried aloud that he was a sick man and knew nothing, but would tell what he knew. And to such purpose did he tell, that Ivan gave the word to his men to march, and on either side of Negore marched the men with the whips, that he might not run away. And when he made that he was weak of his sickness, and stumbled and walked not so fast as they walked, they laid their lashes upon him till he screamed with pain and discovered new strength. And when Karduk told him all would be well with him when they had overtaken his tribe, he asked, "And then may I rest and move not?"

And while he appeared very sick and looked about him with dull eyes, he noted the fighting strength of Ivan's men, and noted with satisfaction that Ivan did not recognize him as the man he had beaten before the gates of the fort. It was a strange following his dull eyes saw. There were Slavonian hunters, fair-skinned and mighty-muscled; short, squat Finns, with flat noses and round faces; Siberian half-breeds, whose noses were more like eagle-beaks; and lean, slant-eyed men, who bore in their veins the Mongol and Tartar blood as well as the blood of the Slav. Wild adventurers they were, forayers and destroyers from the far lands beyond the Sea of Bering, who blasted the new and unknown world with fire and sword and clutched greedily for its wealth of fur and hide. Negore looked upon them with satisfaction, and in his mind's eye he saw them crushed and lifeless at the passage up the rocks. And ever he saw, waiting for him at the passage up the rocks, the face and the form of Oona, and ever he heard her voice in his ears and felt the soft, warm glow of her eyes. But never did he forget to shiver, nor to stumble where the footing was rough, nor to cry aloud at the bite of the lash. Also, he was afraid of Karduk, for he knew him for no true man. His was a false eye, and an easy tongue—a tongue too easy, he judged, for the awkwardness of honest speech.

All that day they marched. And on the next, when Karduk asked him at command of Ivan, he said he doubted they would meet with his tribe till the morrow. But Ivan, who had once been shown the way by Old Kinoos, and had found that way to lead through the white water and a deadly fight, believed no more in anything. So when they came to a passage up the rocks, he halted his forty men, and through Karduk demanded if the way were clear.

Negore looked at it shortly and carelessly. It was a vast slide that broke the straight wall of a cliff, and was overrun with brush and creeping plants, where a score of tribes could have lain well hidden.

He shook his head. "Nay, there be nothing there," he said. "The way is clear."

Again Ivan spoke to Karduk, and Karduk said:

"Know, strange brother, if thy talk be not straight, and if thy people block the way and fall upon Ivan and his men, that thou shalt die, and at once."

"My talk is straight," Negore said. "The way is clear."

Still Ivan doubted, and ordered two of his Slavonian hunters to go up alone. Two other men he ordered to the side of Negore. They placed their guns against his breast and waited. All waited. And Negore knew, should one arrow fly, or one spear be flung, that his death would come upon him. The two Slavonian hunters toiled upward till they grew small and smaller, and when they reached the top and waved their hats that all was well, they were like black specks against the sky.

The guns were lowered from Negore's breast and Ivan gave the order for his men to go forward. Ivan was silent, lost in thought. For an hour he marched, as though puzzled, and then, through Karduk's mouth, he said to Negore:

"How didst thou know the way was clear when thou didst look so briefly upon it?"

Negore thought of the little birds he had seen perched among the rocks and upon the bushes, and smiled, it was so simple; but he shrugged his shoulders and made no answer. For he was thinking, likewise, of another passage up the rocks, to which they would soon come, and where the little birds would all be gone. And he was glad that Karduk came from the Great Fog Sea, where there were no trees or brushes, and where men learned water-craft instead of land-craft and wood-craft.

Three hours later, when the sun rode overhead, they came to another passage up the rocks, and Karduk said:

"Look with all thine eyes, strange brother, and see if the way be clear, for Ivan is not minded this time to wait while men go up before."

Negore looked, and he looked with two men by his side, their guns resting against his breast. He saw that the little birds were all gone, and once he saw the glint of sunlight on a rifle-barrel. And he thought of Oona, and of her words: "And when the fighting begins, it is for thee, Negore, to crawl secretly away so that thou be not slain."

He felt the two guns pressing on his breast. This was not the way she had planned. There would be no crawling secretly away. He would be the first to die when the fighting began. But he said, and his voice was steady, and he still feigned to see with dull eyes and to shiver from his sickness:

"The way is clear."

And they started up, Ivan and his forty men from the far lands beyond the Sea of Bering. And there was Karduk, the man from Pastolik, and Negore, with the two guns always upon him. It was a long climb, and they could not go fast; but very fast to Negore they seemed to approach the midway point where top was no less near than bottom.

A gun cracked among the rocks to the right, and Negore heard the war-yell of all his tribe, and for an instant saw the rocks and bushes bristle alive with his kinfolk. Then he felt torn asunder by a burst of flame hot through his being, and as he fell he knew the sharp pangs of life as it wrenches at the flesh to be free.

But he gripped his life with a miser's clutch and would not let it go. He still breathed the air, which bit his lungs with a painful sweetness; and dimly he saw and heard, with passing spells of blindness and deafness, the flashes of sight and sound again wherein he saw the hunters of Ivan falling to their deaths, and his own brothers fringing the carnage and filling the air with the tumult of their cries and weapons, and, far above, the women and children loosing the great rocks that leaped like things alive and thundered down.

The sun danced above him in the sky, the huge walls reeled and swung, and still he heard and saw dimly. And when the great Ivan fell across his legs, hurled there lifeless and crushed by a down-rushing rock, he remembered the blind eyes of Old Kinoos and was glad.

Then the sounds died down, and the rocks no longer thundered past, and he saw his tribespeople creeping close and closer, spearing the wounded as they came. And near to him he heard the scuffle of a mighty Slavonian hunter, loathe to die, and, half uprisen, borne back and down by the thirsty spears.

Then he saw above him the face of Oona, and felt about him the arms of Oona; and for a moment the sun steadied and stood still, and the great walls were upright and moved not.

"Thou art a brave man, Negore," he heard her say in his ear; "thou art my man, Negore."

And in that moment he lived all the life of gladness of which she had told him, and the laughter and the song, and as the sun went out of the sky above him, as in his old age, he knew the memory of her was sweet. And as even the memories dimmed and died in the darkness that fell upon him, he knew in her arms the fulfilment of all the ease and rest she had promised him. And as black night wrapped around him, his head upon her breast, he felt a great peace steal about him, and he was aware of the hush of many twilights and the mystery of silence.

The Sickness of Lone Chief

THIS IS A TALE that was told to me by two old men. We sat in the smoke of a mosquito-smudge, in the cool of the day, which was midnight; and ever and anon, throughout the telling, we smote lustily and with purpose at such of the winged pests as braved the smoke for a snack at our hides. To the right, beneath us, twenty feet down the crumbling bank, the Yukon gurgled lazily. To the left, on the rose-leaf rim of the low-lying hills, smouldered the sleepy sun, which saw no sleep that night nor was destined to see sleep for many nights to come.

The old men who sat with me and valorously slew mosquitoes were Lone Chief and Mutsak, erstwhile comrades in arms, and now withered repositories of tradition and ancient happening. They were the last of their generation and without honor among the younger set which had grown up on the farthest fringe of a mining civilization. Who cared for tradition in these days, when spirits could be evoked from black bottles, and black bottles could be evoked from the complaisant white men for a few hours' sweat or a mangy fur? Of what potency the fearful rites and masked mysteries of shamanism, when daily that living wonder, the steamboat, coughed and spluttered up and down the Yukon in defiance of all law, a veritable fire-breathing monster? And of what value was hereditary prestige, when he who now chopped the most wood, or best conned a sternwheeler through the island mazes, attained the chiefest consideration of his fellows?

Of a truth, having lived too long, they had fallen on evil days, these two old men, Lone Chief and Mutsak, and in the new order they were without honor or place. So they waited drearily for death, and the while their hearts warmed to the strange white man who shared with them the torments of the mosquito-smudge and lent ready ear to their tales of old time before the steamboat came.

"So a girl was chosen for me," Lone Chief was saying. His voice, shrill and piping, ever and again dropped plummet-like into a hoarse and rattling bass, and, just as one became accustomed to it, soaring upward into the thin treble—alternate cricket chirpings and bullfrog croakings, as it were.

"So a girl was chosen for me," he was saying. "For my father, who was Kask-ta-ka, the Otter, was angered because I looked not with a needful eye upon women. He was an old man, and chief of his tribe. I was the last of his sons to be alive, and through me, only, could he look to see his blood go down among those to come after and as yet unborn. But know, O White Man, that I was very sick; and when neither the hunting nor the fishing delighted me, and by meat my belly was not made warm, how should I look with favor upon women? or prepare for the feast of marriage? or look forward to the prattle and troubles of little children?"

"Ay," Mutsak interrupted. "For had not Lone Chief fought in the arms of a great bear till his head was cracked and blood ran from out his ears?"

Lone Chief nodded vigorously. "Mutsak speaks true. In the time that followed, my head was well, and it was not well. For though the flesh healed and the sore went away, yet was I sick inside. When I walked, my legs shook under me, and when I looked at the light, my eyes became filled with tears. And when I opened my eyes, the world outside went around and around, and when I closed my eyes, my head inside went around and around, and all the things I had ever seen went around and around inside my head. And above my eyes there was a great pain, as though something heavy rested always upon me, or like a band that is drawn tight and gives much hurt. And speech was slow to me, and I waited long for each right word to come to my tongue. And when I waited not long, all manner of words crowded in, and my tongue spoke foolishness. I was very sick, and when my father, the Otter, brought the girl Kasaan before me—"

"Who was a young girl, and strong, my sister's child," Mutsak broke in. "Strong-hipped for children was Kasaan, and straight-legged and quick of foot. She made better moccasins than any of all the young girls, and the bark-rope she braided was the stoutest. And she had a smile in her eyes, and a laugh on her lips; and her temper was not hasty, nor was she unmindful that men give the law and women ever obey."

"As I say, I was very sick," Lone Chief went on. "And when my father, the Otter, brought the girl Kasaan before me, I said rather should they make me ready for burial than for marriage. Whereat the face of my father went black with anger, and he said that I should be served according to my wish, and that I who was yet alive should be made ready for death as one already dead—"

"Which be not the way of our people, O White Man," spoke up Mutsak. "For know that these things that were done to Lone Chief it was our custom to do only to dead men. But the Otter was very angry."

"Ay," said Lone Chief. "My father, the Otter, was a man short of speech and swift of deed. And he commanded the people to gather before the lodge wherein I lay. And when they were gathered, he commanded them to mourn for his son who was dead—"

"And before the lodge they sang the death-song—O-o-o-o-o-o-a-haa-ha-a-ich-klu-kuk-ich-klu-kuk," wailed Mutsak, in so excellent an imitation that all the tendrils of my spine crawled and curved in sympathy.

"And inside the lodge," continued Lone Chief, "my mother blackened her face with soot, and flung ashes upon her head, and mourned for me as one already dead; for so had my father commanded. So Okiakuta, my mother, mourned with much noise, and beat her breast and tore her hair; and likewise Hooniak, my sister, and Seenatah, my mother's sister; and the noise they made caused a great ache in my head, and I felt that I would surely and immediately die.

"And the elders of the tribe gathered about me where I lay and discussed the journey my soul must take. One spoke of the thick and endless forests where lost souls wandered crying, and where I, too, might chance to wander and never see the end. And another spoke of the big rivers, rapid with bad water, where evil spirits shrieked and lifted up their formless arms to drag one down by the hair. For these rivers, all said together, a canoe must be provided me. And yet another spoke of the storms, such as no live man ever saw, when the stars rained down out of the sky, and the earth gaped wide in many cracks, and all the rivers in the heart of the earth rushed out and in. Whereupon they that sat by me flung up their arms and wailed loudly; and those outside heard, and wailed more loudly. And as to them I was as dead, so was I to my own mind dead. I did not know when, or how, yet did I know that I had surely died.

"And Okiakuta, my mother, laid beside me my squirrel-skin parka. Also she laid beside me my parka of caribou hide, and my rain coat of seal gut, and my wet-weather *muclucs*, that my soul should be warm and dry on its long journey. Further, there was mention made of a steep hill, thick with briars and devil's-club, and she fetched heavy moccasins to make the way easy for my feet.

"And when the elders spoke of the great beasts I should have to slay, the young men laid beside me my strongest bow and straightest arrows, my throwing-stick, my spear and knife. And when the elders spoke of the darkness and silence of the great spaces my soul must wander through, my mother wailed yet more loudly and flung yet more ashes upon her head.

"And the girl, Kasaan, crept in, very timid and quiet, and dropped a little bag upon the things for my journey. And in the little bag, I knew, were the flint and steel and the well-dried tinder for the fires my soul must build. And the blankets were chosen which were to be wrapped around me. Also were the slaves selected that were to be killed that my soul might have company. There were seven of these slaves, for my father was rich and powerful, and it was fit that I, his son, should have proper burial. These slaves we had got in war from the Mukumuks, who live down the Yukon. On the morrow, Skolka, the shaman, would kill them, one by one, so that their souls should go questing with mine through the Unknown. Among other things, they would carry my canoe till we came to the big river, rapid with bad water. And there being no room, and their work being done, they would come no farther, but remain and howl forever in the dark and endless forest.

"And as I looked on my fine warm clothes, and my blankets and weapons of war, and as I thought of the seven slaves to be slain, I felt proud of my burial and knew that I must be the envy of many men. And all the while my father, the Otter, sat silent and black. And all that day and night the people sang my death-song and beat the drums, till it seemed that I had surely died a thousand times.

"But in the morning my father arose and made talk. He had been a fighting man all his days, he said, as the people knew. Also the people knew that it were a greater honor to die fighting in battle than on the soft skins by the fire. And since I was to die anyway, it were well that I should go against the Mukumuks and be slain. Thus would I attain honor and chieftainship in the final abode of the dead, and thus would honor remain to my father, who was the Otter. Wherefore he gave command that a war party be made ready to go down the river. And that when we came upon the Mukumuks I was to go forth alone from my party, giving semblance of battle, and so be slain."

"Nay, but hear, O White Man!" cried Mutsak, unable longer to contain himself. "Skolka, the shaman, whispered long that night in the ear of the Otter, and it was his doing that Lone Chief should be sent forth to die. For the Otter being old, and Lone Chief the last of his sons, Skolka had it in mind to become chief himself over the people. And when the people had made great noise for a day and a night and Lone Chief was yet alive, Skolka was become afraid that he would not die. So it was the counsel of Skolka, with fine words of honor and deeds, that spoke through the mouth of the Otter."

"Ay," replied Lone Chief. "Well did I know it was the doing of Skolka, but I was unmindful, being very sick. I had no heart for anger, nor belly for stout words, and I cared little, one way or the other, only I cared to die and have done with it all. So, O White Man, the war party was made ready. No tried fighters were there, nor elders, crafty and wise—naught but five score of young men who had seen little fighting. And all the village gathered together above the bank of the river to see us depart. And we departed amid great rejoicing and the singing of my praises. Even thou, O White Man, wouldst rejoice at sight of a young man going forth to battle, even though doomed to die.

"So we went forth, the five score young men, and Mutsak came also, for he was likewise young and untried. And by command of my father, the Otter, my canoe was lashed on either side to the canoe of Mutsak and the canoe of Kannakut. Thus was my strength saved me from the work of the paddles, so that, for all of my sickness, I might make a brave show at the end. And thus we went down the river.

"Nor will I weary thee with the tale of the journey, which was not long. And not far above the village of the Mukumuks we came upon two of their fighting men in canoes, that fled at the sight of us. And then, according to the command of my father, my canoe was cast loose and I was left to drift down all alone. Also, according to his command, were the young men to see me die, so that they might return and tell the manner of my death. Upon this, my father, the Otter, and Skolka, the shaman, had been very clear, with stern promises of punishment in case they were not obeyed.

"I dipped my paddle and shouted words of scorn after the fleeing warriors. And the vile things I shouted made them turn their heads in anger, when they beheld that the young men held back, and that I came on alone. Whereupon, when they had made a safe distance, the two warriors drew their canoes somewhat apart and waited side by side for me to come between. And I came between, spear in hand, and singing the war-song of my people. Each flung a spear, but I bent my body, and the spears whistled over me, and I was unhurt. Then, and we were all together, we three, I cast my spear at the one to the right, and it drove into his throat and he pitched backward into the water.

"Great to my surprise thereat, for I had killed a man. I turned to the one on the left and drove strong with my paddle, to meet Death face to face; but the man's second spear, which was his last, but bit into the flesh of my shoulder. Then was I upon him, making no cast, but pressing the point into his breast and working it through him with both my hands. And while I worked, pressing with all my strength, he smote me upon the head, once and twice, with the broad of his paddle.

"Even as the point of the spear sprang out beyond his back, he smote me upon the head. There was a flash, as of bright light, and inside my head I felt something give, with a snap—just like that, with a snap. And the weight that pressed above my eyes so long was lifted, and the band that bound my brows so tight was broken. And a great gladness came upon me, and my heart sang with joy.

"This be death, I thought; wherefore I thought that death was very good. And then I saw the two empty canoes, and I knew that I was not dead, but well again. The blows of the man upon my head had made me well. I knew that I had killed, and the taste of the blood made me fierce, and I drove my paddle into the breast of the Yukon and urged my canoe toward the village of the Mukumuks. The young men behind me gave a great cry. I looked over my shoulder and saw the water foaming white from their paddles—"

"Ay, it foamed white from our paddles," said Mutsak. "For we remembered the command of the Otter, and of Skolka, that we behold with our own eyes the manner of Lone Chief's death. A young man of the Mukumuks, on his way to a salmon trap, beheld the coming of Lone Chief, and of the five score men behind him. And the young man fled in his canoe, straight for the village, that alarm might be given and preparation made. But Lone Chief hurried after him, and we hurried after Lone Chief to behold the manner of his death. Only, in the face of the village, as the young man leaped to the shore, Lone Chief rose up in his canoe and made a mighty cast. And the spear entered the body of the young man above the hips, and the young man fell upon his face.

"Whereupon Lone Chief leaped up the bank war-club in hand and a great war-cry on his lips, and dashed into the village. The first man he met was Itwilie, chief over the Mukumuks, and him Lone Chief smote upon the head with his war-club, so that he fell dead upon the ground. And for fear we might not behold the manner of his death, we too, the five score young men, leaped to the shore and followed Lone Chief into the village. Only the Mukumuks did not understand, and thought we had come to fight; so their bow-thongs sang and their arrows whistled among us. Whereat we forgot our errand, and fell upon them with our spears and clubs; and they being unprepared, there was great slaughter—"

"With my own hands I slew their shaman," proclaimed Lone Chief, his withered face a-work with memory of that old-time day. "With my own hands I slew him, who was a greater shaman than Skolka, our own shaman. And each time I faced a man, I thought, 'Now cometh Death'; and each time I slew the man, and Death came not. It seemed the breath of life was strong in my nostrils and I could not die—"

"And we followed Lone Chief the length of the village and back again," continued Mutsak. "Like a pack of wolves we followed him, back and forth, and here and there, till there were no more

Mukumuks left to fight. Then we gathered together five score men-slaves, and double as many women, and countless children, and we set fire and burned all the houses and lodges, and departed. And that was the last of the Mukumuks."

"And that was the last of the Mukumuks," Lone Chief repeated exultantly. "And when we came to our own village, the people were amazed at our burden of wealth and slaves, and in that I was still alive they were more amazed. And my father, the Otter, came trembling with gladness at the things I had done. For he was an old man, and I the last of his sons. And all the tried fighting men came, and the crafty and wise, till all the people were gathered together. And then I arose, and with a voice like thunder, commanded Skolka, the shaman, to stand forth—"

"Ay, O White Man," exclaimed Mutsak. "With a voice like thunder, that made the people shake at the knees and become afraid."

"And when Skolka had stood forth," Lone Chief went on, "I said that I was not minded to die. Also, I said it were not well that disappointment come to the evil spirits that wait beyond the grave. Wherefore I deemed it fit that the soul of Skolka fare forth into the Unknown, where doubtless it would howl forever in the dark and endless forest. And then I slew him, as he stood there, in the face of all the people. Even I, Lone Chief, with my own hands, slew Skolka, the shaman, in the face of all the people. And when a murmuring arose, I cried aloud—"

"With a voice like thunder," prompted Mutsak.

"Ay, with a voice like thunder I cried aloud; 'Behold, O ye people! I am Lone Chief, slayer of Skolka, the false shaman! Alone among men, have I passed down through the gateway of Death and returned again. Mine eyes have looked upon the unseen things. Mine ears have heard the unspoken words. Greater am I than Skolka, the shaman. Greater than all shamans am I. Likewise am I greater chief than my father, the Otter. All his days did he fight with the Mukumuks, and lo, in one day have I destroyed them all. As with the breathing of a breath have I destroyed them. Wherefore, my father, the Otter, being old, and Skolka, the shaman, being dead, I shall be both chief and shaman. Henceforth shall I be both chief and shaman to you, O my people. And if any man dispute my word, let that man stand forth!"

"I waited, but no man stood forth. Then I cried: 'Hoh! I have tasted blood! Now bring meat, for I am hungry. Break open the caches, tear down the fish-racks, and let the feast be big. Let there be merriment, and songs, not of burial, but marriage. And last of all, let the girl Kasaan be brought. The girl Kasaan, who is to be the mother of the children of Lone Chief!'

"And at my words, and because that he was very old, my father, the Otter, wept like a woman, and put his arms about my knees. And from that day I was both chief and shaman. And great honor was mine, and all men yielded me obedience."

"Until the steamboat came," Mutsak prompted.

"Ay," said Lone Chief. "Until the steamboat came."

III.

Treasurehunters

All Gold Canyon

IT WAS THE GREEN HEART of the canyon, where the walls swerved back from the rigid plan and relieved their harshness of line by making a little sheltered nook and filling it to the brim with sweetness and roundness and softness. Here all things rested. Even the narrow stream ceased its turbulent down-rush long enough to form a quiet pool. Knee-deep in the water, with drooping head and half-shut eyes, drowsed a red-coated, many-antlered buck.

On one side, beginning at the very lip of the pool, was a tiny meadow, a cool, resilient surface of green that extended to the base of the frowning wall. Beyond the pool a gentle slope of earth ran up and up to meet the opposing wall. Fine grass covered the slope—grass that was spangled with flowers, with here and there patches of color, orange and purple and golden. Below, the canyon was shut in. There was no view. The walls leaned together abruptly and the canyon ended in a chaos of rocks, moss-covered and hidden by a green screen of vines and creepers and boughs of trees. Up the canyon rose far hills and peaks, the big foothills, pine-covered and remote. And far beyond, like clouds upon the border of the sky, towered minarets of white, where the Sierra's eternal snows flashed austerely the blazes of the sun.

There was no dust in the canyon. The leaves and flowers were clean and virginal. The grass was young velvet. Over the pool three cottonwoods sent their snowy fluffs fluttering down the quiet air. On the slope the blossoms of the wine-wooded manzanita filled the air with springtime odors, while the leaves, wise with experience, were already beginning their vertical twist against the coming aridity of summer. In the open spaces on the slope, beyond the farthest shadow-reach of the manzanita, poised the mariposa lilies, like so many flights of jeweled moths suddenly arrested and on the verge of trembling into flight again. Here and there, that woods harlequin, the madrone, permitting itself to be caught in the act of changing its pea-green trunk to madder-red, breathed its fragrance into the air from great clusters of waxen bells. Creamy white were these bells, shaped like lilies-of-the-valley, with the sweetness of perfume that is of the springtime.

There was not a sigh of wind. The air was drowsy with its weight of perfume. It was a sweetness that would have been cloying had the air been heavy and humid. But the air was sharp and thin. It was as starlight transmuted into atmosphere, shot through and warmed by sunshine, and flower-drenched with sweetness.

An occasional butterfly drifted in and out through the patches of light and shade. And from all about rose the low and sleepy hum of mountain bees—feasting Sybarites that jostled one another good-naturedly at the board, nor found time for rough discourtesy. So quietly did the little stream drip and ripple its way through the canyon that it spoke only in faint and occasional gurgles. The voice of the stream was as a drowsy whisper, ever interrupted by dozings and silences, ever lifted again in the awakenings.

The motion of all things was a drifting in the heart of the canyon. Sunshine and butterflies drifted in and out among the trees. The hum of the bees and the whisper of the stream were a drifting of sound. and the drifting sound and drifting color seemed to weave together in the making of a delicate and intangible fabric which was the spirit of the place. It was a spirit of peace that was not of death, but of smooth-pulsing life, of quietude that was not silence, of movement that was not action, of repose that was quick with existence without being violent with struggle and travail.

The spirit of the place was the spirit of the peace of the living, somnolent with the easement and content of prosperity, and undisturbed by rumors of far wars.

The red-coated, many-antlered buck acknowledged the lordship of the spirit of the place and dozed knee-deep in the cool, shaded pool. There seemed no flies to vex him and he was languid with rest. Sometimes his ears moved when the stream awoke and whispered; but they moved lazily, with foreknowledge that it was merely the stream grown garrulous at discovery that it had slept.

But there came a time when the buck's ears lifted and tensed with swift eagerness for sound. His head was turned down the canyon. His sensitive, quivering nostrils scented the air. His eyes could not pierce the green screen through which the stream rippled away, but to his ears came the voice of a man. It was a steady, monotonous, singsong voice. Once the buck heard the harsh clash of metal upon rock. At the sound he snorted with a sudden start that jerked him through the air from water to meadow, and his feet sank into the young velvet, while he pricked his ears and again scented the air. Then he stole across the tiny meadow, pausing once and again to listen, and faded away out of the canyon like a wraith, soft-footed and without sound.

The clash of steel-shod soles against the rocks began to be heard, and the man's voice grew louder. It was raised in a sort of chant and became distinct with nearness, so that the words could be heard:

"Tu'n around an' tu'n yo' face
Untoe them sweet hills of grace
(D' pow'rs of sin yo' am scornin'!).
Look about an' look aroun',
Fling yo' sin-pack on d' groun'
(Yo' will meet wid d' Lord in d'mornin'!)."

A sound of scrambling accompanied the song, and the spirit of the place fled away on the heels of the red-coated buck. The green screen was burst asunder, and a man peered out at the meadow and the pool and the sloping side-hill. He was a deliberate sort of man. He took in the scene with one embracing glance, then ran his eyes over the details to verify the general impression. Then, and not until then, did he open his mouth in vivid and solemn approval:

"Smoke of life an' snakes of purgatory! Will you just look at that! Wood an' water an' grass an' a side-hill! A pocket-hunter's delight an' a cayuse's paradise! Cool green for tired eyes! Pink pills for pale people ain't in it. A secret pasture for prospectors and a resting-place for tired burros, by damn!"

He was a sandy-complexioned man in whose face geniality and humor seemed the salient characteristics. It was a mobile face, quick-changing to inward mood and thought. Thinking was in him a visible process. Ideas chased across his face like wind-flaws across the surface of a lake. His hair, sparse and unkempt of growth, was as indeterminate and colorless as his complexion. It would seem that all the color of his frame had gone into his eyes, for they were startlingly blue. Also, they were laughing and merry eyes, within them much of the naïveté and wonder of the child; and yet, in an unassertive way, they contained much of calm self-reliance and strength of purpose founded upon self-experience and experience of the world.

From out the screen of vines and creepers he flung ahead of him a miner's pick and shovel and gold-pan. Then he crawled out himself into the open. He was clad in faded overalls and black cotton shirt, with hobnailed brogans on his feet, and on his head a hat whose shapelessness and stains advertised the rough usage of wind and rain and sun and camp-smoke. He stood erect, seeing wide-eyed the secrecy of the scene and sensuously inhaling the warm, sweet breath of the canyon-garden through nostrils that dilated and quivered with delight. His eyes narrowed to laughing slits of blue, his face wreathed itself in joy, and his mouth curled in a smile as he cried aloud:

"Jumping dandelions and happy hollyhocks, but that smells good to me! Talk about your attar o' roses an' cologne factories! They ain't in it!"

He had the habit of soliloquy. His quick-changing facial expressions might tell every thought and mood, but the tongue, perforce, ran hard after, repeating, like a second Boswell.

The man lay down on the lip of the pool and drank long and deep of its water. "Tastes good to me," he murmured, lifting his head and gazing across the pool at the side-hill, while he wiped his mouth with the back of his hand. The side-hill attracted his attention. Still lying on his stomach, he studied the hill formation long and carefully. It was a practised eye that traveled up the slope to the crumbling canyon-wall and back and down again to the edge of the pool. He scrambled to his feet and favored the side-hill with a second survey.

"Looks good to me," he concluded, picking up his pick and shovel and gold-pan.

He crossed the stream below the pool, stepping agilely from stone to stone. Where the side-hill touched the water he dug up a shovelful of dirt and put it into the gold-pan. He squatted down, holding the pan in his two hands, and partly immersing it in the stream. Then he imparted to the pan a deft circular motion that sent the water sluicing in and out through the dirt and gravel. The larger and the lighter particles worked to the surface, and these, by a skillful dipping movement of the pan, he spilled out and over the edge. Occasionally, to expedite matters, he rested the pan and with his fingers raked out the large pebbles and pieces of rock.

The contents of the pan diminished rapidly until only fine dirt and the smallest bits of gravel remained. At this stage he began to work very deliberately and carefully. It was fine washing, and he washed fine and finer, with a keen scrutiny and delicate and fastidious touch. At last the pan seemed empty of everything but water; but with a quick semicircular flirt that sent the water flying over the shallow rim into the stream, he disclosed a layer of black sand on the bottom of the pan. So thin was this layer that it was like a streak of paint. He examined it closely. In the midst of it was a tiny golden speck. He dribbled a little water in over the depressed edge of the pan. With a quick flirt he sent the water sluicing across the bottom, turning the grains of black sand over and over. A second tiny golden speck rewarded his effort.

The washing had now become very fine—fine beyond all need of ordinary placer-mining. He worked the black sand, a small portion at a time, up the shallow rim of the pan. Each small portion he examined sharply, so that his eyes saw every grain of it before he allowed it to slide over the edge and away. Jealously, bit by bit, he let the black sand slip away. A golden speck, no larger than a pin-point, appeared on the rim, and by his manipulation of the water it returned to the bottom of the pan. And in such fashion another speck was disclosed, and another. Great was his care of them. Like a shepherd he herded his flock of golden specks so that not one should be lost. At last, of the pan of dirt nothing remained but his golden herd. He counted it, and then, after all his labor, sent it flying out of the pan with one final swirl of water.

But his blue eyes were shining with desire as he rose to his feet. "Seven," he muttered aloud, asserting the sum of the specks for which he had toiled so hard and which he had so wantonly thrown away. "Seven," he repeated, with the emphasis of one trying to impress a number on his memory.

He stood still a long while, surveying the hillside. In his eyes was a curiosity, new-aroused and burning. There was an exultance about his bearing and a keenness like that of a hunting animal catching the fresh scent of game.

He moved down the stream a few steps and took a second panful of dirt.

Again came the careful washing, the jealous herding of the golden specks, and the wantonness with which he sent them flying into the stream when he had counted their number.

"Five," he muttered, and repeated, "five."

He could not forbear another survey of the hill before filling the pan farther down the stream. His golden herds diminished. "Four, three, two, two, one," were his memory-tabulations as he moved down the stream. When but one speck of gold rewarded his washing, he stopped and built a fire of dry twigs. Into this he thrust the gold-pan and burned it till it was blue-black. He held up the pan and examined it critically. Then he nodded approbation. Against such a color-background he could defy the tiniest yellow speck to elude him.

Still moving down the stream, he panned again. A single speck was his reward. A third pan contained no gold at all. Not satisfied with this, he panned three times again, taking his shovels of dirt within a foot of one another. Each pan proved empty of gold, and the fact, instead of discouraging him, seemed to give him satisfaction. His elation increased with each barren washing, until he arose, exclaiming jubilantly:

"If it ain't the real thing, may God knock off my head with sour apples!"

Returning to where he had started operations, he began to pan up the stream. At first his golden herds increased—increased prodigiously. "Fourteen, eighteen, twenty-one, twenty-six," ran his memory tabulations. Just above the pool he struck his richest pan—thirty-five colors.

"Almost enough to save," he remarked regretfully as he allowed the water to sweep them away.

The sun climbed to the top of the sky. The man worked on. Pan by pan, he went up the stream, the tally of results steadily decreasing.

"It's just booful, the way it peters out," he exulted when a shovelful of dirt contained no more than a single speck of gold.

And when no specks at all were found in several pans, he straightened up and favored the hillside with a confident glance.

"Ah ha! Mr. Pocket!" he cried out, as though to an auditor

hidden somewhere above him beneath the surface of the slope. "Ah, ha! Mr. Pocket! I'm a-comin', I'm a-comin', an' I'm shorely gwine to get yer! You heah me, Mr. Pocket? I'm gwine to get yer as shore as punkins ain't cauliflowers!"

He turned and flung a measuring glance at the sun poised above him in the azure of the cloudless sky. Then he went down the canyon, following the line of shovel-holes he had made in filling the pans. He crossed the stream below the pool and disappeared through the green screen. There was little opportunity for the spirit of the place to return with its quietude and repose, for the man's voice, raised in ragtime song, still dominated the canyon with possession.

After a time, with a greater clashing of steel-shod feet on rock, he returned. The green screen was tremendously agitated. It surged back and forth in the throes of a struggle. There was a loud grating and clanging of metal. The man's voice leaped to a higher pitch and was sharp with imperativeness. A large body plunged and panted. There was a snapping and ripping and rending, and amid a shower of falling leaves a horse burst through the screen. On its back was a pack, and from this trailed broken vines and torn creepers. The animal gazed with astonished eyes at the scene into which it had been precipitated, then dropped its head to the grass and began contentedly to graze. A second horse scrambled into view, slipping once on the mossy rocks and regaining equilibrium when its hoofs sank into the yielding surface of the meadow. It was riderless, though on its back was a high-horned Mexican saddle, scarred and discolored by long usage.

The man brought up the rear. He threw off pack and saddle, with an eye to camp location, and gave the animals their freedom to graze. He unpacked his food and got out frying-pan and coffee-pot. He gathered an armful of dry wood, and with a few stones made a place for his fire.

"My!" he said, "but I've got an appetite. I could scoff iron-filings an' horseshoe nails an' thank you kindly, ma'am, for a second helpin'."

He straightened up, and, while he reached for matches in the pocket of his overalls, his eyes traveled across the pool to the side-hill. His fingers had clutched the match-box, but they relaxed their hold and the hand came out empty. The man wavered perceptibly. He looked at his preparations for cooking and he looked at the hill.

"Guess I'll take another whack at her," he concluded, starting to cross the stream.

"They ain't no sense in it, I know," he mumbled apologetically. "But keepin' grub back an hour ain't goin' to hurt none, I reckon."

A few feet back from his first line of test-pans he started a second line. The sun dropped down the western sky, the shadows lengthened, but the man worked on. He began a third line of test-pans. He was cross-cutting the hillside, line by line, as he ascended. The center of each line produced the richest pans, while the ends came where no colors showed in the pan. And as he ascended the hillside the lines grew perceptibly shorter. The regularity with which their length diminished served to indicate that somewhere up the slope the last line would be so short as to have scarcely length at all, and that beyond could come only a point. The design was growing into an inverted "V." The converging sides of this "V" marked the boundaries of the gold-bearing dirt.

The apex of the "V" was evidently the man's goal. Often he ran his eye along the converging sides and on up the hill, trying to divine the apex, the point where the gold-bearing dirt must cease. Here resided "Mr. Pocket"—for so the man familiarly addressed the imaginary point above him on the slope, crying out:

"Come down out o' that, Mr. Pocket! Be right smart an' agreeable, an' come down!"

"All right," he would add later, in a voice resigned to determination. "All right, Mr. Pocket. It's plain to me I got to come right up an' snatch you out bald-headed. An' I'll do it! I'll do it!" he would threaten still later.

Each pan he carried down to the water to wash, and as he went higher up the hill the pans grew richer, until he began to save the gold in an empty baking-powder can which he carried carelessly in his hip-pocket. So engrossed was he in his toil that he did not notice the long twilight of oncoming night. It was not until he tried vainly to see the gold colors in the bottom of the pan that he realized the passage of time. He straightened up abruptly. An expression of whimsical wonderment and awe overspread his face as he drawled:

"Gosh darn my buttons! if I didn't plumb forget dinner!"

He stumbled across the stream in the darkness and lighted his long-delayed fire. Flapjacks and bacon and warmed-over beans constituted his supper. Then he smoked a pipe by the smouldering coals, listening to the night noises and watching the moonlight stream through the canyon. After that he unrolled his bed, took off his heavy shoes, and pulled the blankets up to his chin. His face showed white in the moonlight, like the face of a corpse. But it was a corpse that knew its resurrection, for the man rose suddenly on one elbow and gazed across at his hillside.

"Good night, Mr Pocket," he called sleepily. "Good night."

He slept through the early gray of morning until the direct rays of the sun smote his closed eyelids, when he awoke with a start and looked about him until he had established the continuity of his existence and identified his present self with the days previously lived.

To dress, he had merely to buckle on his shoes. He glanced at his fireplace and at his hillside, wavered, but fought down the temptation and started the fire.

"Keep yer shirt on, Bill; keep yer shirt on," he admonished himself. "What's the good of rushin'? No use in gettin' all het up an' sweaty. Mr. Pocket'll wait for you. He ain't a-runnin' away before you can get yer breakfast. Now, what you want, Bill, is something fresh in yer bill o' fare. So it's up to you to go an' get it."

He cut a short pole at the water's edge and drew from one of his pockets a bit of line and a draggled fly that had once been a royal coachman.

"Mebbe they'll bite in the early morning," he muttered, as he made his first cast into the pool. And a moment later he was gleefully crying: "What'd I tell you, eh? What'd I tell you?"

He had no reel, nor any inclination to waste time, and by main strength, and swiftly, he drew out of the water a flashing ten-inch trout. Three more, caught in rapid succession, furnished his breakfast. When he came to the stepping-stones on his way to his hillside, he was struck by a sudden thought, and paused.

"I'd just better take a hike down-stream a ways," he said. "There's no tellin' what cuss may be snoopin' around."

But he crossed over on the stones, and with a "I really oughter take that hike," the need of the precaution passed out of his mind and he fell to work.

At nightfall he straightened up. The small of his back was stiff from stooping toil, and as he put his hand behind him to soothe the protesting muscles, he said:

"Now what d'ye think of that, by damn? I clean forgot my dinner again! If I don't watch out, I'll sure be degeneratin' into a two-meal-a-day crank."

"Pockets is the damnedest things I ever see for makin' a man absent-minded," he communed that night, as he crawled into his blankets. Nor did he forget to call up the hillside, "Good night, Mr. Pocket! Good night!"

Rising with the sun, and snatching a hasty breakfast, he was early at work. A fever seemed to be growing in him, nor did the increasing richness of the test-pans allay this fever. There was a flush in his cheek other than that made by the heat of the sun, and he was oblivious to fatigue and the passage of time. When he filled a pan with dirt, he ran down the hill to wash it; nor could he forbear running up the hill again, panting and stumbling profanely, to refill the pan.

He was now a hundred yards from the water, and the inverted "V" was assuming definite proportions. The width of the pay-dirt steadily decreased, and the man extended in his mind's eye the sides of the "V" to their meeting-place far up the hill. This was his goal, the apex of the "V," and he panned many times to locate it.

"Just about two yards above that manzanita bush an' a yard to the right," he finally concluded.

Then the temptation seized him. "As plain as the nose on your face," he said, as he abandoned his laborious cross-cutting and climbed to the indicated apex. He filled a pan and carried it down the hill to wash. It contained no trace of gold. He dug deep, and he dug shallow, filling and washing a dozen pans, and was unrewarded even by the tiniest golden speck. He was enraged at having yielded to the temptation, and cursed himself blasphemously and pridelessly. Then he went down the hill and took up the cross-cutting.

"Slow an' certain, Bill; slow an' certain," he crooned. "Short-cuts to fortune ain't in your line, an' it's about time you know it. Get wise, Bill; get wise. Slow an' certain's the only hand you can play; so go to it, an' keep to it, too."

As the cross-cuts decreased, showing that the sides of the "V" were converging, the depth of the "V" increased. The gold-trace was dipping into the hill. It was only at thirty inches beneath the surface that he could get colors in his pan. The dirt he found at twenty-five inches from the surface, and at thirty-five inches, yielded barren pans. At the base of the "V," by the water's edge, he had found the gold colors at the grass roots. The higher he went up the hill, the deeper the gold dipped. To dig a hole three feet deep in order to get one test-pan was a task of no mean magnitude; while between the man and the apex intervened an untold number of such holes to be dug. "An' there's no tellin' how much deeper it'll pitch," he sighed, in a moment's pause, while his fingers soothed his aching back.

Feverish with desire, with aching back and stiffening muscles, with pick and shovel gouging and mauling the soft brown earth, the man toiled up the hill. Before him was the smooth slope, spangled with flowers and made sweet with their breath. Behind him was devastation. It looked like some terrible eruption breaking out on the smooth skin of the hill. His slow progress was like that of a slug, befouling beauty with a monstrous trail.

Though the dipping gold-trace increased the man's work, he found consolation in the increasing richness of the pans. Twenty cents, thirty cents, fifty cents, sixty cents, were the values of the gold found in the pans, and at nightfall he washed his banner pan, which gave him a dollar's worth of gold-dust from a shovelful of dirt.

"I'll just bet it's my luck to have some inquisitive cuss come buttin' in here on my pasture," he mumbled sleepily that night as he pulled the blankets up to his chin.

Suddenly he sat upright. "Bill!" he called sharply. "Now, listen to me, Bill; d'ye hear! It's up to you, to-morrow mornin', to mosey round an' see what you can see. Understand? To-morrow morning, an' don't you forget it!"

He yawned and glanced across at his side-hill. "Good night, Mr. Pocket," he called.

In the morning he stole a march on the sun, for he had finished breakfast when its first rays caught him, and he was climbing the wall of the canyon where it crumbled away and gave footing. From the outlook at the top he found himself in the midst of loneliness. As far as he could see, chain after chain of mountains heaved themselves into his vision. To the east his eyes, leaping the miles between range and range and between many ranges, brought up at last against the white-peaked Sierras—the main crest, where the backbone of the Western world reared itself against the sky. To the north and south he could see more distinctly the cross-systems that broke through the main trend of the sea of mountains. To the west the ranges fell away, one behind the other, diminishing and fading into the gentle foothills that, in turn, descended into the great valley which he could not see.

And in all that mighty sweep of earth he saw no sign of man nor of the handiwork of man—save only the torn bosom of the hillside at his feet. The man looked long and carefully. Once, far down his own canyon, he thought he saw in the air a faint hint of smoke. He looked again and decided that it was the purple haze of the hills made dark by a convolution of the canyon wall at its back.

"Hey, you, Mr. Pocket!" he called down into the canyon. "Stand out from under! I'm a-comin', Mr. Pocket! I'm a-comin!"

The heavy brogans on the man's feet made him appear clumsy-footed, but he swung down from the giddy height as lightly and airily as a mountain goat. A rock, turning under his foot on the edge of the precipice, did not disconcert him. He seemed to know the precise time required for the turn to culminate in disaster, and in the meantime he utilized the false footing itself for the momentary earth-contact necessary to carry him on into safety. Where the earth sloped so steeply that it was impossible to stand for a second upright, the man did not hesitate. His foot pressed the impossible surface for but a fraction of the fatal second and gave him the bound that carried him onward. Again, where even the fraction of a second's footing was out of the question, he would swing his body past by a moment's hand-grip on a jutting knob of rock, a crevice, or a precariously rooted shrub. At last, with a wild leap and yell, he exchanged the face of the wall for an earth-slide and finished the descent in the midst of several tons of sliding earth and gravel.

His first pan of the morning washed out over two dollars in coarse gold. It was from the center of the "V." To either side the diminution in the values of the pans was swift. His lines of cross-cutting holes were growing very short. The converging sides of the inverted "V" were only a few yards apart. Their meeting-point was only a few yards above him. But the pay-streak was dipping deeper and deeper into the earth. By early afternoon he was sinking the test-holes five feet before the pans could show the gold-trace.

For that matter, the gold-trace had become something more than a trace; it was a placer mine in itself, and the man resolved to come back after he had found the pocket and work over the ground. But the increasing richness of the pans began to worry him. By late afternoon the worth of the pans had grown to three and four dollars. The man scratched his head perplexedly and looked a few feet up the hill at the manzanita bush that marked approximately the apex of the "V." He nodded his head and said oracularly:

"It's one o' two things, Bill; one o' two things. Either Mr. Pocket's spilled himself all out an' down the hill, or else Mr. Pocket's that damned rich you maybe won't be able to carry him all away with you. And that 'd be hell, wouldn't it, now?" He chuckled at contemplation of so pleasant a dilemma.

Nightfall found him by the edge of the stream, his eyes wrestling with the gathering darkness over the washing of a five-dollar pan.

"Wisht I had an electric light to go on working," he said.

He found sleep difficult that night. Many times he composed himself and closed his eyes for slumber to overtake him; but his blood pounded with too strong desire, and as many times his eyes opened and he murmured wearily, "Wisht it was sun-up."

Sleep came to him in the end, but his eyes were open with the first paling of the stars, and the gray of dawn caught him with breakfast finished and climbing the hillside in the direction of the secret abiding-place of Mr. Pocket.

The first cross-cut the man made, there was space for only three holes, so narrow had become the pay-streak and so close was he to the fountainhead of the golden stream he had been following for four days.

"Be ca'm, Bill; be ca'm," he admonished himself, as he broke ground for the final hole where the sides of the "V" had at last come together in a point.

"I've got the almighty cinch on you, Mr. Pocket, an' you can't lose me," he said many times as he sank the hole deeper and deeper.

Four feet, five feet, six feet, he dug his way down into the earth. The digging grew harder. His pick grated on broken rock. He examined the rock. "Rotten quartz" was his conclusion as, with the shovel, he cleared the bottom of the hole of loose dirt. He attacked the crumbling quartz with the pick, bursting the disintegrating rock asunder with every stroke.

He thrust his shovel into the loose mass. His eye caught a gleam of yellow. He dropped the shovel and squatted suddenly on his heels. As a farmer rubs the clinging earth from fresh-dug potatoes, so the man, a piece of rotten quartz held in both hands, rubbed the dirt away.

"Sufferin' Sardanopolis!" he cried. "Lumps an' chunks of it!"

It was only half rock he held in his hand. The other half was virgin gold. He dropped it into his pan and examined another piece. Little yellow was to be seen, but with his strong fingers he crumbled the rotten quartz away till both hands were filled with glowing yellow. He rubbed the dirt away from fragment after fragment, tossing them into the gold-pan. It was a treasure-hole. So much had the quartz rotted away that there was less of it than there was of gold. Now and again he found a piece to which no rock clung—a piece that was all gold. A chunk, where the pick had laid open the heart of the gold, glittered like a handful of yellow jewels, and he cocked his head at it and slowly turned it around and over to observe the rich play of the light upon it.

"Talk about yer Too Much Gold diggin's!" the man snorted contemptuously. "Why, this diggin' 'd make it look like thirty cents. This diggin' is All Gold. An' right here an' now I name this yere canyon 'All Gold Canyon,' b' gosh!"

Still squatting on his heels, he continued examining the

fragments and tossing them into the pan. Suddenly there came to him a premonition of danger. It seemed a shadow had fallen upon him. But there was no shadow. His heart had given a great jump up into his throat and was choking him. Then his blood slowly chilled and he felt the sweat of his shirt cold against his flesh.

He did not spring up nor look around. He did not move. He was considering the nature of the premonition he had received, trying to locate the source of the mysterious force that had warned him, striving to sense the imperative presence of the unseen thing that threatened him. There is an aura of things hostile, made manifest by messengers too refined for the senses to know; and this aura he felt, but knew not how he felt it. His was the feeling as when a cloud passes over the sun. It seemed that between him and life had passed something dark and smothering and menacing; a gloom, as it were, that swallowed up life and made for death—his death.

Every force of his being impelled him to spring up and confront the unseen danger, but his soul dominated the panic, and he remained squatting on his heels, in his hands a chunk of gold. He did not dare to look around, but he knew by now that there was something behind him and above him. He made believe to be interested in the gold in his hand. He examined it critically, turned it over and over, and rubbed the dirt from it. And all the time he knew that something behind him was looking at the gold over his shoulder.

Still feigning interest in the chunk of gold in his hand, he listened intently and he heard the breathing of the thing behind him. His eyes searched the ground in front of him for a weapon, but they saw only the uprooted gold, worthless to him now in his extremity. There was his pick, a handy weapon on occasion; but this was not such an occasion. The man realized his predicament. He was in a narrow hole that was seven feet deep. His head did not come to the surface of the ground. He was in a trap.

He remained squatting on his heels. He was quite cool and

collected; but his mind, considering every factor, showed him only his helplessness. He continued rubbing the dirt from the quartz fragments and throwing the gold into the pan. There was nothing else for him to do. Yet he knew that he would have to rise up, sooner or later, and face the danger that breathed at his back. The minutes passed, and with the passage of each minute he knew that by so much he was nearer the time when he must stand up, or else—and his wet shirt went cold against his flesh again at the thought—or else he might receive death as he stooped there over his treasure.

Still he squatted on his heels, rubbing dirt from gold and debating in just what manner he should rise up. He might rise up with a rush and claw his way out of the hole to meet whatever threatened on the even footing above ground. Or he might rise up slowly and carelessly, and feign casually to discover the thing that breathed at his back. His instinct and every fighting fiber of his body favored the mad, clawing rush to the surface. His intellect, and the craft thereof, favored the slow and cautious meeting with the thing that menaced and which he could not see. And while he debated, a loud, crashing noise burst on his ear. At the same instant he received a stunning blow on the left side of the back, and from the point of impact felt a rush of flame through his flesh. He sprang up in the air, but halfway to his feet collapsed. His body crumpled in like a leaf withered in sudden heat, and he came down, his chest across his pan of gold, his face in the dirt and rock, his legs tangled and twisted because of the restricted space at the bottom of the hole. His legs twitched convulsively several times. His body was shaken as with a mighty ague. There was a slow expansion of the lungs, accompanied by a deep sigh. Then the air was slowly, very slowly, exhaled, and his body as slowly flattened itself down into inertness.

Above, revolver in hand, a man was peering down over the edge of the hole. He peered for a long time at the prone and motionless body beneath him. After a while the stranger sat down on the edge of the hole so that he could see into it, and rested the revolver on his knee. Reaching his hand into a pocket, he drew out a wisp of brown paper. Into this he dropped a few crumbs of tobacco. The combination became a cigarette, brown and squat, with the ends turned in. Not once did he take his eyes from the body at the bottom of the hole. He lighted the cigarette and drew its smoke into his lungs with a caressing intake of the breath. He smoked slowly. Once the cigarette went out and he relighted it. And all the while he studied the body beneath him.

In the end he tossed the cigarette stub away and rose to his feet. He moved to the edge of the hole. Spanning it, a hand resting on each edge, and with the revolver still in the right hand, he muscled his body down into the hole. While his feet were yet a yard from the bottom he released his hands and dropped down.

At the instant his feet struck bottom he saw the pocket-miner's arm leap out, and his own legs knew a swift, jerking grip that overthrew him. In the nature of the jump his revolver-hand was above his head. Swiftly as the grip had flashed about his legs, just as swiftly he brought the revolver down. He was still in the air, his fall in process of completion, when he pulled the trigger. The explosion was deafening in the confined space. The smoke filled the hole so that he could see nothing. He struck the bottom on his back, and like a cat's the pocket-miner's body was on top of him. Even as the miner's body passed on top, the stranger crooked in his right arm to fire; and even in that instant the miner, with a quick thrust of elbow, struck his wrist. The muzzle was thrown up and the bullet thudded into the dirt of the side of the hole.

The next instant the stranger felt the miner's hand grip his wrist. The struggle was now for the revolver. Each man strove to turn it against the other's body. The smoke in the hole was clearing. The stranger, lying on his back, was beginning to see dimly. But suddenly he was blinded by a handful of dirt deliberately flung into his eyes by his antagonist. In that moment of shock his grip on the revolver was broken. In the next moment he felt a smashing darkness descend upon his brain, and in the midst of the darkness even the darkness ceased.

But the pocket-miner fired again and again, until the revolver was empty. Then he tossed it from him and, breathing heavily, sat down on the dead man's legs.

The miner was sobbing and struggling for breath. "Measly skunk!" he panted; "a-campin' on my tail an' lettin' me do the work, an' then shootin' me in the back!"

He was half-crying from anger and exhaustion. He peered at the face of the dead man. It was sprinkled with loose dirt and gravel, and it was difficult to distinguish the features.

"Never laid eyes on him before," the miner concluded his scrutiny. "Just a common an' ordinary thief, damn him! An' he shot me in the back! He shot me in the back!"

He opened his shirt and felt himself, front and back, on his left side.

"Went clean through, and no harm done!" he cried jubilantly. "I'll bet he aimed all right all right; but he drew the gun over when he pulled the trigger—the cuss! But I fixed 'm! Oh, I fixed 'm!"

His fingers were investigating the bullet-hole in his side, and a shade of regret passed over his face. "It's goin' to be stiffer'n hell," he said. "An' it's up to me to get mended an' get out o' here."

He crawled out of the hole and went down the hill to his camp. Half an hour later he returned, leading his pack-horse. His open shirt disclosed the rude bandages with which he had dressed his wound. He was slow and awkward with his left-hand movements, but that did not prevent his using the arm.

The bight of the pack-rope under the dead man's shoulders enabled him to heave the body out of the hole. Then he set to work gathering up his gold. He worked steadily for several hours, pausing often to rest his stiffening shoulder and to exclaim:

"He shot me in the back, the measly skunk! He shot me in the back!"

When his treasure was quite cleaned up and wrapped securely into a number of blanket-covered parcels, he made an estimate of its value.

"Four hundred pounds, or I'm a Hottentot," he concluded. "Say two hundred in quartz an' dirt—that leaves two hundred pounds of gold. Bill! Wake up! Two hundred pounds of gold! Forty thousand dollars! An' it's yourn—all yourn!"

He scratched his head delightedly and his fingers blundered into an unfamiliar groove. They quested along it for several inches. It was a crease through his scalp where the second bullet had ploughed.

He walked angrily over to the dead man.

"You would, would you?" he bullied. "You would, eh? Well, I fixed you good an' plenty, an' I'll give you decent burial, too. That's more'n you'd have done for me."

He dragged the body to the edge of the hole and toppled it in. It struck the bottom with a dull crash, on its side, the face twisted up to the light. The miner peered down at it.

"An' you shot me in the back!" he said accusingly.

With pick and shovel he filled the hole. Then he loaded the gold on his horse. It was too great a load for the animal, and when he had gained his camp he transferred part of it to his saddle-horse. Even so, he was compelled to abandon a portion of his outfit—pick and shovel and gold-pan, extra food and cooking utensils, and divers odds and ends.

The sun was at the zenith when the man forced the horses at the screen of vines and creepers. To climb the huge boulders the animals were compelled to uprear and struggle blindly through the tangled mass of vegetation. Once the saddle-horse fell heavily and the man removed the pack to get the animal on its feet. After it started on its way again the man thrust his head out from among the leaves and peered up at the hillside.

"The measly skunk!" he said, and disappeared.

There was a ripping and tearing of vines and boughs. The trees surged back and forth, marking the passage of the animals through the midst of them. There was a clashing of steel-shod hoofs on stone, and now and again an oath or a sharp cry of command. Then the voice of the man was raised in song:—

"Tu'n around an' tu'n yo' face
Untoe them sweet hills of grace
(D' pow'rs of sin yo' am scornin'!).
Look about an' look aroun',
Fling yo' sin-pack on d' groun'
(Yo' will meet wid d' Lord in d' mornin'!)."

The song grew faint and fainter, and through the silence crept back the spirit of the place. The stream once more drowsed and whispered; the hum of the mountain bees rose sleepily. Down through the perfume-weighted air fluttered the snowy fluffs of the cottonwoods. The butterflies drifted in an out among the trees, and over all blazed the quiet sunshine. Only remained the hoof-marks in the meadow and the torn hillside to mark the boisterous trail of the life that had broken the peace of the place and passed on.

At The Rainbow's End

IT WAS FOR TWO reasons that Montana Kid discarded his "chaps" and Mexican spurs, and shook the dust of the Idaho ranges from his feet. In the first place, the encroachments of a steady, sober, and sternly moral civilization had destroyed the primeval status of the western cattle ranges, and refined society turned the cold eye of disfavor upon him and his ilk. In the second place, in one of its cyclopean moments the race had arisen and shoved back its frontier several thousand miles. Thus, with unconscious foresight, did mature society make room for its adolescent members. True, the new territory was mostly barren; but its several hundred thousand square miles of frigidity at least gave breathing space to those who else would have suffocated at home.

Montana Kid was such a one. Heading for the sea-coast, with a haste several sheriff's posses might possibly have explained, and with more nerve than coin of the realm, he succeeded in shipping from a Puget Sound port, and managed to survive the contingent miseries of steerage seasickness and steerage grub. He was rather sallow and drawn, but still his own indomitable self, when he landed on the Dyea beach one day in the spring of the year. Between the cost of dogs, grub, and outfits, and the customs exactions of the two clashing governments, it speedily penetrated to his understanding that the Northland was anything save a poor man's Mecca. So he cast about him in search of quick harvests. Between the beach and the passes were scattered many thousands of passionate pilgrims. These pilgrims Montana Kid proceeded to farm. At first he dealt faro in a pine-board gambling shack; but disagreeable necessity forced him to drop a sudden period into a man's life, and to move on up trail. Then he effected a corner in horseshoe nails, and they circulated at par with legal tender, four to the dollar, till an unexpected consignment of a hundred barrels or so broke the market and forced him to disgorge his stock at a loss. After that he located at Sheep Camp, organized the professional packers, and jumped the freight ten cents a pound in a single day. In token of their gratitude, the packers patronized his faro and roulette layouts and were mulcted cheerfully of their earnings. But his commercialism was of too lusty a growth to be long endured; so they rushed him one night, burned his shanty, divided the bank, and headed him up the trail with empty pockets.

Ill-luck was his running mate. He engaged with responsible parties to run whisky across the line by way of precarious and unknown trails, lost his Indian guides, and had the very first outfit confiscated by the Mounted Police. Numerous other misfortunes tended to make him bitter of heart and wanton of action, and he celebrated his arrival at Lake Bennett by terrorizing the camp for twenty straight hours. Then a miners' meeting took him in hand, and commanded him to make himself scarce. He had a wholesome respect for such assemblages, and he obeyed in such haste that he inadvertently removed himself at the tail-end of another man's dog team. This was equivalent to horse-stealing in a more mellow clime, so he hit only the high places across Bennett and down Tagish, and made his first camp a full hundred miles to the north.

Now it happened that the break of spring was at hand, and many of the principal citizens of Dawson were traveling south on the last ice. These he met and talked with, noted their names and possessions, and passed on. He had a good memory, also a fair imagination; nor was veracity one of his virtues.

DAWSON, ALWAYS EAGER for news, beheld Montana Kid's sled heading down the Yukon, and went out on the ice to meet him.

No, he hadn't any newspapers; didn't know whether Durrant was hanged yet, nor who had won the Thanksgiving game; hadn't heard whether the United States and Spain had gone to fighting; didn't know who Dreyfus was; but O'Brien? Hadn't they heard? O'Brien, why, he was drowned in the White Horse; Sitka Charley the only one of the party who escaped. Joe Ladue? Both legs frozen and amputated at the Five Fingers. And Jack Dalton? Blown up on the *Sea Lion* with all hands. And Bettles? Wrecked on the *Carthagina*, in Seymour Narrows—twenty survivors out of three hundred. And Swiftwater Bill? Gone through the rotten ice of Lake LeBarge with six female members of the opera troupe he was convoying. Governor Walsh? Lost with all hands and eight sleds on the Thirty Mile. Devereaux? Who was Devereaux? Oh, the courier! Shot by Indians on Lake Marsh.

So it went. The word was passed along. Men shouldered in to ask after friends and partners, and in turn were shouldered out, too stunned for blasphemy. By the time Montana Kid gained the bank he was surrounded by several hundred fur-clad miners. When he passed the Barracks he was the center of a procession. At the Opera House he was the nucleus of an excited mob, each member struggling for a chance to ask after some absent comrade. On every side he was being invited to drink. Never before had the Klondike thus opened its arms to a *che-cha-qua*. All Dawson was humming. Such a series of catastrophes had never occurred in its history. Every man of note who had gone south in the spring had been wiped out. The cabins vomited forth their occupants. Wild-eyed men hurried down from the creeks and gulches to seek out this man who had told a tale of such disaster. The Russian half-breed wife of Bettles sought the fireplace, inconsolable, and rocked back and forth, and ever and anon flung white wood-ashes upon her raven hair. The flag at the Barracks flopped dismally at half-mast. Dawson mourned its dead.

Why Montana Kid did this thing no man may know. Nor, beyond the fact that the truth was not in him, can explanation be hazarded. But for five whole days he plunged the land in wailing and sorrow, and for five whole days he was the only man in the Klondike. The country gave him its best of bed and board. The saloons granted him the freedom of their bars. Men sought him continuously. The high officials bowed down to him for further information, and he was feasted at the Barracks by Constantine and his brother officers. And then, one day, Devereaux, the government courier, halted his tired dogs before the gold commissioner's office. Dead? Who said so? Give him a moose steak and he'd show them how dead he was. Why, Governor Walsh was in camp on the Little Salmon, and O'Brien coming in on the first water. Dead? Give him a moose steak and he'd show them.

And forthwith Dawson hummed. The Barracks' flag rose to the masthead, and Bettles' wife washed herself and put on clean raiment. The community subtly signified its desire that Montana Kid obliterate himself from the landscape. And Montana Kid obliterated; as usual, at the tail-end of some one else's dog team. Dawson rejoiced when he headed down the Yukon, and wished him godspeed to the ultimate destination of the case-hardened sinner. After that the owner of the dogs bestirred himself, made complaint to Constantine, and from him received the loan of a policeman.

WITH CIRCLE CITY in prospect and the last ice crumbling under his runners, Montana Kid took advantage of the lengthening days and traveled his dogs late and early. Further, he had but little doubt that the owner of the dogs in question had taken his trail, and he wished to make American territory before the river broke. But by the afternoon of the third day it became evident that he had lost in his race with spring. The Yukon was growling and straining at its fetters. Long detours became necessary, for the trail had begun to fall through into the swift current beneath, while the ice, in constant unrest, was thundering apart in great gaping fissures. Through these and through countless airholes, the water began to sweep across the surface of the ice, and by the time he pulled into a woodchopper's cabin on the point of an island, the dogs were being rushed off their feet and were swimming more often than not. He was greeted sourly by the two residents, but he unharnessed and proceeded to cook up.

Donald and Davy were fair specimens of frontier inefficients. Canadian-born, city-bred Scots, in a foolish moment they had resigned their counting-house desks, drawn upon their savings, and gone Klondiking. And now they were feeling the rough edge of the country. Grubless, spiritless, with a lust for home in their hearts, they had been staked by the P.C. Company to cut wood for its steamers, with the promise at the end of a passage home. Disregarding the possibilities of the ice-run, they had fittingly demonstrated their inefficiency by their choice of the island on which they located. Montana Kid, though possessing little knowledge of the break-up of a great river, looked about him dubiously, and cast yearning glances at the distant bank where the towering bluffs promised immunity from all the ice of the Northland.

After feeding himself and dogs, he lighted his pipe and strolled out to get a better idea of the situation. The island, like all its river brethren, stood higher at the upper end, and it was here that Donald and Davy had built their cabin and piled many cords of wood. The far shore was a full mile away, while between the island and the near shore lay a back-channel perhaps a hundred yards across. At first sight of this, Montana Kid was tempted to take his dogs and escape to the mainland, but on closer inspection he discovered a rapid current flooding on top. Below, the river twisted sharply to the west, and in this turn its breast was studded by a maze of tiny islands.

"That's where she'll jam," he remarked to himself.

Half a dozen sleds, evidently bound upstream to Dawson, were splashing through the chill water to the tail of the island. Travel on the river was passing from the precarious to the impossible, and it was nip and tuck with them till they gained the island and came up the path of the wood-choppers toward the cabin. One of them, snow-blind, towed helplessly at the rear of a sled. Husky young fellows they were, rough-garmented and trail-worn, yet Montana Kid had met the breed before and knew at once that it was not his kind.

"Hello! How's things up Dawson-way?" queried the foremost, passing his eye over Donald and Davy and settling it upon the Kid.

A first meeting in the wilderness is not characterized by formality. The talk quickly became general, and the news of the Upper and Lower Countries was swapped equitably back and forth. But the little the new-comers had was soon over with, for they had wintered at Minook, a thousand miles below, where nothing was doing. Montana Kid, however, was fresh from Salt Water, and they annexed him while they pitched camp, swamping him with questions concerning the outside, from which they had been cut off for a twelvemonth.

A shrieking split, suddenly lifting itself above the general uproar on the river, drew everybody to the bank. The surface water had increased in depth, and the ice, assailed from above and below, was struggling to tear itself from the grip of the shores. Fissures reverberated into life before their eyes, and the air was filled with multitudinous crackling, crisp and sharp, like the sound that goes up on a clear day from the firing line.

From up the river two men were racing a dog team toward them on an uncovered stretch of ice. But even as they looked, the pair struck the water and began to flounder through. Behind, where their feet had sped the moment before, the ice broke up and turned turtle. Through this opening the river rushed out upon them to their waists, burying the sled and swinging the dogs off at right angles in a drowning tangle. But the men stopped their flight to give the animals a fighting chance, and they groped hurriedly in the cold confusion, slashing at the detaining traces with their sheath-knives. Then they fought their way to the bank through swirling water and grinding ice, where, foremost in leaping to the rescue among the jarring fragments, was the Kid.

"Why, blime me, if it ain't Montana Kid!" exclaimed one of the men whom the Kid was just placing upon his feet at the top of the bank. He wore the scarlet tunic of the Mounted Police and jocularly raised his right hand in salute.

"Got a warrant for you, Kid," he continued, drawing a bedraggled paper from his breast pocket, "an' I 'ope as you'll come along peaceable."

Montana Kid looked at the chaotic river and shrugged his shoulders, and the policeman, following his glance, smiled.

"Where are the dogs?" his companion asked.

"Gentlemen," interrupted the policeman, "this 'ere mate o' mine is Jack Sutherland, owner of Twenty-Two Eldorado—"

"Not Sutherland of '92?" broke in the snow-blinded Minook man, groping feebly toward him.

"The same." Sutherland gripped his hand.

"And you?"

"Oh, I'm after your time, but I remember you in my freshman year—you were doing P.G. work then. Boys," he called, turning half about, "this is Sutherland, Jack Sutherland, erstwhile fullback on the Varsity. Come up, you gold-chasers, and fall upon him! Sutherland, this is Greenwich—played quarter two seasons back."

"Yes, I read of the game," Sutherland said, shaking hands. "And I remember that big run of yours for the first touchdown."

Greenwich flushed darkly under his tanned skin and awkwardly made room for another.

"And here's Matthews—Berkeley man. And we've got some Eastern cracks knocking about, too. Come up, you Princeton men! Come up! This is Sutherland, Jack Sutherland!"

Then they fell upon him heavily, carried him into camp, and supplied him with dry clothes and numerous mugs of black tea.

Donald and Davy, overlooked, had retired to their nightly game of crib. Montana Kid followed them with the policeman.

"Here, get into some dry togs," he said, pulling them from out his scanty kit. "Guess you'll have to bunk with me, too."

"Well, I say, you're a good 'un," the policeman remarked as he pulled on the other man's socks. "Sorry I've got to take you back to Dawson, but I only 'ope they won't be 'ard on you."

"Not so fast." The Kid smiled curiously. "We ain't under way yet. When I go I'm going down river, and I guess the chances are you'll go along."

"Not if I know myself—"

"Come on outside, and I'll show you, then. These damn fools," thrusting a thumb over his shoulder at the two Scots, "played smash when they located here. Fill your pipe, first—this is pretty good plug—and enjoy yourself while you can. You haven't many smokes before you."

The policeman went with him wonderingly while Donald and Davy dropped their cards and followed. The Minook men noticed Montana Kid pointing now up the river, now down, and came over.

"What's up?" Sutherland demanded.

"Nothing much." Nonchalance sat well upon the Kid. "Just a case of raising hell and putting a chunk under. See that bend down there? That's where she'll jam millions of tons of ice. Then she'll jam in the bends up above, millions of tons. Upper jam breaks first, lower jam holds, pouf!" He dramatically swept the island with his hand. "Millions of tons," he added reflectively.

"And what of the woodpiles?" Davy questioned.

The Kid repeated his sweeping gesture, and Davy wailed, "The labor of months! It canna be! Na, na, lad, it canna be. I doot not it's a jowk. Ay, say that it is," he appealed.

But when the Kid laughed harshly and turned on his heel, Davy flung himself upon the piles and began frantically to toss the cordwood back from the bank.

"Lend a hand, Donald!" he cried. "Can ye no lend a hand? 'Tis the labor of months and the passage home!"

Donald caught him by the arm and shook him, but he tore free. "Did ye no hear, man? Millions of tons, and the island shall be sweepit clean."

"Straighten yersel' up, man," said Donald. "It's a bit fashed ye are."

But Davy fell upon the cordwood. Donald stalked back to the cabin, buckled on his money belt and Davy's, and went out to the point of the island where the ground was highest and where a huge pine towered above its fellows.

The men before the cabin heard the ringing of his axe and smiled. Greenwich returned from across the island with the word that they were penned in. It was impossible to cross the back-channel. The blind Minook man began to sing, and the rest joined in with—

"Wonder if it's true?
Does it seem so to you?
Seems to me he's lying—
Oh, I wonder if it's true?"

"It's ay sinfu'," Davy moaned, lifting his head and watching them dance in the slanting rays of the sun. "And my guid wood a' going to waste."

"Oh, I wonder if it's true."

was flaunted back.

The noise of the river ceased suddenly. A strange calm wrapped about them. The ice had ripped from the shores and was floating higher on the surface of the river, which was rising. Up it came, swift and silent, for twenty feet, till the huge cakes rubbed softly against the crest of the bank. The tail of the island, being lower, was overrun. Then, without effort, the white flood started down-stream. But the sound increased with the momentum, and soon the whole island was shaking and quivering with the shock of the grinding bergs. Under pressure, the mighty cakes, weighing hundreds of tons, were shot into the air like peas. The frigid anarchy increased its riot, and the men had to shout into one another's ears to be heard. Occasionally the racket from the back channel could be heard above the tumult.

The island shuddered with the impact of an enormous cake which drove in squarely upon its point. It ripped a score of pines out by the roots, then swinging around and over, lifted its muddy base from the bottom of the river and bore down upon the cabin, slicing the bank and trees away like a gigantic knife. It seemed barely to graze the corner of the cabin, but the cribbed logs tilted up like matches, and the structure, like a toy house, fell backward in ruin.

"The labor of months! The labor of months, and the passage home!" Davy wailed, while Montana Kid and the policeman dragged him backward from the woodpiles.

"You'll 'ave plenty o' hoppertunity all in good time for yer passage 'ome," the policeman growled, clouting him alongside the head and sending him flying into safety.

Donald, from the top of the pine, saw the devastating berg sweep away the cordwood and disappear down-stream. As though satisfied with this damage, the ice-flood quickly dropped to its old level and began to slacken its pace. The noise likewise eased down, and the others could hear Donald shouting from his eyrie to look down-stream. As forecast, the jam had come among the islands in the bend, and the ice was piling up in a great barrier which stretched from shore to shore. The river came to a standstill, and the water finding no outlet began to rise. It rushed up till the island was awash, the men splashing around up to their knees, and the dogs swimming to the ruins of the cabin. At this stage it abruptly became stationary, with no perceptible rise or fall.

Montana Kid shook his head. "It's jammed above, and no more's coming down."

"And the gamble is, which jam will break first," Sutherland added.

"Exactly," the Kid affirmed. "If the upper jam breaks first, we haven't a chance. Nothing will stand before it."

The Minook men turned away in silence, but soon "Rumsky Ho" floated upon the quiet air, followed by "The Orange and the Black." Room was made in the circle for Montana Kid and the policeman, and they quickly caught the ringing rhythm of the choruses as they drifted on from song to song.

"Oh, Donald, will ye no lend a hand?" Davy sobbed at the foot of the tree into which his comrade had climbed. "Oh, Donald, man, will ye no lend a hand?" he sobbed again, his hands bleeding from vain attempts to scale the slippery trunk.

But Donald had fixed his gaze up river, and now his voice rang out, vibrant with fear:—

"God Almighty, here she comes!"

Standing knee-deep in the icy water, the Minook men, with Montana Kid and the policeman, gripped hands and raised their voices in the terrible "Battle Hymn of the Republic." But the words were drowned in the advancing roar.

And to Donald was vouchsafed a sight such as no man may see and live. A great wall of white flung itself upon the island. Trees, dogs, men, were blotted out, as though the hand of God had wiped the face of nature clean. This much he saw, then swayed an instant longer in his lofty perch and hurtled far out into the frozen hell.

The One Thousand Dozen

DAVID RASMUNSEN was a hustler, and, like many a greater man, a man of the one idea. Wherefore, when the clarion call of the North rang on his ear, he conceived an adventure in eggs and bent all his energy to its achievement. He figured brieffly and to the point, and the adventure became iridescent-hued, splendid. That eggs would sell at Dawson for five dollars a dozen was a safe working premise. Whence it was incontrovertible that one thousand dozen would bring, in the Golden Metropolis, five thousand dollars.

On the other hand, expense was to be considered, and he considered it well, for he was a careful man, keenly practical, with a hard head and a heart that imagination never warmed. At fifteen cents a dozen, the initial cost of his thousand dozen would be one hundred and fifty dollars, a mere bagatelle in face of the enormous profit. And suppose, just suppose, to be wildly extravagant for once, that transportation for himself and eggs should run up eight hundred and fifty more; he would still have four thousand clear cash and clean when the last egg was disposed of and the last dust had rippled into his sack.

"You see, Alma,"—he figured it over with his wife, the cosy dining room submerged in a sea of maps, government surveys, guidebooks, and Alaskan itineraries—"you see, expenses don't really begin till you make Dyea—fifty dollars'll cover it with a first-class passage thrown in. Now from Dyea to Lake Linderman, Indian packers take your goods over for twelve cents a pound, twelve dollars a hundred, or one hundred and twenty dollars a thousand. Say I have fifteen hundred pounds, it'll cost one hundred and eighty dollars—call it two hundred and be safe. I am creditably informed by a Klondiker just come out that I can buy a boat for three hundred. But the same man says I'm sure to get a couple passengers for one hundred and fifty each, which will give me the boat for nothing, and, further, they can help me manage it. And. . . that's all; I put my eggs ashore from the boat at Dawson. Now let me see how much is that?"

"Fifty dollars from San Francisco to Dyea, two hundred from Dyea to Linderman, passengers pay for the boat—two hundred and fifty all told," she summed up swiftly.

"And a hundred for my clothes and personal outfit," he went on happily; "that leaves a margin of five hundred for emergencies. And what possible emergencies can arise?"

Alma shrugged her shoulders and elevated her brows. If that vast Northland was capable of swallowing up a man and a thousand dozen eggs, surely there was room and to spare for whatever else he might happen to possess. So she thought, but she said nothing. She knew David Rasmunsen too well to say anything.

"Doubling the time because of chance delays, I should make the trip in two months. Think of it, Alma! Four thousand in two months! Beats the paltry hundred a month I'm getting now. Why, we'll build further out where we'll have more space, gas in every room, and a view, and the rent of the cottage'll pay taxes, insurance, and water, and leave something over. And then there's always the chance of my striking it and coming out a millionnaire. Now tell me, Alma, don't you think I'm very moderate?"

And Alma could hardly think otherwise. Besides, had not her own cousin—though a remote and distant one to be sure, the black sheep, the harum-scarum, the ne'er-do-well—had not he come down out of that weird North country with a hundred thousand in yellow dust, to say nothing of a half-ownership in the hole from which it came?

David Rasmunsen's grocer was surprised when he found him

weighing eggs in the scales at the end of the counter, and Rasmunsen himself was more surprised when he found that a dozen eggs weighed a pound and a half—fifteen hundred pounds for his thousand dozen! There would be no weight left for his clothes, blankets, and cooking utensils, to say nothing of the grub he must necessarily consume by the way. His calculations were all thrown out, and he was just proceeding to recast them when he hit upon the idea of weighing small eggs. "For whether they be large or small, a dozen eggs is a dozen eggs," he observed sagely to himself; and a dozen small ones he found to weigh but a pound and a quarter. Thereat the city of San Francisco was overrun by anxious-eyed emissaries, and commission houses and dairy associations were startled by a sudden demand for eggs running not more than twenty ounces to the dozen.

Rasmunsen mortgaged the little cottage for a thousand dollars, arranged for his wife to make a prolonged stay among her own people, threw up his job, and started North. To keep within his schedule he compromised on a second-class passage, which, because of the rush, was worse than steerage; and in the late summer, a pale and wabbly man, he disembarked with his eggs on the Dyea beach. But it did not take him long to recover his land legs and appetite. His first interview with the Chilkoot packers straightened him up and stiffened his backbone. Forty cents a pound they demanded for the twenty-eight-mile portage, and while he caught his breath and swallowed, the price went up to forty-three. Fifteen husky Indians put the straps on his packs at forty-five, but took them off at an offer of forty-seven from a Skaguay Croesus in dirty shirt and ragged overalls who had lost his horses on the White Pass Trail and was now making a last desperate drive at the country by way of Chilkoot.

But Rasmunsen was clean grit, and at fifty cents found takers, who, two days later, set his eggs down intact at Linderman. But fifty cents a pound is a thousand dollars a ton, and his fifteen hundred pounds had exhausted his emergency fund and left him stranded at the Tantalus point where each day he saw the fresh-whipsawed boats departing for Dawson. Further, a great anxiety brooded over the camp where the boats were built. Men worked frantically, early and late, at the height of their endurance, calking, nailing, and pitching in a frenzy of haste for which adequate explanation was not far to seek. Each day the snow-line crept farther down the bleak, rock-shouldered peaks, and gale followed gale, with sleet and slush and snow, and in the eddies and quiet places young ice formed and thickened through the fleeting hours. And each morn, toil-stiffened men turned wan faces across the lake to see if the freeze-up had come. For the freeze-up heralded the death of their hope—the hope that they would be floating down the swift river ere navigation closed on the chain of lakes.

To harrow Rasmunsen's soul further, he discovered three competitors in the egg business. It was true that one, a little German, had gone broke and was himself forlornly back-tripping the last pack of the portage; but the other two had boats nearly completed and were daily supplicating the god of merchants and traders to stay the iron hand of winter for just another day. But the iron hand closed down over the land. Men were being frozen in the blizzard, which swept Chilkoot, and Rasmunsen frosted his toes ere he was aware. He found a chance to go passenger with his freight in a boat just shoving off through the rubble, but two hundred, hard cash, was required, and he had no money.

"Ay tank you yust wait one leedle w'ile," said the Swedish boat-builder, who had struck his Klondike right there and was wise enough to know it—"one leedle w'ile und I make you a tam fine skiff boat, sure Pete."

With this unpledged word to go on. Rasmunsen hit the back trail to Crater Lake, where he fell in with two press correspondents whose tangled baggage was strewn from Stone House, over across the Pass, and as far as Happy Camp.

"Yes," he said with consequence. "I've a thousand dozen eggs at Linderman, and my boat's just about got the last seam calked.

Consider myself in luck to get it. Boats are at a premium, you know, and none to be had."

Whereupon and almost with bodily violence the correspondents clamored to go with him, fluttered greenbacks before his eyes, and spilled yellow twenties from hand to hand. He could not hear of it, but they overpersuaded him, and he reluctantly consented to take them at three hundred apiece. Also they pressed upon him the passage money in advance. And while they wrote to their respective journals concerning the good Samaritan with the thousand dozen eggs, the good Samaritan was hurrying back to the Swede at Linderman.

"Here, you! Gimme that boat!" was his salutation, his hand jingling the correspondents' gold pieces and his eyes hungrily bent upon the finished craft.

The Swede regarded him stolidly and shook his head.

"How much is the other fellow paying? Three hundred? Well, here's four. Take it."

He tried to press it upon him, but the man backed away.

"Ay tank not. Ay say him get der skiff boat. You yust wait—"

"Here's six hundred. Last call. Take it or leave it. Tell'm it's a mistake."

The Swede wavered. "Ay tank yes," he finally said, and the last Rasmunsen saw of him his vocabulary was going to wreck in a vain effort to explain the mistake to the other fellows.

The German slipped and broke his ankle on the steep hogback above Deep Lake, sold out his stock for a dollar a dozen, and with the proceeds hired Indian packers to carry him back to Dyea. But on the morning Rasmunsen shoved off with his correspondents, his two rivals followed suit.

"How many you got?" one of them, a lean little New Englander, called out.

"One thousand dozen," Rasmunsen answered proudly.

"Huh! I'll go you even stakes I beat you in with my eight hundred."

The correspondents offered to lend him the money; but Rasmunsen declined, and the Yankee closed with the remaining rival, a brawny son of the sea and sailor of ships and things, who promised to show them all a wrinkle or two when it came to cracking on. And crack on he did, with a large tarpaulin squaresail which pressed the bow half under at every jump. He was the first to run out of Linderman, but, disdaining the portage, piled his loaded boat on the rocks in the boiling rapids. Rasmunsen and the Yankee, who likewise had two passengers, portaged across on their backs and then lined their empty boats down through the bad water to Bennett.

Bennett was a twenty-five-mile lake, narrow and deep, a funnel between the mountains through which storms ever romped. Rasmunsen camped on the sand-pit at its head, where were many men and boats bound north in the teeth of the Arctic winter. He awoke in the morning to find a piping gale from the south, which caught the chill from the whited peaks and glacial valleys and blew as cold as north wind ever blew. But it was fair, and he also found the Yankee staggering past the first bold headland with all sail set. Boat after boat was getting under way, and the correspondents fell to with enthusiasm.

"We'll catch him before Caribou Crossing," they assured Rasmunsen, as they ran up the sail and the *Alma* took the first icy spray over her bow.

Now Rasmunsen all his life had been prone to cowardice on water, but he clung to the kicking steering-oar with set face and determined jaw. His thousand dozen were there in the boat before his eyes, safely secured beneath the correspondents' baggage, and somehow, before his eyes, were the little cottage and the mortgage for a thousand dollars.

It was bitter cold. Now and again he hauled in the steering-sweep and put out a fresh one while his passengers chopped the ice from the blade. Wherever the spray struck, it turned instantly to frost, and the dipping boom of the spritsail was quickly fringed with icicles. The *Alma* strained and hammered through the big seas till the seams and butts began to spread, but in lieu of bailing the correspondents chopped ice and flung it overboard. There was no let-up. The mad race with winter was on, and the boats tore along in a desperate string.

"W-w-we can't stop to save our souls!" one of the correspondents chattered, from cold, not fright.

"That's right! Keep her down the middle, old man!" the other encouraged.

Rasmunsen replied with an idiotic grin. The iron-bound shores were in a lather of foam, and even down the middle the only hope was to keep running away from the big seas. To lower sail was to be overtaken and swamped. Time and again they passed boats pounding among the rocks, and once they saw one on the edge of the breakers about to strike. A little craft behind them, with two men, jibed over and turned bottom up.

"W-w-watch out, old man!" cried he of the chattering teeth.

Rasmunsen grinned and tightened his aching grip on the sweep. Scores of times had the send of the sea caught the big square stern of the *Alma* and thrown her off from dead before it till the after leach of the spritsail fluttered hollowly, and each time, and only with all his strength, had he forced her back. His grin by then had become fixed, and it disturbed the correspondents to look at him.

They roared down past an isolated rock a hundred yards from shore. From its wave-drenched top a man shrieked wildly, for the instant cutting the storm with his voice. But the next instant the *Alma* was by, and the rock growing a black speck in the troubled froth.

"That settles the Yankee! Where's the sailor?" shouted one of his passengers.

Rasmunsen shot a glance over his shoulder at a black squaresail.

He had seen it leap up out of the gray to windward, and for an hour, off and on, had been watching it grow. The sailor had evidently repaired damages and was making up for lost time.

"Look at him come!"

Both passengers stopped chopping ice to watch. Twenty miles of Bennett were behind them—room and to spare for the sea to toss up its mountains toward the sky. Sinking and soaring like a storm god, the sailor drove by them. The huge sail seemed to grip the boat from the crests of the waves, to tear it bodily out of the water, and fling it crashing and smothering down into the yawning troughs.

"The sea'll never catch him!"

"But he'll r-r-run her nose under!"

Even as they spoke, the black tarpaulin swooped from sight behind a big comber. The next wave rolled over the spot, and the next, but the boat did not reappear. The *Alma* rushed by the place. A little riffraff of oars and boxes was seen. An arm thrust up and a shaggy head broke surface a score of yards away.

For a time there was silence. As the end of the lake came in sight, the waves began to leap aboard with such steady recurrence that the correspondents no longer chopped ice but flung the water out with buckets. Even this would not do, and, after a shouted conference with Rasmunsen, they attacked the baggage. Flour, bacon, beans, blankets, cooking stove, ropes, odds and ends, everything they could get hands on, flew overboard. The boat acknowledged it at once, taking less water and rising more buoyantly.

"That'll do!" Rasmunsen called sternly, as they applied themselves to the top layer of eggs.

"The h-hell it will!" answered the shivering one, savagely. With the exception of their notes, films, and cameras, they had sacrificed their outfit. He bent over, laid hold of an egg-box, and began to worry it out from under the lashing.

"Drop it! Drop it, I say!"

Rasmunsen had managed to draw his revolver, and with the crook of his arm over the sweep head was taking aim. The correspondent stood up on the thwart, balancing back and forth, his face twisted with menace and speechless anger.

"My God!"

So cried his brother correspondent, hurling himself, face downward, into the bottom of the boat. The *Alma*, under the divided attention of Rasmunsen, had been caught by a great mass of water and whirled around. The after leach hollowed, the sail emptied and jibed, and the boom, sweeping with terrific force across the boat, carried the angry correspondent overboard with a broken back. Mast and sail had gone over the side as well. A drenching sea followed, as the boat lost headway, and Rasmunsen sprang to the bailing bucket.

Several boats hurtled past them in the next half-hour—small boats, boats of their own size, boats afraid, unable to do aught but run madly on. Then a ten-ton barge, at imminent risk of destruction, lowered sail to windward and lumbered down upon them.

"Keep off! Keep off!" Rasmunsen screamed.

But his low gunwale ground against the heavy craft, and the remaining correspondent clambered aboard. Rasmunsen was over the eggs like a cat and in the bow of the *Alma*, striving with numb fingers to bend the hauling-lines together.

"Come on!" a red-whiskered man yelled at him.

"I've a thousand dozen eggs here," he shouted back. "Gimme a two! I'll pay you!"

"Come on!" they howled in chorus.

A big whitecap broke just beyond, washing over the barge and leaving the *Alma* half swamped. The men cast off, cursing him as they ran up their sail. Rasmunsen cursed back and fell to bailing. The mast and sail, like a sea anchor, still fast by the halyards, held the boat head on to wind and sea and gave him a chance to fight the water out.

Three hours later, numbed, exhausted, blathering like a lunatic, but still bailing, he went ashore on an ice-strewn beach near Caribou Crossing. Two men, a government courier and a half-breed voyageur, dragged him out of the surf, saved his cargo, and beached the *Alma.* They were paddling out of the country in a Peterborough, and gave him shelter for the night in their storm-bound camp. Next morning they departed, but he elected to stay by his eggs. And thereafter the name and fame of the man with the thousand dozen eggs began to spread through the land. Gold-seekers who made in before the freeze-up carried the news of his coming. Grizzled old-timers of Forty Mile and Circle City, sour doughs with leathern jaws and bean-calloused stomachs, called up dream memories of chickens and green things at mention of his name. Dyea and Skaguay took an interest in his being, and questioned his progress from every man who came over the passes, while Dawson—golden, omeletless Dawson—fretted and worried, and waylaid every chance arrival for word of him.

But of this, Rasmunsen knew nothing. The day after the wreck he patched up the *Alma* and pulled out. A cruel east wind blew in his teeth from Tagish, but he got the oars over the side and bucked manfully into it, though half the time he was drifting backward and chopping ice from the blades. According to the custom of the country, he was driven ashore at Windy Arm; three times on Tagish saw him swamped and beached; and Lake Marsh held him at the freeze-up. The *Alma* was crushed in the jamming of the floes, but the eggs were intact. These he back-tripped two miles across the ice to the shore, where he built a cache, which stood for years after and was pointed out by men who knew.

Half a thousand frozen miles stretched between him and Dawson, and the waterway was closed. But Rasmunsen, with a peculiar tense look in his face, struck back up the lakes on foot. What he suffered on that lone trip, with naught but a single blanket, an axe, and a handful of beans, is not given to ordinary mortals to know. Only the Arctic adventurer may understand. Suffice that he was caught in a blizzard on Chilkoot and left two of his toes with the surgeon at Sheep Camp. Yet he stood on his feet and washed dishes in the scullery of the *Pawona* to the Puget Sound, and from there passed coal on a P.S. boat to San Francisco.

It was a haggard, unkempt man who limped across the shining office floor to raise a second mortgage from the bank people. His hollow cheeks betrayed themselves through the scraggly beard, and his eyes seemed to have retired into deep caverns where they burned with cold fires. His hands were grained from exposure and hard work, and the nails were rimmed with tight-packed dirt and coal dust. He spoke vaguely of eggs and ice-packs, winds and tides; but when they declined to let him have more than a second thousand, his talk became incoherent, concerning itself chiefly with the price of dogs and dog-food, and such things as snowshoes and moccasins and winter trails. They let him have fifteen hundred, which was more than the cottage warranted, and breathed easier when he scrawled his signature and passed out the door.

Two weeks later he went over Chilkoot with three dog sleds of five dogs each. One team he drove, the two Indians with him driving the others. At Lake Marsh they broke out the cache and loaded up. But there was no trail. He was the first in over the ice, and to him fell the task of packing the snow and hammering away through the rough river jams. Behind him he often observed a camp-fire smoke trickling thinly up through the quiet air, and he wondered why the people did not overtake him. For he was a stranger to the land and did not understand. Nor could he understand his Indians when they tried to explain. This they conceived to be a hardship, but when they balked and refused to break camp of mornings, he drove them to their work at pistol point.

When he slipped through an ice bridge near the White Horse and froze his foot, tender yet and oversensitive from the previous freezing, the Indians looked for him to lie up. But he sacrificed a blanket, and, with his foot incased in an enormous moccasin, big as a water-bucket, continued to take his regular turn with the front sled. Here was the cruelest work, and they respected him, though on the side they rapped their foreheads with their knuckles and significantly shook their heads. One night they tried to run away, but the zip-zip of his bullets in the snow brought them back, snarling but convinced. Whereupon, being only savage Chilkat men, they put their heads together to kill him; but he slept like a cat, and, waking or sleeping, the chance never came. Often they tried to tell him the import of the smoke wreath in the rear, but he could not comprehend and grew suspicious of them. And when they sulked or shirked, he was quick to let drive at them between the eyes, and quick to cool their heated souls with sight of his ready revolver.

And so it went—with mutinous men, wild dogs, and a trail that broke the heart. He fought the men to stay with him, fought the dogs to keep them away from the eggs, fought the ice, the cold, and the pain of his foot, which would not heal. As fast as the young tissue renewed, it was bitten and seared by the frost, so that a running sore developed, into which he could almost shove his fist. In the mornings, when he first put his weight upon it, his head went dizzy, and he was near to fainting from the pain; but later on in the day it usually grew numb, to recommence when he crawled into his blankets and tried to sleep. Yet he, who had been a clerk and sat at a desk all his days, toiled till the Indians were exhausted, and even outworked the dogs. How hard he worked, how much he suffered, he did not know. Being a man of the one idea, now that the idea had come, it mastered him. In the foreground of his consciousness was Dawson, in the background his thousand dozen eggs, and midway between the two his ego fluttered, striving always to draw them together to a glittering golden point. This golden point was the five thousand dollars, the consummation of the idea and the point of departure for whatever new idea might present itself. For the rest, he was a mere automaton. He was unaware of other things, seeing them as through a glass darkly, and giving them no thought. The work of his hands he did with machine-like wisdom; likewise the work of his head. So the look on his face grew very tense, till even the Indians were afraid of it, and marvelled at the strange white man who had made them slaves and forced them to toil with such foolishness.

Then came a snap on Lake Le Barge, when the cold of outer space smote the tip of the planet, and the frost ranged sixty and odd degrees below zero. Here, laboring with open mouth that he might breathe more freely, he chilled his lungs, and for the rest of the trip he was troubled with a dry, hacking cough, especially irritable in smoke of camp or under stress of undue exertion. On the Thirty Mile river he found much open water, spanned by precarious ice bridges and fringed with narrow rim ice, tricky and uncertain. The rim ice was impossible to reckon on, and he dared it without reckoning, falling back on his revolver when his drivers demurred. But on the ice bridges, covered with snow though they were, precautions could be taken. These they crossed on their snowshoes, with long poles, held crosswise in their hands, to which to cling in case of accident. Once over, the dogs were called to follow. And on such a bridge, where the absence of the center ice was masked by the snow, one of the Indians met his end. He went through as quickly and neatly as a knife through thin cream, and the current swept him from view down under the stream ice.

That night his mate fled away through the pale moonlight, Rasmunsen futilely puncturing the silence with his revolver—a thing that he handled with more celerity than cleverness. Thirty-six hours later the Indian made a police camp on the Big Salmon.

"Um—um—um funny mans—what you call?—top um head all loose," the interpreter explained to the puzzled captain. "Eh? Yep, clazy, much clazy mans. Eggs, eggs, all a time eggs—savvy? Come bimeby."

It was several days before Rasmunsen arrived, the three sleds lashed together, and all the dogs in a single team. It was awkward, and where the going was bad he was compelled to back-trip it sled by sled, though he managed most of the time, through herculean efforts, to bring all along on the one haul. He did not seem moved when the captain of police told him his man was hitting the high places for Dawson, and was by that time, probably, halfway between Selkirk and Stewart. Nor did he appear interested when informed that the police had broken the trail as far as Pelly; for he had attained to a fatalistic acceptance of all natural dispensations, good or ill. But when they told him that Dawson was in the bitter clutch of famine, he smiled, threw the harness on his dogs, and pulled out.

But it was at his next halt that the mystery of the smoke was explained. With the word at Big Salmon that the trail was broken to Pelly, there was no longer any need for the smoke wreath to linger in his wake; and Rasmunsen, crouching over his lonely fire, saw a motley string of sleds go by. First came the courier and the half-breed who had hauled him out from Bennett; then mail-carriers for Circle City, two sleds of them, and a mixed following of ingoing Klondikers. Dogs and men were fresh and fat, while Rasmunsen and his brutes were jaded and worn down to the skin and bone. They of the smoke wreath had traveled one day in three, resting and reserving their strength for the dash to come when broken trail was met with; while each day he had plunged and floundered forward, breaking the spirit of his dogs and robbing them of their mettle.

As for himself, he was unbreakable. They thanked him kindly for his efforts in their behalf, those fat, fresh men—thanked him kindly, with broad grins and ribald laughter; and now, when he understood, he made no answer. Nor did he cherish silent bitterness. It was immaterial. The idea—the fact behind the idea—was not changed. Here he was and his thousand dozen; there was Dawson; the problem was unaltered.

At the Little Salmon, being short of dog food, the dogs got into his grub, and from there to Selkirk he lived on beans—coarse, brown beans, big beans, grossly nutritive, which griped his stomach and doubled him up at two-hour intervals. But the Factor at Selkirk had a notice on the door of the Post to the effect that no steamer had been up the Yukon for two years, and in consequence grub was beyond price. He offered to swap flour, however, at the rate of a cupful for each egg, but Rasmunsen shook his head and hit the trail. Below the Post he managed to buy frozen horse hide for the dogs, the horses having been slain by the Chilkat cattle men, and the scraps and offal preserved by the Indians. He tackled the hide himself, but the hair worked into the bean sores of his mouth, and was beyond endurance.

Here at Selkirk, he met the forerunners of the hungry exodux of Dawson, and from there on they crept over the trail, a dismal throng. "No grub!" was the song they sang. "No grub, and had to go." "Everybody holding candles for a rise in the spring." "Flour dollar'n a half a pound, and no sellers."

"Eggs?" one of them answered. "Dollar apiece, but they ain't none."

Rasmunsen made a rapid calculation. "Twelve thousand dollars," he said aloud.

"Hey?" the man asked.

"Nothing," he answered, and *mushed* the dogs along.

When he arrived at Stewart River, seventy miles from Dawson, five of his dogs were gone, and the remainder were falling in the traces. He, also, was in the traces, hauling with what little strength was left in him. Even then he was barely crawling along ten miles a day. His cheek-bones and nose, frostbitten again and again, were turned to bloody-black and hideous. The thumb, which was separated from the fingers by the gee-pole, had likewise been nipped and gave him great pain. The monstrous moccasin still incased his foot, and strange pains were beginning to rack the leg. At Six Mile, the last beans, which he had been rationing for some time, were finished; yet he steadfastly refused to touch the eggs. He could not reconcile his mind to the legitimacy of it, and staggered and fell along the way to Indian River. Here a fresh-killed moose and an open-handed old-timer gave him and his dogs new strength, and at Ainslie's he felt repaid for it all when a stampede, ripe from Dawson in five hours, was sure he could get a dollar and a quarter for every egg he possessed.

He came up the steep bank by the Dawson barracks with fluttering heart and shaking knees. The dogs were so weak that he was forced to rest them, and, waiting, he leaned limply against the gee-pole. A man, an eminently decorous-looking man, came sauntering by in a great bearskin coat. He glanced at Rasmunsen curiously, then stopped and ran a speculative eye over the dogs and the three lashed sleds.

"What you got?" he asked.

"Eggs," Rasmunsen answered huskily, hardly able to pitch his voice above a whisper.

"Eggs! Whoopee! Whoopee!" He sprang up into the air, gyrated madly, and finished with half a dozen war steps. "You don't say—all of 'em?"

"All of 'em."

"Say, you must be the Egg Man." He walked around and viewed Rasmunsen from the other side. "Come, now, ain't you the Egg Man?"

Rasmunsen didn't know, but supposed he was, and the man sobered down a bit.

"What d'ye expect to get for 'em?" he asked cautiously.

Rasmunsen became audacious. "Dollar'n a half," he said.

"Done!" the man came back promptly. "Gimme a dozen."

"I—I mean a dollar'n a half apiece," Rasmunsen hesitatingly explained.

"Sure. I heard you. Make it two dozen. Here's the dust."

The man pulled out a healthy gold sack the size of a small sausage and knocked it negligently against the gee-pole. Rasmunsen felt a strange trembling in the pit of his stomach, a tickling of the nostrils, and an almost overwhelming desire to sit down and cry. But a curious, wide-eyed crowd was beginning to collect, and man after man was calling out for eggs. He was without scales, but the man with the bearskin coat fetched a pair and obligingly weighed in the dust while Rasmunsen passed out the goods. Soon there was a pushing and shoving and shouldering, and a great clamor. Everybody wanted to buy and be served first. And as the excitement grew, Rasmunsen cooled down. This would never do. There must be something behind the fact of their buying so eagerly. It would be wiser if he rested first and sized up the market. Perhaps eggs were worth two dollars apiece. Anyway, whenever he wished to sell, he was sure of a dollar and a half. "Stop!" he cried, when a couple of hundred had been sold. "No more now. I'm played out. I've got to get a cabin, and then you can come and see me."

A groan went up at this, but the man with the bearskin coat approved. Twenty-four of the frozen eggs went rattling in his capacious pockets and he didn't care whether the rest of the town ate or not. Besides, he could see Rasmunsen was on his last legs.

"There's a cabin right around the second corner from the Monte Carlo," he told him—"the one with the sody-bottle window. It ain't mine, but I've got charge of it. Rents for ten a day and cheap for the money. You move right in, and I'll see you later. Don't forget the sody-bottle window."

"Tra-la-loo!" he called back a moment later. "I'm goin' up the hill to eat eggs and dream of home."

On his way to the cabin, Rasmunsen recollected he was hungry and bought a small supply of provisions at the N.A.T.&T. store—also a beefsteak at the butcher shop and dried salmon for the dogs. He found the cabin without difficulty and left the dogs in the harness while he started the fire and got the coffee under way.

"A dollar'n a half apiece—one thousand dozen—eighteen thousand dollars!" He kept muttering it to himself, over and over, as he went about his work.

As he flopped the steak into the frying-pan the door opened. He turned. It was the man with the bearskin coat. He seemed to come in with determination, as though bound on some explicit errand, but as he looked at Rasmunsen an expression of perplexity came into his face.

"I say—now I say—" he began, then halted.

Rasmunsen wondered if he wanted the rent.

"I say, damn it, you know, them eggs is bad."

Rasmunsen staggered. He felt as though some one had struck him an astounding blow between the eyes. The walls of the cabin reeled and tilted up. He put out his hand to steady himself and rested it on the stove. The sharp pain and the smell of the burning flesh brought him back to himself.

"I see," he said slowly, fumbling in his pocket for the sack. "You want your money back."

"It ain't the money," the man said, "but hain't you got any eggs—good?"

Rasmunsen shook his head. "You'd better take the money."

But the man refused and backed away.

"I'll come back," he said, "when you've taken stock, and get what's comin'."

Rasmunsen rolled the chopping-block into the cabin and carried in the eggs. He went about it quite calmly. He took up the handaxe, and, one by one, chopped the eggs in half. These halves he examined carefully and let fall to the floor. At first he sampled from the different cases, then deliberately emptied one case at a time. The heap on the floor grew larger. The coffee boiled over and the smoke of the burning beefsteak filled the cabin. He chopped steadfastly and monotonously till the last case was finished.

Somebody knocked at the door, knocked again, and let himself in.

"What a mess!" he remarked, as he paused and surveyed the scene.

The severed eggs were beginning to thaw in the heat of the stove, and a miserable odor was growing stronger.

"Must a-happened on the steamer," he suggested.

Rasmunsen looked at him long and blankly.

"I'm Murray, Big Jim Murray, everybody knows me," the man volunteered. "I'm just hearin' your eggs is rotten, and I'm offerin' you two hundred for the batch. They ain't good as salmon, but still they're fair scoffin's for dogs."

Rasmunsen seemed turned to stone. He did not move. "You go to hell," he said passionlessly.

"Now just consider. I pride myself it's a decent price for a mess like that, and it's better'n nothin'. Two hundred. What you say?"

"You go to hell," Rasmunsen repeated softly, "and get out of here."

Murray gaped with a great awe, then went out carefully, backward, with his eyes fixed on the other's face.

Rasmunsen followed him out and turned the dogs loose. He threw them all the salmon he had bought, and coiled a sled-lashing up in his hand. Then he reentered the cabin and drew the latch in after him. The smoke from the cindered steak made his eyes smart. He stood on the bunk, passed the lashing over the ridgepole, and measured the swing-off with his eye. It did not seem to satisfy, for he put the stool on the bunk and climbed upon the stool. He drove a noose in the end of the lashing and slipped his head through. The other end he made fast. Then he kicked the stool out from under.

Which Make Men Remember

FORTUNE LA PEARLE crushed his way through the snow, sobbing, straining, cursing his luck, Alaska, Nome, the cards, and the man who had felt his knife. The hot blood was freezing on his hands, and the scene yet bright in his eyes—the man, clutching the table and sinking slowly to the floor; the rolling counters and the scattered deck; the swift shiver throughout the room, and the pause; the game-keepers no longer calling, and the clatter of the chips dying away; the startled faces; the infinite instant of silence; and then the great blood-roar and the tide of vengeance which lapped his heels and turned the town mad behind him.

"All hell's broke loose," he sneered, turning aside in the darkness and heading for the beach.

Lights were flashing from open doors, and tent, cabin, and dance-hall let slip their denizens upon the chase. The clamour of men and howling of dogs smote his ears and quickened his feet. He ran on and on. The sounds grew dim, and the pursuit dissipated itself in vain rage and aimless groping. But a flitting shadow clung to him. Head thrust over shoulder, he caught glimpses of it, now taking vague shape on an open expanse of snow, now merging into the deeper shadows of some darkened cabin or beach-listed craft.

Fortune La Pearle swore like a woman, weakly, with the hint of tears that comes of exhaustion, and plunged deeper into the maze of heaped ice, tents, and prospect holes. He stumbled over taut hawsers and piles of dunnage, tripped on crazy guy-ropes and insanely planted pegs, and fell again and again upon frozen dumps and mounds of hoarded driftwood. At times, when he deemed he had drawn clear, his head dizzy with the painful pounding of his heart and the suffocating intake of his breath, he slackened down; and ever the shadow leaped out of the gloom and forced him on in heart-breaking flight. A swift intuition flashed upon him, leaving in its trail the cold chill of superstition. The persistence of the shadow he invested with his gambler's symbolism. Silent, inexorable, not to be shaken off, he took it as the fate which waited at the last turn when chips were cashed in and gains and losses counted up. Fortune La Pearle believed in those rare, illuminating moments, when the intelligence flung from it time and space, to rise naked through eternity and read the facts of life from the open book of chance. That this was such a moment he had no doubt; and when he turned inland and sped across the snow-covered tundra he was not startled because the shadow took upon it greater definiteness and drew in closer. Oppressed with his own impotence, he halted in the midst of the white waste and whirled about. His right hand slipped from its mitten, and a revolver, at level, glistened in the pale light of the stars.

"Don't shoot. I haven't a gun."

The shadow had assumed tangible shape, and at the sound of its human voice a trepidation affected Fortune La Pearle's knees, and his stomach was stricken with the qualms of sudden relief.

Perhaps things fell out differently because Uri Bram had no gun that night when he sat on the hard benches of the El Dorado and saw murder done. To that fact also might be attributed the trip on the Long Trail which he took subsequently with a most unlikely comrade. But be it as it may, he repeated a second time, "Don't shoot. Can't you see I haven't a gun?"

"Then what the flaming hell did you take after me for?" demanded the gambler, lowering his revolver.

Uri Bram shrugged his shoulders. "It don't matter much, anyhow. I want you to come with me."

"Where?"

"To my shack, over on the edge of the camp."

But Fortune La Pearle drove the heel of his moccasin into the snow and attested by his various deities to the madness of Uri Bram.

"Who are you," he perorated, "and what am I, that I should put my neck into the rope at your bidding?"

"I am Uri Bram," the other said simply, "and my shack is over there on the edge of camp. I don't know who you are, but you've thrust the soul from a living man's body—there's the blood red on your sleeve—and, like a second Cain, the hand of all mankind is against you, and there is no place you may lay your head. Now, I have a shack—"

"For the love of your mother, hold your say, man," interrupted Fortune La Pearle, "or I'll make you a second Abel for the joy of it. So help me, I will! With a thousand men to lay me by the heels, looking high and low, what do I want with your shack? I want to get out of here—away! away! away! Cursed swine! I've half a mind to go back and run amuck, and settle for a few of them, the pigs! One gorgeous, glorious fight, and end the whole damn business! It's a skin game, that's what life is, and I'm sick of it!"

He stopped, appalled, crushed by his great desolation, and Uri Bram seized the moment. He was not given to speech, this man, and that which followed was the longest in his life, save one long afterward in another place.

"That's why I told you about my shack. I can stow you there so they'll never find you, and I've got grub in plenty. Elsewise you can't get away. No dogs, no nothing, the sea closed, St. Michael the nearest post, runners to carry the news before you, the same over the portage to Anvik—not a chance in the world for you! Now wait with me till it blows over. They'll forget all about you in a month or less, what of stampeding to York and what not, and you can hit the trail under their noses and they won't bother. I've got my own ideas of justice. When I ran after you, out of the El

Dorado and along the beach, it wasn't to catch you or give you up. My ideas are my own, and that's not one of them."

He ceased as the murderer drew a prayer-book from his pocket. With the aurora borealis glimmering yellow in the northeast, heads bared to the frost and naked hands grasping the sacred book, Fortune La Pearle swore him to the words he had spoken—an oath which Uri Bram never intended breaking, and never broke.

At the door of the shack the gambler hesitated for an instant, marveling at the strangeness of this man who had befriended him, and doubting.

But by the candlelight he found the cabin comfortable and without occupants, and he was quickly rolling a cigarette while the other man made coffee. His muscles relaxed in the warmth and he lay back with half-assumed indolence, intently studying Uri's face through the curling wisps of smoke. It was a powerful face, but its strength was of that peculiar sort which stands girt in and unrelated. The seams were deep graven, more like scars, while the stern features were in no way softened by hints of sympathy or humour. Under prominent bushy brows the eyes shone cold and grey. The cheekbones, high and forbidding, were undermined by deep hollows. The chin and jaw displayed a steadiness of purpose which the narrow forehead advertised as single, and, if needs be, pitiless. Everything was harsh, the nose, the lips, the voice, the lines about the mouth. It was the face of one who communed much with himself, unused to seeking counsel from the world; the face of one who wrestled oft of nights with angels, and rose to face the day with shut lips that no man might know. He was narrow but deep; and Fortune, his own humanity broad and shallow, could make nothing of him. Did Uri sing when merry and sigh when sad, he could have understood; but as it was, the cryptic features were undecipherable; he could not measure the soul they concealed.

"Lend a hand, Mister Man," Uri ordered when the cups had been emptied. "We've got to fix up for visitors."

Fortune purred his name for the other's benefit, and assisted understandingly. The bunk was built against a side and end of the cabin. It was a rude affair, the bottom being composed of driftwood logs overlaid with moss. At the foot the rough ends of these timbers projected in an uneven row. From the side next the wall Uri ripped back the moss and removed three of the logs. The jagged ends he sawed off and replaced so that the projecting row remained unbroken.

Fortune carried in sacks of flour from the cache and piled them on the floor beneath the aperture. On these Uri laid a pair of long seabags, and over all spread several thicknesses of moss and blankets. Upon this Fortune could lie, with the sleeping furs stretching over him from one side of the bunk to the other, and all men could look upon it and declare it empty.

In the weeks which followed, several domiciliary visits were paid, not a shack or tent in Nome escaping, but Fortune lay in his cranny undisturbed. In fact, little attention was given to Uri Bram's cabin; for it was the last place under the sun to expect to find the murderer of John Randolph. Except during such interruptions, Fortune lolled about the cabin, playing long games of solitaire and smoking endless cigarettes. Though his volatile nature loved geniality and play of words and laughter, he quickly accommodated himself to Uri's taciturnity. Beyond the actions and plans of his pursuers, the state of the trails, and the price of dogs, they never talked; and these things were only discussed at rare intervals and briefly.

But Fortune fell to working out a system, and hour after hour, and day after day, he shuffled and dealt, shuffled and dealt, noted the combinations of the cards in long columns, and shuffled and dealt again. Toward the end even this absorption failed him, and, head bowed upon the table, he visioned the lively all-night houses of Nome, where the gamekeepers and lookouts worked in shifts and the clattering roulette ball never slept. At such times his loneliness and bankruptcy stunned him till he sat for hours in the same unblinking, unchanging position. At other times, his long-pent bitterness found voice in passionate outbursts; for he had rubbed the world the wrong way and did not like the feel of it.

"Life's a skin game," he was fond of repeating, and on this one note he rang the changes.

"I never had half a chance," he complained. "I was faked in my birth and flim-flammed with my mother's milk. The dice were loaded when she tossed the box, and I was born to prove the loss.

"But that was no reason she should blame me for it, and look on me as a cold deck; but she did—ay, she did. Why didn't she give me a show? Why didn't the world? Why did I go broke in Seattle? Why did I take the steerage, and live like a hoy to Nome? Why did I go to the El Dorado? I was heading for Big Pete's and only went for matches. Why didn't I have matches? Why did I want to smoke? Don't you see? All worked out, every bit of it, all parts fitting snug. Before I was born, like as not. I'll put the sack I never hope to get on it, before I was born. That's why! That's why John Randolph passed the word and his checks in at the same time. Damn him! It served him well right! Why didn't he keep his tongue between his teeth and give me a chance? He knew I was next to broke. Why didn't I hold my hand? Oh, why? Why? Why?"

And Fortune La Pearle would roll upon the floor, vainly interrogating the scheme of things.

At such outbreaks Uri said no word, gave no sign, save that his grey eyes seemed to turn dull and muddy, as though from lack of interest.

There was nothing in common between these two men, and this fact Fortune grasped sufficiently to wonder sometimes why Uri had stood by him.

But the time of waiting came to an end. Even a community's blood lust cannot stand before its gold lust. The murder of John Randolph had already passed into the annals of the camp, and there it rested. Had the murderer appeared, the men of Nome would certainly have stopped stampeding long enough to see justice done, whereas the whereabouts of Fortune La Pearle was no longer an insistent problem. There was gold in the creek beds and ruby beaches, and when the sea opened, the men with healthy sacks would sail away to where the good things of life were sold absurdly cheap.

So, one night, Fortune helped Uri Bram harness the dogs and lash and sled, and the twain took the winter trail south on the ice. But it was not all south; for they left the sea east from St. Michael's, crossed the divide, and struck the Yukon at Anvik, many hundred miles from its mouth. Then on, into the northeast, past Koyukuk, Tanana, and Minook, till they rounded the Great Curve at Fort Yukon, crossed and recrossed the Arctic Circle, and headed south through the Flats. It was a weary journey, and Fortune would have wondered why the man went with him, had not Uri told him that he owned claims and had men working at Eagle. Eagle lay on the edge of the line; a few miles farther on, the British flag waved over the barracks at Fort Cudahy. Then came Dawson, Pelly, the Five Fingers, Windy Arm, Caribou Crossing, Linderman, the Chilcoot and Dyea.

On the morning after passing Eagle, they rose early. This was their last camp, and they were now to part. Fortune's heart was light. There was a promise of spring in the land, and the days were growing longer. The way was passing into Canadian territory. Liberty was at hand, the sun was returning, and each day saw him nearer to the Great Outside. The world was big, and he could once again paint his future in royal red. He whistled about the breakfast and hummed snatches of light song while Uri put the dogs in harness and packed up. But when all was ready, Fortune's feet itching to be off, Uri pulled an unused backlog to the fire and sat down.

"Ever hear of the Dead Horse Trail?

He glanced up meditatively and Fortune shook his head, inwardly chafing at the delay.

"Sometimes there are meetings under circumstances which make men remember," Uri continued, speaking in a low voice and very slowly, "and I met a man under such circumstances on the Dead Horse Trail. Freighting an outfit over the White Pass in '97 broke many a man's heart, for there was a world of reason when they gave that trail its name. The horses died like mosquitoes in the first frost, and from Skaguay to Bennett they rotted in heaps. They died at the Rocks, they were poisoned at the Summit, and they starved at the Lakes; they fell off the trail, what there was of it, or they went through it; in the river they drowned under their loads, or were smashed to pieces against the boulders; they snapped their legs in the crevices and broke their backs falling backwards with their packs; in the sloughs they sunk from sight or smothered in the slime, and they were disembowelled in the bogs where the corduroy logs turned end up in the mud; men shot them, worked them to death, and when they were gone, went back to the beach and bought more. Some did not bother to shoot them—stripping the saddles off and the shoes and leaving them where they fell. Their hearts turned to stone—those which did not break—and they became beasts, the men on Dead Horse Trail.

"It was there I met a man with the heart of a Christ and the patience. And he was honest. When he rested at midday he took the packs from the horses so that they, too, might rest. He paid fifty dollars a hundred-weight for their fodder, and more. He used his own bed to blanket their backs when they rubbed raw. Other men let the saddles eat holes the size of water-buckets. Other men, when the shoes gave out, let them wear their hoofs down to the bleeding stumps. He spent his last dollar for horseshoe nails. I know this because we slept in the one bed and ate from the one pot, and became blood brothers where men lost their grip of things and died blaspheming God. He was never too tired to ease a strap or tighten a cinch, and often there were tears in his eyes when he looked on all that waste of misery. At a passage in the rocks, where the brutes upreared hindlegged and stretched their forelegs upward like cats to clear the wall, the way was piled with carcasses where they had toppled back. And here he stood, in the stench of hell, with a cheery word and a hand on the rump at the right time, till the string passed by. And when one bogged he blocked the trail till it was clear again; nor did the man live who crowded him at such time.

"At the end of the trail a man who had killed fifty horses wanted to buy, but we looked at him and at our own—mountain cayuses from eastern Oregon. Five thousand he offered, and we were broke, but we remembered the poison grass of the Summit and the passage in the Rocks, and the man who was my brother spoke no word, but divided the cayuses into two bunches—his in the one and mine in the other—and he looked at me and we understood each other. So he drove mine to the one side and I drove his to the other, and we took with us our rifles and shot them to the last one, while the man who had killed fifty horses cursed us till his throat cracked. But that man, with whom I wielded blood-brothership on the Dead Horse Trail—"

"Why, that man was John Randolph," Fortune, sneering the while, completed the climax for him.

Uri nodded, and said, "I am glad you understand."

"I am ready," Fortune answered, the old weary bitterness strong in his face again. "Go ahead, but hurry."

Uri Bram rose to his feet.

"I have had faith in God all the days of my life. I believe He loves justice. I believe He is looking down upon us now, choosing between us. I believe He waits to work His will through my own right arm. And such is my belief, that we will take equal chance and let Him speak His own judgment."

Fortune's heart leaped at the words. He did not know much concerning Uri's God, but he believed in Chance, and Chance had been coming his way ever since the night he ran down the beach and across the snow. "But there is only one gun," he objected.

"We will fire turn about," Uri replied, at the same time throwing out the cylinder of the other man's Colt and examining it.

"And the cards to decide! One hand seven up!"

Fortune's blood was warming to the game, and he drew the deck from his pocket as Uri nodded. Surely Chance would not desert him now! He thought of the returning sun as he cut for deal, and he thrilled when he found the deal was his. He shuffled and dealt, and Uri cut him the Jack of Spades. They laid down their hands. Uri's was bare of trumps, while he held ace, deuce. The outside seemed very near to him as they stepped off the fifty paces.

"If God withholds His hand and you drop me, the dogs and outfit are yours. You'll find a bill of sale, already made out, in my pocket," Uri explained, facing the path of the bullet, straight and broad-breasted.

Fortune shook a vision of the sun shining on the ocean from the eyes and took aim. He was very careful. Twice he lowered as the spring breeze shook the pines. But the third time he dropped on one knee, gripped the revolver steadily in both hands, and fired. Uri whirled half about, threw up his arms, swayed wildly for a moment, and sank into the snow. But Fortune knew he had fired too far to one side, else the man would not have whirled.

When Uri, mastering the flesh and struggling to his feet, beckoned for the weapon, Fortune was minded to fire again. But he thrust the idea from him. Chance had been very good to him already, he felt, and if he tricked now he would have to pay for it afterward. No, he would play fair. Besides Uri was hard hit and could not possibly hold the heavy Colt long enough to draw a bead.

"And where is your God now?" he taunted, as he gave the wounded man the revolver. And Uri answered: "God has not yet spoken. Prepare that he may speak."

Fortune faced him, but twisted his chest sideways in order to present less surface. Uri tottered about drunkenly, but waited, too, for the moment's calm between the cats-paws. The revolver was very heavy, and he doubted, like Fortune, because of its weight. But he held it, arm extended, above his head, and then let it slowly drop forward and down. At the instant Fortune's left breast and the sight flashed into line with his eyes, he pulled the trigger. Fortune did not whirl, but gay San Francisco dimmed and faded, and as the sun-bright snow turned black and blacker, he breathed his last malediction on the Chance he had misplayed.

IV.

Wolf Dogs of the North

A Daughter of the Aurora

"YOU—WHAT YOU CALL—lazy mans, you lazy mans would desire me to haf for wife. It is not good. Nevaire, no, nevaire, will lazy mans my hoosband be."

Thus Joy Molineau spoke her mind to Jack Harrington, even as she had spoken it, but more tritely and in his own tongue, to Louis Savoy the previous night.

"Listen, Joy—"

"No, no; why moos' I listen to lazy mans? It is vaire bad, you hang rount, make visitation to my cabin and do nothing. How you get grub for the famille? Why haf not you the dust? Odder mans haf plentee."

"But I work hard, Joy. Never a day am I not on trail or up creek. Even now have I just come off. My dogs are yet tired. Other men have luck and find plenty of gold; but I—I have no luck."

"Ah! But when this mans with the wife which is Indian, this mans McCormack, when him discovaire the Klondike, you go not. Odder mans go; odder mans now rich."

"You know I was prospecting over on the head-reaches of the Tanana," Harrington protested, "and knew nothing of the Eldorado or Bonanza until it was too late."

"That is deeferent; only you are—what you call—way off."

"What?"

"Way off. In the—yes—in the dark. It is nevaire too late. One vaire rich mine is there, on the creek which is Eldorado. The mans drive the stake and him go 'way. No odder mans know what of him become. The mans, him which drive the stake, is nevaire no more. Sixty days no mans on that claim file the papaire. Then odder mans, plentee odder mans—what you call—jump that claim. Then they race, O so queek, like the wind, to file the papaire. Him be vaire rich. Him get grub for famille."

Harrington hid the major portion of his interest.

"When's the time up?" he asked. "What claim is it?"

"So I speak Louis Savoy last night," she continued, ignoring him. "Him I think the winnaire."

"Hang Louis Savoy!"

"So Louis Savoy speak in my cabin last night. Him say, 'Joy, I am strong mans. I haf good dogs. I haf long wind. I will be winnaire. Then you will haf me for hoosband?' And I say to him, I say—"

"What'd you say?"

"I say, 'If Louis Savoy is winnaire, then will he haf me for wife.'"

"And if he don't win?"

"Then Louis Savoy, him will not be—what you call—the father of my children."

"And if I win?"

"You winnaire? Ha! Ha! Nevaire!"

Exasperating as it was, Joy Molineau's laughter was pretty to hear. Harrington did not mind it. He had long since been broken in. Besides, he was no exception. She had forced all her lovers to suffer in kind. And very enticing she was just then, her lips parted, her color heightened by the sharp kiss of the frost, her eyes vibrant with the lure which is the greatest of all lures which may be seen nowhere save in woman's eyes. Her sled-dogs clustered about her in hirsute masses, and the leader, Wolf Fang, laid his long snout softly in her lap.

"If I do win?" Harrington pressed.

She looked from dog to lover and back again.

"What you say, Wolf Fang? If him strong mans and file the papaire, shall we his wife become? Eh? What you say?"

Wolf Fang pricked up his ears and growled at Harrington.

"It is vaire cold," she suddenly added with feminine irrelevance, rising to her feet and straightening out the team.

Her lover looked on stolidly. She had kept him guessing from the first time they met, and patience had been joined unto his virtues.

"Hi! Wolf Fang!" she cried, springing upon the sled as it leaped into sudden motion. "Ai! Ya! Mush-on!"

From the corner of his eye Harrington watched her swinging down the trail to Forty Mile. Where the road forked and crossed the river to Fort Cudahy, she halted the dogs and turned about.

"O Mistaire Lazy Mans!" she called back. "Wolf Fang, him say yes—if you winnaire!"

BUT SOMEHOW, as such things will, it leaked out, and all Forty Mile, which had hitherto speculated on Joy Molineau's choice between her two latest lovers, now hazarded bets and guesses as to which would win in the forthcoming race. The camp divided itself into two factions, and every effort was put forth in order that their respective favourites might be the first in at the finish. There was a scramble for the best dogs the country could afford, for dogs, and good ones, were essential, above all, to success. And it meant much to the victor. Besides the possession of a wife, the like of which had yet to be created, it stood for a mine worth a million at least.

That fall, when news came down of McCormack's discovery on Bonanza, all the Lower Country, Circle City and Forty Mile included, had stampeded up the Yukon—at least all save those who, like Jack Harrington and Louis Savoy, were away prospecting in the west. Moose pastures and creeks were staked indiscriminately and promiscuously; and incidentally, one of the unlikeliest of creeks, Eldorado. Olaf Nelson laid claim to five hundred of its linear feet, duly posted his notice, and as duly disappeared. At that time the nearest recording office was in the police barracks at Fort Cudahy, just across the river from Forty Mile; but when it became bruited abroad that Eldorado Creek was a treasure-house, it was quickly discovered that Olaf Nelson had failed to make the down-Yukon trip to file upon his property. Men cast hungry eyes upon the ownerless claim, where they knew a thousand-thousand dollars waited but shovel and sluice-box. Yet they dared not touch it; for there was a law which permitted sixty days to lapse between the staking and the filing, during which time a claim was immune. The whole country knew of Olaf Nelson's disappearance, and scores of men made preparation for the jumping and for the consequent race to Fort Cudahy.

But competition at Forty Mile was limited. With the camp devoting its energies to the equipping either of Jack Harrington or Louis Savoy, no man was unwise enough to enter the contest single-handed. It was a stretch of a hundred miles to the Recorder's office, and it was planned that the two favorites should have four relays of dogs stationed along the trail. Naturally, the last relay was to be the crucial one, and for these twenty-five miles their respective partisans strove to obtain the strongest possible animals. So bitter did the factions wax, and so high did they bid, that dogs brought stiffer prices than ever before in the annals of the country. And, as it chanced, this scramble for dogs turned the public eye still more searchingly upon Joy Molineau. Not only was she the cause of it all, but she possessed the finest sled-dog from Chilcoot to Bering Sea. As wheel or leader, Wolf Fang had no equal. The man whose sled he led down the last stretch was bound to win. There could be no doubt of it. But the community had an innate sense of the fitness of things, and not once was Joy vexed by overtures for his use. And the factions drew consolation from the fact that if one man did not profit by him, neither should the other.

However, since man, in the individual or in the aggregate, has been so fashioned that he goes through life blissfully obtuse to the deeper subtleties of his womankind, so the men of Forty Mile failed to divine the inner deviltry of Joy Molineau. They confessed, afterward, that they had failed to appreciate this dark-eyed daughter of the aurora, whose father had traded furs in the country before ever they dreamed of invading it, and who had herself first opened eyes on the scintillant northern lights. Nay, accident of birth had not rendered her less the woman, nor had it limited her woman's understanding of men. They knew she played with them, but they did not know the wisdom of her play, its deepness and its deftness. They failed to see more than the exposed card, so that to the very last Forty Mile was in a state of pleasant obfuscation, and it was not until she cast her final trump that it came to reckon up the score.

Early in the week the camp turned out to start Jack Harrington and Louis Savoy on their way. They had taken a shrewd margin of time, for it was their wish to arrive at Olaf Nelson's claim some days previous to the expiration of its immunity, that they might rest themselves, and their dogs be fresh for the first relay. On the way up they found the men of Dawson already stationing spare dog teams along the trail, and it was manifest that little expense had been spared in view of the millions at stake.

A couple of days after the departure of their champions, Forty Mile began sending up their relays—first to the seventy-five station, then to the fifty, and last to the twenty-five. The teams for the last stretch were magnificent, and so equally matched that the camp discussed their relative merits for a full hour at fifty below before they were permitted to pull out. At the last moment Joy Molineau dashed in among them on her sled. She drew Lon McFane, who had charge of Harrington's team, to one side, and hardly had the first words left her lips when it was noticed that his lower jaw dropped with a celerity and emphasis suggestive of great things. He unhitched Wolf Fang from her sled, put him at the head of Harrington's team, and mushed the string of animals into the Yukon trail.

"Poor Louis Savoy!" men said; but Joy Molineau flashed her black eyes defiantly and drove back to her father's cabin.

MIDNIGHT DREW NEAR on Olaf Nelson's claim. A few hundred fur-clad men had preferred sixty below and the jumping, to the inducements of warm cabins and comfortable bunks. Several score of them had their notices prepared for posting and their dogs at hand. A bunch of Captain Constantine's mounted police had been ordered on duty that fair play might rule. The command had gone forth that no man should place a stake till the last second of the day had ticked itself into the past. In the northland such commands are equal to Jehovah's in the matter of potency; the dum-dum as rapid and effective as the thunderbolt. It was clear and cold. The aurora borealis painted palpitating color revels on the sky. Rosy waves of cold brilliancy swept across the zenith, while great coruscating bars of greenish white blotted out the stars, or a Titan's hand reared mighty arches above the Pole. And at this mighty display the wolf-dogs howled as had their ancestors of old time.

A bearskin-coated policeman stepped prominently to the fore, watch in hand. Men hurried among the dogs, rousing them to their feet, untangling their traces, straightening them out. The entries came to the mark, firmly gripping stakes and notices. They had gone over the boundaries of the claim so often that they could now have done it blindfolded. The policeman raised his hand. Casting off their superfluous furs and blankets, and with a final cinching of belts, they came to attention.

"Time!"

Sixty pairs of hands unmitted; as many pairs of moccasins gripped hard upon the snow.

"Go!"

They shot across the wide expanse, round the four sides, sticking notices at every corner, and down the middle where the two center stakes were to be planted. Then they sprang for the sleds on the frozen bed of the creek. An anarchy of sound and motion broke out. Sled collided with sled, and dog-team fastened upon dog-team with bristling manes and screaming fangs. The narrow creek was glutted with the struggling mass. Lashes and butts of dog-whips were distributed impartially among men and brutes. And to make it of greater moment, each participant had a bunch of comrades intent on breaking him out of jam. But one by one, and by sheer strength, the sleds crept out and shot from sight in the darkness of the overhanging banks.

Jack Harrington had anticipated this crush and waited by his sled until it untangled. Louis Savoy, aware of his rival's greater wisdom in the matter of dog-driving, had followed his lead and also waited. The rout had passed beyond ear-shot when they took the trail, and it was not till they had traveled the ten miles or so down to Bonanza that they came upon it, speeding along in single file, but well bunched. There was little noise, and less chance of one passing another at that stage. The sleds, from runner to runner, measured sixteen inches, the trail eighteen; but the trail, packed down fully a foot by the traffic, was like a gutter. On either side spread the blanket of soft snow crystals. If a man turned into this in an endeavour to pass, his dogs would wallow perforce to their bellies and slow down to a snail's pace. So the men lay close to their leaping sleds and waited. No alteration in position occurred down the fifteen miles of Bonanza and Klondike to Dawson, where the Yukon was encountered. Here the first relays waited. But here, intent to kill their first teams, if necessary, Harrington and Savoy had had their fresh teams placed a couple of miles beyond those of the others. In the confusion of changing sleds they passed full half the bunch. Perhaps thirty men were still leading them when they shot on to the broad breast of the Yukon. Here was the tug. When the river froze in the fall, a mile of open water had been left between two mighty jams. This had but recently crusted, the current being swift, and now it was as level, hard, and slippery as a dance floor. The instant they struck this glare ice Harrington came to his knees, holding precariously on with one hand, his whip singing fiercely among his dogs and fearsome abjurations hurtling about their ears. The teams spread out on the smooth surface, each straining to the uttermost. But few men in the North could lift their dogs as did Jack Harrington. At once he began to pull ahead, and Louis Savoy, taking the pace, hung on desperately, his leaders running even with the tail of his rival's sled.

Midway on the glassy stretch their relays shot out from the bank. But Harrington did not slacken. Watching his chance when the new sled swung in close, he leaped across, shouting as he did so and jumping up the pace of his fresh dogs. The other driver fell off somehow. Savoy did likewise with his relay, and the abandoned teams, swerving to right and left, collided with the others and piled the ice with confusion. Harrington cut out the pace; Savoy hung on. As they neared the end of the glare ice, they swept abreast of the leading sled. When they shot into the narrow trail between the soft snowbanks, they led the race; and Dawson, watching by the light of the aurora, swore that it was neatly done.

When the frost grows lusty at sixty below, men cannot long remain without fire or excessive exercise, and live. So Harrington and Savoy now fell to the ancient custom of "ride and run." Leaping from their sleds, tow-thongs in hand, they ran behind till the blood resumed its wonted channels and expelled the frost, then back to the sleds till the heat again ebbed away. Thus, riding and running, they covered the second and third relays. Several times, on smooth ice, Savoy spurted his dogs, and as often failed to gain past. Strung along for five miles in the rear, the remainder of the race strove to overtake them, but vainly, for to Louis Savoy alone was the glory given of keeping Jack Harrington's killing pace.

As they swung into the seventy-five mile station, Lon McFane dashed alongside; Wolf Fang in the lead caught Harrington's eye, and he knew that the race was his. No team in the North could pass him on those twenty-five miles. And when Savoy saw Wolf Fang heading his rival's team, he knew that he was out of the running, and he cursed softly to himself, in the way woman is most frequently cursed. But he still clung to the other's smoking trail, gambling on chance to the last. And as they churned along, the day breaking in the southeast, they marveled in joy and sorrow at that which Joy Molineau had done.

FORTY MILE had early crawled out of its sleeping furs and congregated near the edge of the trail. From this point it could view the up-Yukon course to its first bend several miles away. Here it could also see across the river to the finish at Fort Cudahy, where the Gold Recorder nervously awaited. Joy Molineau had taken her position several rods back from the trail, and under the circumstances, the rest of Forty Mile forbore interposing itself. So the space was clear between her and the slender line of the course. Fires had been built, and around these men wagered dust and dogs, the long odds on Wolf Fang.

"Here they come!" shrilled an Indian boy from the top of a pine.

Up the Yukon a black speck appeared against the snow, closely followed by a second. As these grew larger, more black specks manifested themselves, but at a goodly distance to the rear. Gradually they resolved themselves into dogs and sleds, and men lying flat upon them.

"Wolf Fang leads," a lieutenant of police whispered to Joy. She smiled her interest back.

"Ten to one on Harrington!" cried a Birch Creek King, dragging out his sack.

"The Queen, her pay you not mooch?" queried Joy.

The lieutenant shook his head.

"You have some dust, ah, how mooch?" she continued.

He exposed his sack. She gauged it with a rapid eye.

"Mebbe—say—two hundred, eh? Good. Now I give—what you call—the tip. Covaire the bet." Joy smiled inscrutably. The lieutenant pondered. He glanced up the trail. The two men had risen to their knees and were lashing their dogs furiously, Harrington in the lead.

"Ten to one on Harrington!" bawled the Birch Creek King, flourishing his sack in the lieutenant's face.

"Covaire the bet," Joy prompted.

He obeyed, shrugging his shoulders in token that he yielded, not to the dictate of his reason, but to her charm. Joy nodded to reassure him.

All noise ceased. Men paused in the placing of bets.

Yawing and reeling and plunging, like luggers before the wind, the sleds swept wildly upon them. Though he still kept his leader up to the tail of Harrington's sled, Louis Savoy's face was without hope. Harrington's mouth was set. He looked neither to the right nor the left. His dogs were leaping in perfect rhythm, firm-footed, close to the trail, and Wolf Fang, head low and unseeing, whining softly, was leading his comrades magnificently.

Forty Mile stood breathless. Not a sound, save the roar of the runners and the voice of the whips.

Then the clear voice of Joy Molineau rose on the air. "Ai! Ya! Wolf Fang! Wolf Fang!"

Wolf Fang heard. He left the trail sharply, heading directly for his mistress. The team dashed after him, and the sled poised an instant on a single runner, then shot Harrington into the snow. Savoy was by like a flash. Harrington pulled to his feet and watched him skimming across the river to the Gold Recorder's. He could not help hearing what was said.

"Ah, him do vaire well," Joy Molineau was explaining to the lieutenant. "Him—what you call—set the pace. Yes, him set the pace vaire well."

Brown Wolf

SHE HAD DELAYED, because of the dew-wet grass, in order to put on her overshoes, and when she emerged from the house found her waiting husband absorbed in the wonder of a bursting almond-bud. She sent a questing glance across the tall grass and in and out among the orchard trees.

"Where's Wolf?" she asked.

"He was here a moment ago." Walt Irvine drew himself away with a jerk from the metaphysics and poetry of the organic miracle of blossom and surveyed the landscape. "He was running a rabbit the last I saw of him."

"Wolf! Wolf! Here Wolf!" she called, as they left the clearing and took the trail that led down through the waxen-belled manzanita jungle to the county road.

Irvine thrust between his lips the little finger of each hand and lent to her efforts a shrill whistling.

She covered her ears hastily and made a wry grimace.

"My! for a poet, delicately attuned and all the rest of it, you can make unlovely noises. My eardrums are pierced. You outwhistle—"

"Orpheus."

"I was about to say a street-arab," she concluded severely.

"Poesy does not prevent one from being practical—at least it doesn't prevent *me*. Mine is no futility of genius that can't sell gems to the magazines."

He assumed a mock extravagance, and went on:

"I am no attic singer, no ballroom warbler. And why? Because I am practical. Mine is no squalor of song that cannot transmute itself, with proper exchange value, into a flower-crowned cottage, a sweet mountain-meadow, a grove of redwoods, an orchard of thirty-seven trees, one long row of blackberries and two short rows of strawberries, to say nothing of a quarter of a mile of gurgling brook. I am a beauty-merchant, a trader in song, and I pursue utility, dear Madge. I sing a song, and thanks to the magazine editors I transmute my song into a waft of the west wind sighing through our redwoods, into a murmur of waters over mossy stones that sings back to me another song than the one I sang and yet the same song wonderfully—er—transmuted."

"O that all your song-transmutations were as successful!" she laughed.

"Name one that wasn't."

"Those two beautiful sonnets that you transmuted into the cow that was accounted the worst milker in the township."

"She was beautiful—" he began,

"But she didn't give milk," Madge interrupted.

"But she *was* beautiful, now, wasn't she?" he insisted.

"And here's where beauty and utility fall out" was her reply. "And there's the Wolf!"

From the thicket-covered hillside came a crashing of underbrush, and then, forty feet above them, on the edge of the sheer wall of rock, appeared a wolf's head and shoulders. His braced forepaws dislodged a pebble, and with sharp-pricked ears and peering eyes he watched the fall of the pebble till it struck at their feet. Then he transferred his gaze and with open mouth laughed down at them.

"You Wolf, you!" and "You blessed Wolf!" the man and woman called out to him.

The ears flattened back and down at the sound, and the head seemed to snuggle under the caress of an invisible hand.

They watched him scramble backward into the thicket, then proceeded on their way. Several minutes later, rounding a turn in the trail where the descent was less precipitious, he joined them in the midst of a miniature avalanche of pebbles and loose soil.

He was not demonstrative. A pat and a rub around the ears from the man, and a more prolonged caressing from the woman, and he was away down the trail in front of them, gliding effortlessly over the ground in true wolf fashion.

In build and coat and brush he was a huge timber-wolf; but the lie was given to his wolfhood by his color and marking. There the dog unmistakably advertised itself. No wolf was ever colored like him. He was brown, deep brown, red-brown, an orgy of browns. Back and shoulders were a warm brown that paled on the sides and underneath to a yellow that was dingy because of the brown that lingered in it. The white of the throat and paws and of the spots over the eyes was dirty because of the persistent and ineradicable brown, while the eyes themselves were twin topazes, golden and brown.

The man and woman loved the dog very much; perhaps this was because it had been such a task to win his love. It had been no easy matter when he first drifted in mysteriously out of nowhere to their little mountain cottage. Footsore and famished, he had killed a rabbit under their very noses and under their very windows, and then crawled away and slept by the spring at the foot of the blackberry bushes. When Walt Irvine went down to inspect the intruder, he was snarled at for his pains, and Madge likewise was snarled at when she went down to present, as a peace-offering, a large pan of bread and milk.

A most unsociable dog he proved to be, resenting all their advances, refusing to let them lay hands on him, menacing them with bared fangs and bristling hair. Nevertheless he remained, sleeping and resting by the spring, and eating the food they gave him after they set it down at a safe distance and retreated. His wretched physical condition explained why he lingered; and when he had recuperated, after several days' sojourn, he disappeared.

And this would have been the end of him, so far as Irvine and his wife were concerned, had not Irvine at that particular time been called away into the northern part of the state. Riding along on the train, near to the line between California and Oregon, he chanced to look out of the window and saw his unsociable guest sliding along the wagon road, brown and wolfish, tired yet tireless, dust-covered and soiled with two hundred miles of travel.

Now Irvine was a man of impulse, a poet. He got off the train at the next station, bought a piece of meat at a butcher shop, and captured the vagrant on the outskirts of the town. The return trip was made in the baggage car, and so Wolf came a second time to the mountain cottage. Here he was tied up for a week and made love to by the man and woman. But it was very circumspect love-making. Remote and alien as a traveler from another planet, he snarled down their soft-spoken love-words. He never barked. In all the time they had him he was never known to bark.

To win him became a problem. Irvine liked problems. He had a metal plate made, on which was stamped: RETURN TO WALT IRVINE, GLEN ELLEN, SONOMA COUNTY, CALIFORNIA. This was riveted to a collar and strapped about the dog's neck. Then he was turned loose, and promptly he disappeared. A day later came a telegram from Mendocino County. In twenty hours he had made over a hundred miles to the north, and was still going when captured.

He came back by Wells Fargo Express, was tied up three days, and was loosed on the fourth and lost. This time he gained southern Oregon before he was caught and returned. Always, as soon as he received his liberty, he fled away, and always he fled north. He was possessed of an obsession that drove him north. The homing instinct, Irvine called it, after he had expended the selling price of a sonnet in getting the animal back from northern Oregon.

Another time the brown wanderer succeeded in traversing half the length of California, all of Oregon, and most of Washington, before he was picked up and returned "Collect." A remarkable thing was the speed with which he traveled. Fed up and rested, as soon as he was loosed he devoted all his energy to getting over the ground. On the first day's run he was known to cover as high as a hundred and fifty miles a day until caught. He always arrived back lean and hungry and savage, and always departed fresh and vigorous, cleaving his way northward in response to some prompting of his being that no one could understand.

But at last, after a futile year of flight, he accepted the inevitable and elected to remain at the cottage where first he had killed the rabbit and slept by the spring. Even after that, a long time elapsed before the man and woman succeeded in patting him. It was a great victory, for they alone were allowed to put hands on him. He was fastidiously exclusive, and no guest at the cottage ever succeeded in making up to him. A low growl greeted such approach; if any one had the hardihood to come nearer, the lips lifted, the naked fangs appeared, and the growl became a snarl—a snarl so terrible and malignant that it awed the stoutest of them, as it likewise awed the farmers' dogs that knew ordinary dog-snarling, but had never seen wolf-snarling before.

He was without antecedents. His history began with Walt and Madge. He had come up from the south, but never a clue did they get of the owner from whom he had evidently fled. Mrs. Johnson, their nearest neighbor and the one who supplied them with milk, proclaimed him a Klondike dog. Her brother was burrowing for frozen pay-streaks in that far country, and so she constituted herself an authority on the subject.

But they did not dispute her. There were the tips of Wolf's ears, obviously so severely frozen at some time that they would never quite heal again. Besides, he looked like the photographs of the Alaskan dogs they saw published in magazines and newspapers. They often speculated over his past, and tried to conjure up (from what they had read and heard) what his northland life had been. That the northland still drew him, they knew; for at night they sometimes heard him cry softly; and when the north wind blew and the bit of frost was in the air, a great restlessness would come upon him and he would lift a mournful lament which they knew to be the long wolf-howl. Yet he never barked. No provocation was great enough to draw from him that canine cry.

Long discussions they had, during the time of winning him, as to whose dog he was. Each claimed him, and each proclaimed loudly any expression of affection made by him. But the man had the better of it at first, chiefly because he was a man. It was patent that Wolf had had no experience with women. He did not understand women. Madge's skirts were something he never quite accepted. The swish of them was enough to set him a-bristle with suspicion, and on a windy day she could not approach him at all.

On the other hand, it was Madge who fed him; also it was she who ruled the kitchen, and it was by her favor, and her favor alone, that he was permitted to come within that sacred precinct. It was because of these things that she bade fair to overcome the handicap of her garments. Then it was that Walt put forth special effort, making it a practice to have Wolf lie at his feet while he wrote, and, between petting and talking, losing much time from his work. Walt won in the end, and his victory was most probably due to the fact that he was a man, though Madge averred that they would have had another quarter of a mile of gurgling brook, and at least two west winds sighing through their redwoods, had Walt properly devoted his energies to song-transmutation and left Wolf alone to exercise a natural taste and an unbiassed judgment.

"It's about time I heard from those triolets," Walt said, after a silence of five minutes, during which they had swung steadily down the trail. "There'll be a check at the post-office, I know, and we'll transmute it into beautiful buckwheat flour, a gallon of maple syrup, and a new pair of overshoes for you."

"And into beautiful milk from Mrs. Johnson's beautiful cow," Madge added. "To-morrow's the first of the month, you know."

Walt scowled unconsciously; then his face brightened, and he clapped his hand to his breast pocket.

"Never mind. I have here a nice beautiful new cow, the best milker in California."

"When did you write it?" she demanded eagerly. Then, reproachfully, "And you never showed it to me."

"I saved it to read to you on the way to the post-office, in a spot remarkably like this one," he answered, indicating, with a wave of his hand, a dry log on which to sit.

A tiny stream flowed out of a dense fern-brake, slipped down a mossy-lipped stone, and ran across the path at their feet. From the valley arose the mellow song of meadow-larks, while about them, in and out, through sunshine and shadow, fluttered great yellow butterflies.

Up from below came another sound that broke in upon Walt reading softly from his manuscript. It was a crunching of heavy feet, punctuated now and again by the clattering of a displaced stone. As Walt finished and looked to his wife for approval, a man came into view around the turn of the trail. He was bare-headed and sweaty. With a handkerchief in one hand he mopped his face, while in the other hand he carried a new hat and a wilted starched collar which he had removed from his neck. He was a well-built man, and his muscles seemed on the point of bursting out of the painfully new and ready-made black clothes he wore.

"Warm day," Walt greeted him. Walt believed in country democracy, and never missed an opportunity to practise it.

The man paused and nodded.

"I guess I ain't used much to the warm," he vouchsafed half apologetically. "I'm more accustomed to zero weather."

"You don't find any of that in this country," Walt laughed.

"Should say not," the man answered. "An' I ain't here a-lookin' for it neither. I'm tryin' to find my sister. Mebbe you know where she lives. Her name's Johnson, Mrs. William Johnson."

"You're not her Klondike brother!" Madge cried, her eyes bright with interest, "about whom we've heard so much?"

"Yes'm, that's me," he answered modestly. "My name's Miller, Skiff Miller. I just thought I'd s'prise her."

"You are on the right track then. Only you've come by the

foot-path." Madge stood up to direct him, pointing up the canyon a quarter of a mile. "You see that blasted redwood? Take the little trail turning off to the right. It's the short cut to her house. You can't miss it."

"Yes'm, thank you, ma'am," he said.

He made tentative efforts to go, but seemed awkwardly rooted to the spot. He was gazing at her with an open admiration of which he was quite unconscious, and which was drowning, along with him, in the rising sea of embarrassment in which he floundered.

"We'd like to hear you tell about the Klondike," Madge said. "Mayn't we come over some day while you are at your sister's? Or, better yet, won't you come over and have dinner with us?"

"Yes'm, thank you, ma'am," he mumbled mechanically. Then he caught himself up and added: "I ain't stoppin' long. I got to be pullin' north again. I go out on to-night's train. You see, I've got a mail contract with the government."

When Madge had said that it was too bad, he made another futile effort to go. But he could not take his eyes from her face. He forgot his embarrassment in his admiration, and it was her turn to flush and feel uncomfortable.

It was at this juncture, when Walt had just decided it was time for him to be saying something to relieve the strain, that Wolf, who had been away nosing through the brush, trotted wolf-like into view.

Skiff Miller's abstraction disappeared. The pretty woman before him passed out of his field of vision. He had eyes only for the dog, and a great wonder came into his face.

"Well, I'll be damned!" he enunciated slowly and solemnly.

He sat down ponderingly on the log, leaving Madge standing. At the sound of his voice, Wolf's ears had flattened down, then his mouth had opened in a laugh. He trotted slowly up to the stranger and first smelled his hands, then licked them with his tongue.

Skiff Miller patted the dog's head, and slowly and solemnly repeated, "Well, I'll be damned!"

"Excuse me, ma'am," he said the next moment, "I was just s'prised some, that was all."

"We're surprised, too," she answered lightly. "We never saw Wolf make up to a stranger before."

"Is that what you call him—Wolf?" the man asked.

Madge nodded. "But I can't understand his friendliness toward you—unless it's because you're from the Klondike. He's a Klondike dog, you know."

"Yes'm," Miller said absently. He lifted one of Wolf's fore legs and examined the foot-pads, pressing them and denting them with his thumb. "Kind of soft," he remarked. "He ain't been on trail for a long time."

"I say," Walt broke in, "it is remarkable the way he lets you handle him."

Skiff Miller arose, no longer awkward with admiration of Madge, and in a sharp, businesslike manner asked, "How long have you had him?"

But just then the dog, squirming and rubbing against the newcomer's legs, opened his mouth and barked. It was an explosive bark, brief and joyous, but a bark.

"That's a new one on me," Skiff Miller remarked.

Walt and Madge stared at each other. The miracle had happened. Wolf had barked.

"It's the first time he ever barked," Madge said.

"First time I ever heard him, too," Miller volunteered.

Madge smiled at him. The man was evidently a humorist.

"Of course," she said, "since you have only seen him for five minutes."

Skiff Miller looked at her sharply, seeking in her face the guile her words had led him to suspect.

"I thought you understood," he said slowly. "I thought you'd tumbled to it from his makin' up to me. He's my dog. His name ain't Wolf. It's Brown."

"Oh, Walt!" was Madge's instinctive cry to her husband.

Walt was on the defensive at once.

"How do you know he's your dog?" he demanded.

"Because he is," was the reply.

"Mere assertion," Walt said sharply.

In his slow and pondering way, Skiff Miller looked at him, then asked, with a nod of his head toward Madge:

"How d'you know she's your wife? You just say, 'Because she is,' and I'll say it's mere assertion. The dog's mine. I bred 'm an' raised 'm, an' I guess I ought to know. Look here. I'll prove it to you."

Skiff Miller turned to the dog. "Brown!" His voice rang out sharply, and at the sound the dog's ears flattened down as to a caress. "Gee!" The dog made a swinging turn to the right. "Now mush-on!" And the dog ceased his swing abruptly and started straight ahead, halting obediently at command.

"I can do it with whistles," Skiff Miller said proudly. "He was my lead dog."

"But you are not going to take him away with you?" Madge asked tremulously.

The man nodded.

"Back into that awful Klondike world of suffering?"

He nodded and added: "Oh, it ain't so bad as all that. Look at me. Pretty healthy specimen, ain't I?"

"But the dogs! The terrible hardship, the heart-breaking toil, the starvation, the frost! Oh, I've read about it and I know."

"I nearly ate him once, over on Little Fish River," Miller volunteered grimly. "If I hadn't got a moose that day was all that saved 'm."

"I'd have died first!" Madge cried.

"Things is different down here," Miller explained. "You don't have to eat dogs. You think different just about the time you're all in. You've never ben all in, so you don't know anything about it."

"That's the very point," she argued warmly. "Dogs are not eaten in California. Why not leave him here? He is happy. He'll never want for food—you know that. He'll never suffer from cold and hardship. Here all is softness and gentleness. Neither the human nor nature is savage. He will never know a whip-lash again. And as for the weather—why, it never snows here."

"But it's all-fired hot in summer, beggin' your pardon," Skiff Miller laughed.

"But you do not answer," Madge continued passionately. "What have you to offer him in that northland life?"

"Grub, when I've got it, and that's most of the time," came the answer.

"And the rest of the time?"

"No grub."

"And the work?"

"Yes, plenty of work," Miller blurted out impatiently. "Work without end, an' famine, an' frost, an all the rest of the miseries—that's what he'll get when he comes with me. But he likes it. He is used to it. He knows that life. He was born to it an' brought up to it. An' you don't know anything about it. You don't know what you're talking about. That's where the dog belongs, and that's where he'll be happiest."

"The dog doesn't go," Walt announced in a determined voice. "So there is no need of further discussion."

"What's that?" Skiff Miller demanded, his brows lowering and an obstinate flush of blood reddening his forehead.

"I said the dog doesn't go, and that settles it. I don't believe he's your dog. You may have seen him sometime. You may even sometime have driven him for his owner. But his obeying the ordinary driving commands of the Alaskan trail is no demonstration that he is yours. Any dog in Alaska would obey you as he obeyed. Besides, he is undoubtedly a valuable dog, as dogs go in

Alaska, and that is sufficient explanation of your desire to get possession of him. Anyway, you've got to prove property."

Skiff Miller, cool and collected, the obstinate flush a trifle deeper on his forehead, his huge muscles bulging under the black cloth of his coat, carefully looked the poet up and down as though measuring the strength of his slenderness.

The Klondiker's face took on a contemptuous expression as he said finally, "I reckon there's nothin' in sight to prevent me takin' the dog right here an' now."

Walt's face reddened, and the striking-muscles of his arms and shoulders seemed to stiffen and grow tense. His wife fluttered apprehensively into the breach.

"Maybe Mr. Miller is right," she said. "I am afraid that he is. Wolf does seem to know him, and certainly he answers to the name of 'Brown.' He made friends with him instantly, and you know that's something he never did with anybody before. Besides, look at the way he barked. He was just bursting with joy. Joy over what? Without doubt at finding Mr. Miller."

Walt's striking-muscles relaxed, and his shoulders seemed to droop with hopelessness.

"I guess you're right, Madge," he said. "Wolf isn't Wolf, but Brown, and he must belong to Mr. Miller."

"Perhaps Mr. Miller will sell him," she suggested. "We can buy him."

Skiff Miller shook his head, no longer belligerent, but kindly, quick to be generous in response to generousness.

"I had five dogs," he said, casting about for the easiest way to temper his refusal. "He was the leader. They was the crack team of Alaska. Nothin' could touch 'em. In 1898 I refused five thousand dollars for the bunch. Dogs was high, then, anyway; but that wasn't what made the fancy price. It was the team itself. Brown was the best in the team. That winter I refused twelve hundred for 'm. I didn't sell 'm then, an' I ain't a-sellin' 'm now. Besides, I think a mighty lot of that dog. I've ben lookin' for 'm for three years. It made me fair sick when I found he'd ben stole—not the value of him, but the—well, I liked 'm like hell, that's all, beggin' your pardon. I couldn't believe my eyes when I seen 'm just now. I thought I was dreamin'. It was too good to be true. Why, I was his wet-nurse. I put 'm to bed, snug every night. His mother died, and I brought 'm up on condensed milk at two dollars a can when I couldn't afford it in my own coffee. He never knew any mother but me. He used to suck my finger regular, the darn little cuss—that finger right there!"

And Skiff Miller, too overwrought for speech, held up a fore finger for them to see.

"That very finger," he managed to articulate, as though it somehow clinched the proof of ownership and the bond of affection.

He was still gazing at his extended finger when Madge began to speak.

"But the dog," she said. "You haven't considered the dog."

Skiff Miller looked puzzled.

"Have you thought about him?" she asked.

"Don't know what you're drivin' at," was the response.

"Maybe the dog has some choice in the matter," Madge went on. "Maybe he has his likes and desires. You have not considered him. You give him no choice. It has never entered your mind that possibly he might prefer California to Alaska. You consider only what you like. You do with him as you would with a sack of potatoes or a bale of hay."

This was a new way of looking at it, and Miller was visibly impressed as he debated it in his mind. Madge took advantage of his indecision.

"If you really love him, what would be happiness to him would be your happiness also," she urged.

Skiff Miller continued to debate with himself, and Madge stole a glance of exultation to her husband, who looked back warm approval.

"What do you think?" the Klondiker suddenly demanded.

It was her turn to be puzzled. "What do you mean?" she asked.

"D'ye think he'd sooner stay in California?"

She nodded her head with positiveness. "I am sure of it."

Skiff Miller again debated with himself, though this time aloud, at the same time running his gaze in a judicial way over the mooted animal.

"He was a good worker. He's done a heap of work for me. He never loafed on me, an' he was a joe-dandy at hammerin' a raw team into shape. He's got a head on him. He can do everything but talk. He knows what you say to him. Look at 'm now. He knows we're talkin' about him."

The dog was lying at Skiff Miller's feet, head close down on paws, ears erect and listening, and eyes that were quick and eager to follow the sound of speech as it fell from the lips of first one and then the other.

"An' there's a lot of work in 'm yet. He's good for years to come. An' I do like him. I like him like hell."

Once or twice after that Skiff Miller opened his mouth and closed it again without speaking. Finally he said:

"I'll tell you what I'll do. Your remarks, ma'am, has some weight in them. The dog's worked hard, and maybe he's earned a soft berth an' has got a right to choose. Anyway, we'll leave it up to him. Whatever he says, goes. You people stay right here settin' down. I'll say good-by and walk off casual-like. If he wants to stay, he can stay. If he wants to come with me, let 'm come. I won't call 'm to come an' don't you call 'm to come back."

He looked with sudden suspicion at Madge, and added, "Only you must play fair. No persuadin' after my back is turned."

"We'll play fair," Madge began, but Skiff Miller broke in on her assurances.

"I know the ways of women," he announced. "Their hearts is soft. When their hearts is touched they're likely to stack the cards, look at the bottom of the deck, an' lie like the devil—beggin' your pardon, ma'am. I'm only discoursin' about women in general."

"I don't know how to thank you," Madge quavered.

"I don't see as you've got any call to thank me," he replied. "Brown ain't decided yet. Now you won't mind if I go away slow? It's no more'n fair, seein' I'll be out of sight inside a hundred yards."

Madge agreed, and added, "And I promise you faithfully that we won't do anything to influence him."

"Well, then, I might as well be gettin' along," Skiff Miller said in the ordinary tones of one departing.

At this change in his voice, Wolf lifted his head quickly, and still more quickly got to his feet when the man and woman shook hands. He sprang up on his hind legs, resting his fore paws on her hip and at the same time licking Skiff Miller's hand. When the latter shook hands with Walt, Wolf repeated his act, resting his weight on Walt and licking both men's hands.

"It ain't no picnic, I can tell you that," were the Klondiker's last words, as he turned and went slowly up the trail.

For the distance of twenty feet Wolf watched him go, himself all eagerness and expectancy, as though waiting for the man to turn and retrace his steps. Then, with a quick low whine, Wolf sprang after him, overtook him, caught his hand between his teeth with reluctant tenderness, and strove gently to make him pause.

Failing in this, Wolf raced back to where Walt Irvine sat, catching his coat-sleeve in his teeth and trying vainly to drag him after the retreating man.

Wolf's perturbation began to wax. He desired ubiquity. He wanted to be in two places at the same time, with the old master and the new, and steadily the distances between them was increasing. He sprang about excitedly, making short nervous leaps and twists, now toward one, now toward the other, in painful indecision, not knowing his own mind, desiring both and unable to choose, uttering quick sharp whines and beginning to pant.

He sat down abruptly on his haunches, thrusting his nose upward, the mouth opening and closing with jerking movements, each time opening wider. These jerking movements were in unison with the recurrent spasms that attacked the throat, each pasm severer and more intense than the preceding one. And in accord with jerks and spasms the larynx began to vibrate, at first silently, accompanied by the rush of air expelled from the lungs, then sounding a low, deep note, the lowest in the register of the human ear. All this was the nervous and muscular preliminary to howling.

But just as the howl was on the verge of bursting from the full throat, the wide-opened mouth was closed, the paroxysms ceased, and he looked long and steadily at the retreating man. Suddenly Wolf turned his head, and over his shoulder just as steadily regarded Walt. The appeal was unanswered. Not a word nor a sign did the dog receive, no suggestion and no clue as to what his conduct should be.

A glance ahead to where the old master was nearing the curve of the trail excited him again. He sprang to his feet with a whine, and then, struck by a new idea, turned his attention to Madge. Hitherto he had ignored her, but now, both masters failing him, she alone was left. He went over to her and snuggled his head in her lap, nudging her arm with his nose—an old trick of his when begging for favors. He backed away from her and began writhing and twisting playfully, curvetting and prancing, half rearing and striking his fore paws to the earth, struggling with all his body, from the wheedling eyes and flattening ears to the wagging tail, to express the thought that was in him and that was denied him utterance.

This, too, he soon abandoned. He was depressed by the coldness of these humans who had never been cold before. No response could he draw from them, no help could he get. They did not consider him. They were as dead.

He turned and silently gazed after the old master. Skiff Miller was rounding the curve. In a moment he would be gone from view. Yet he never turned his head, plodding straight onward, slowly and methodically, as though possessed of no interest in what was occurring behind his back.

And in this fashion he went out of view. Wolf waited for him to reappear. He waited a long minute, silently, quietly, without movement, as though turned to stone—withal stone quick with eagerness and desire. He barked once, and waited. Then he turned and trotted back to Walt Irvine. He sniffed his hand and dropped down heavily at his feet, watching the trail where it curved emptily from view.

The tiny stream slipping down the mossy-lipped stone seemed suddenly to increase the volume of its gurgling noise. Save for the meadow-larks, there was no other sound. The great yellow butterflies drifted silently through the sunshine and lost themselves in the drowsy shadows. Madge gazed triumphantly at her husband.

A few minutes later Wolf got upon his feet. Decision and deliberation marked his movements. He did not glance at the man and woman. His eyes were fixed up the trail. He had made up his mind. They knew it. And they knew, so far as they were concerned, that the ordeal had just begun.

He broke into a trot, and Madge's lips pursed, forming an avenue for the caressing sound that it was the will of her to send forth. But the caressing sound was not made. She was impelled to look at her husband, and she saw the sternness with which he watched her. The pursed lips relaxed, and she sighed inaudibly.

Wolf's trot broke into a run. Wider and wider were the leaps he made. Not once did he turn his head, his wolf's brush standing out straight behind him. He cut sharply across the curve of the trail and was gone.

Diable: A Dog

THE DOG was a devil.

This was recognized throughout the northland. "Hell's Spawn" he was called by many men, but his master, Black Leclère, chose for him the shameful name, "Diable." Now Black Leclère was also a devil, and the twain were well matched. The first they met, Diable was a puppy, lean and hungry and with bitter eyes; and they met with snap and snarl and wicked looks, for Leclère's upper lip had a wolfish way of lifting and showing the cruel white teeth. And it lifted then and his eyes glinted viciously as he reached for Diable and dragged him out from the squirming litter. It was certain that they divined each other, for on the instant Diable had buried his puppy fangs in Leclère's hand and Leclère, with thumb and finger, was coolly choking his young life out of him.

"*Sacré*dam!" the Frenchman said softly, flirting the quick blood from his bitten hand and gazing down on the little puppy choking and gasping in the snow.

Leclère turned to John Hamlin, storekeeper of the Sixty Mile Post. "Dat fo' w'at Ah lak heem. 'Ow moch, eh, you, m'sieu? 'Ow moch? Ah buy heem, now."

And because he hated him with an exceeding bitter hate, Leclère bought Diable. And for five years the twain adventured across the northland, from St. Michael's and the Yukon Delta to the head-reaches of the Pelly and even so far as the Peace River, Athabasca and the Great Slave. And they acquired a reputation for uncompromising wickedness the like of which never before had attached itself to man and dog.

Diable's father was a great gray timberwolf. But the mother of Diable, as he dimly remembered her, was a snarling, bickering husky, full-fronted and heavy-chested, with a malign eye, a cat-like grip of life, and a genius for trickery and evil. There was neither faith nor trust in her. Much of evil and much of strength were there in these, Diable's progenitors, and, bone and flesh of their bone and flesh, he had inherited it all. And then came Black Leclère, to lay his heavy hand on the bit of pulsating puppy-life, to press and prod and mold it till it became a big, bristling beast, acute in knavery, overspilling with hate, sinister, malignant, diabolical. With a proper master the puppy might have made a fairly ordinary, efficient sled-dog. He never got the chance. Leclère but confirmed him in his congenital iniquity.

The history of Leclère and the dog is a history of war—of five cruel, relentless years, of which their first meeting is fit summary. To begin with, it was Leclère's fault, for he hated with understanding and intelligence, while the long-legged, ungainly puppy hated only blindly, instinctively, without reason or method. At first there were no refinements of cruelty (these were to come later), but simple beatings and crude brutalities. In one of these, Diable had an ear injured. He never regained control of the riven muscles, and ever after the ear drooped limply down to keep keen the memory of his tormentor. And he never forgot.

His puppyhood was a period of foolish rebellion. He was always worsted, but he fought back because it was his nature to fight back. And he was unconquerable. Yelping shrilly from the pain of lash and club, he nonetheless always contrived to throw in the defiant snarl, the bitter, vindictive menace of his soul, which fetched without fail more blows and beatings. But his was his mother's tenacious grip on life. Nothing could kill him. He flourished under misfortune, grew fat with famine, and out of his terrible struggle for life developed a preternatural intelligence. His was the stealth and cunning of his mother, the fierceness and valor of his wolf sire.

Possibly it was because of his father that he never wailed. His puppy yelps passed with his lanky legs, so that he became grim and taciturn, quick to strike, slow to warn. He answered curse with snarl and blow with snap, grinning the while his implacable hatred; but never again, under the extremest agony, did Leclère bring from him the cry of fear or pain. This unconquerableness only fanned Leclère's wrath and stirred him to greater deviltries. Did Leclère give Diable half a fish and to his mates whole ones, Diable went forth to rob other dogs of their fish. Also he robbed caches and expressed himself in a thousand rogueries till he became a terror to all dogs and the masters of dogs. Did Leclère beat Diable and fondle Babette—Babette, who was not half the worker he was—why, Diable threw her down in the snow and broke her hind leg in his heavy jaws, so that Leclère was forced to shoot her. Likewise, in bloody battles Diable mastered all his team-mates, set them the law of trail and forage, and made them live to the law he set.

In five years he heard but one kind word, received but one soft stroke of a hand, and then he did not know what manner of things they were. He leaped like the untamed thing he was, and his jaws were together in a flash. It was the missionary at Sunrise, a newcomer in the country, who spoke the kind word and gave the soft stroke of the hand. And for six months after, he wrote no letters home to the States, and the surgeon at McQuestion traveled two hundred miles on the ice to save him from blood-poisoning.

Men and dogs looked askance at Diable when he drifted into their camps and posts, and they greeted him with feet threateningly lifted for the kick, or with bristling manes and bared fangs. Once a man did kick Diable, and Diable, with quick wolf-snap, closed his jaws like a steel trap on the man's leg and crunched down to the bone. Whereat the man was determined to have his life, only Black Leclère, with ominous eyes and naked hunting-knife, stepped in between. The killing of Diable—ah, *sacrédam*!

that was a pleasure Leclère reserved for himself. Some day it would happen, or else—bah! who was to know? Anyway, the problem would be solved.

For they had become problems to each other, this man and beast, or rather, they had become a problem, the pair of them. The very breath each drew was a challenge and a menace to the other. Their hate bound them together as love could never bind. Leclère was bent on the coming of the day when Diable should wilt in spirit and cringe and whimper at his feet. And Diable—Leclère knew what was in Diable's mind, and more than once had read it in his eyes. And so clearly had he read that when the dog was at his back he made it a point to glance often over his shoulder.

Men marveled when Leclère refused large money for the dog. "Some day you'll kill him and be out his price," said John Hamlin, once, when Diable lay panting in the snow where Leclère had kicked him and no one knew whether his ribs were broken and no one dared look to see.

"Dat," said Leclère dryly, "dat is my biz'ness, m'sieu'."

And the men marveled that Diable did not run away. They did not understand. But Leclère understood. He was a man who had lived much in the open, beyond the sound of human tongue, and he had learned the voices of wind and storm, the sigh of night, the whisper of dawn, the clash of day. In a dim way he could hear the green things growing, the running of the sap, the bursting of the bud. And he knew the subtle speech of the things that moved, of the rabbit in the snare, the moody raven beating the air with hollow wing, the baldface shuffling under the moon, the wolf like a gray shadow gliding betwixt the twilight and the dark. And to him Diable spoke clear and direct. Full well he understood why Diable did not run away, and he looked more often over his shoulder.

When in anger, Diable was not nice to look upon, and more than once had he leaped for Leclère's throat, to be stretched quivering and senseless in the snow by the butt of the ever-ready dog-whip. And so Diable learned to bide his time. When he reached his full strength and prime of youth, he thought the time had come. He was broad-chested, powerfully muscled, of far more than ordinary size, and his neck from head to shoulders was a mass of bristling hair—to all appearances a full-blooded wolf. Leclère was lying asleep in his furs when Diable deemed the time to be ripe. He crept upon him stealthily, head low to earth and lone ear laid back, with a feline softness of tread to which even Leclère's delicate tympanum could not responsively vibrate. The dog breathed gently, very gently, and not till he was close at hand did he raise his head. He paused for a moment and looked at the bronzed bull-throat, naked and knotty and swelling to a deep and steady pulse. The slaver dripped down his fangs and slid off his tongue at the sight, and in that moment he remembered his drooping ear, his uncounted blows and wrongs, and without a sound sprang on the sleeping man.

Leclère awoke to the pang of the fangs in his throat, and, perfect animal that he was, he awoke clear-headed and with full comprehension. He closed on the hound's windpipe with both his hands and rolled out of his furs to get his weight uppermost. But the thousands of Diable's ancestors had clung at the throats of unnumbered moose and caribou and dragged them down, and the wisdom of those ancestors was his. When Leclère's weight came on top of him, he drove his hind legs upward and in and clawed down chest and abdomen, ripping and tearing through skin and muscle. and when he felt the man's body wince above him and lift, he worried and shook at the man's throat. His team-mates closed around in a snarling, slavering circle, and Diable, with falling breath and fading sense, knew that their jaws were hungry for him. But that did not matter—it was the man, the man above him, and he ripped and clawed and shook and worried to the last ounce of his strength. But Leclère choked him with both his hands till Diable's chest heaved and writhed for the air denied, and his eyes glazed and his jaws slowly loosened and his tongue protruded black and swollen.

"Eh? Bon, you devil!" Leclère gurgled, mouth and throat clogged with his own blood, as he shoved the dizzy dog from him.

And then Leclère cursed the other dogs off as they fell upon Diable. They drew back into a wide circle, squatting alertly on their haunches and licking their chops, each individual hair on every neck bristling and erect.

Diable recovered quickly, and at sound of Leclère's voice, tottered to his feet and swayed weakly back and forth.

"A-h-ah! You beeg devil!" Leclère spluttered. "Ah fix you. Ah fix you plentee, by Gar!"

Diable, the air biting into his exhausted lungs like wine, flashed full into the man's face, his jaws missing and coming together with a metallic clip. They rolled over and over in the snow, Leclère striking madly with his fists. They they separated, face to face, and circled back and forth before each other for an opening. Leclère could have drawn his knife. His rifle was at his feet. But the beast in him was up and raging. He would do the thing with his hands—and his teeth. The dog sprang in, but Leclère knocked him over with a blow of his fist, fell upon him, and buried his teeth to the bone in the dog's shoulder.

It was a primordial setting and a primordial scene, such as might have been in the savage youth of the world. An open space in a dark forest, a ring of grinning wolf-dogs, and in the center two beasts, locked in combat, snapping and snarling, raging madly about, panting, sobbing, cursing, straining, wild with passion, blind with lust, in a fury of murder, ripping, tearing and clawing in elemental brutishness.

But Leclère caught the dog behind the ear with a blow from his fist, knocking him over and for an instant stunning him. Then Leclère leaped upon him with his feet, and sprang up and down, striving to grind him into the earth. Both Diable's hind legs were broken ere Leclère ceased that he might catch breath.

"A-a-ah! A-a-ah!" he screamed, incapable of articulate speech, shaking his fist through sheer impotence of throat and larynx.

But Diable was indomitable. He lay their in a hideous, helpless welter, his lip feebly lifting and writhing to the snarl he had not the strength to utter. Leclère kicked him, and the tired jaws closed on the ankle but could not break the skin.

Then Leclère picked up the whip and proceeded almost to cut him to pieces, at each stroke of the lash crying: "Dis taim Ah break you! Eh? By Gar, Ah break you!"

In the end, exhausted, fainting from loss of blood, he crumpled up and fell by his victim, and, when the wolf-dogs closed in to take vengeance, with his last consciousness dragged his body on top of Diable to shield him from their fangs.

This occurred not far from Sunrise, and the missionary, opening the door to Leclère a few hours later, was surprised to note the absence of Diable from the team. Nor did his surprise lessen when Leclère threw back the robes from the sled, gathered Diable into his arms, and staggered across the threshold. It happened that the surgeon of McQuestion was up on a gossip, and between them they proceeded to repair Leclère.

"Merci, non," said he. "Do you fix firs' de dog. To die? Non. Eet is not good. Becos' heem Ah mus' yet break. Dat Do' w'at he mus' not die."

The surgeon called it a marvel, the missionary a miracle, that Leclère lived through at all; but so weakened was he that in the spring the fever got him and he went on his back again. The dog had been in even worse plight, but his grip on life prevailed, and the bones of his hind legs knitted and his internal organs righted themselves during the several weeks he lay strapped to the floor. And by the time Leclère, finally convalescent, sallow and shaky, took the sun by the cabin door, Diable had reasserted his supremacy and brought not only his own team-mates but the missionary's dogs into subjection.

He moved never a muscle nor twitched a hair when for the

first time Leclère tottered out on the missionary's arm and sank down slowly and with infinite caution on the three-legged stool.

"Bon!" he said. "*Bon!* De good sun!" And he stretched out his wasted hands and washed them in the warmth.

Then his gaze fell on the dog, and the old light blazed back in his eyes. He touched the missionary lightly on the arm. "*Mon père*, dat is one beeg devil, dat Diable. You will bring me one pistol, so dat Ah drink the sun in peace."

And thereforth, for many days, he sat in the sun before the cabin door. He never dozed, and the pistol lay always across his knees. The dog had a way, the first thing each day, of looking for the weapon in its wonted place. At sight of it he would lift his lip faintly in token that he understood, and Leclère would lift his own lip in an answering grin. One day the missionary took note of the trick. "Bless me!" he said. "I really believe the brute comprehends."

Leclère laughed softly. "Look you, *mon père*. Dat w'at Ah now spik, to dat does he lissen."

As if in confirmation, Diable just perceptibly wriggled his lone ear up to catch the sound.

"Ah say 'keel'—"

Diable growled deep down in his throat, the hair bristled along his neck, and every muscle went tense and expectant.

"Ah lift de gun, so, like dat—" And suiting action to word, he sighted the pistol at the dog.

Diable, with a single leap sidewise, landed around the corner of the cabin out of sight.

"Bless me!" the missionary remarked. "Bless me!" he repeated at intervals, unconscious of his paucity of expression.

Leclère grinned proudly.

"But why does he not run away?"

The Frenchman's shoulders went up in a racial shrug which means all things from total ignorance to infinite understanding.

"Then why do you not kill him?"

Again the shoulders went up.

"Mon père," he said, after a pause, "de taim is not yet. He is one beeg devil. Some taim Ah break heem, so, an' so, all to leetle bits. Some taim. *Bon!*"

A day came when Leclère gathered his dogs together and floated down in a bateau to Forty Mile and on to the Porcupine, where he took a commission from the P.C. Company and went exploring for the better part of a year. After that he poled up the Koyokuk to deserted Arctic City, and later came drifting back, from camp to camp, along the Yukon. And during the long months Diable was well lessoned. He learned many tortures—the torture of hunger, the torture of thirst, the torture of fire, and, worst of all, the torture of muscle.

Like the rest of his kind, he did not enjoy music. It gave him exquisite anguish, racking him nerve by nerve and ripping apart every fiber of his being. It made him howl, long and wolf-like, as when the wolves bay the stars on frosty nights. He could not help howling. It was his one weakness in the contest with Leclère, and it was his shame. Leclère, on the other hand, passionately loved music—as passionately as he loved strong drink. And when his soul clamored for expression, it usually uttered itself in one or both of the two ways. And when he had drunk, not too much but just enough for the perfect poise of exaltation, his brain alilt with unsung song and the devil in him aroused and rampant, his soul found its supreme utterance in the bearding of Diable.

"Now we will haf a leetle museek," he would say. "Eh? W'at you t'ink, Diable?"

It was only an old and battered harmonica, tenderly treasured and patiently repaired; but it was the best that money could buy, and out of its silver reeds he drew weird, vagrant airs which men had never heard before. Then the dog, dumb of throat, with teeth tight-clenched, would back away, inch by inch, to the farthest cabin corner. And Leclère, playing, playing, a stout club tucked handily under his arm, followed the animal up, inch by inch, step by step, till there was no further retreat.

At first Diable would crowd himself into the smallest possible space, groveling close to the floor; but as the music came nearer and nearer he was forced to uprear, his back jammed into the logs, his fore legs fanning the air as though to beat off the rippling waves of sound. He still kept his teeth together, but severe muscular contractions attacked his body, strange twitchings and jerkings, till he was all aquiver and writhing in silent torment. As he lost control, his jaws spasmodically wrenched apart and deep, throaty vibrations issued forth, too low in the register of sound for human ear to catch. And then, as he stood reared with nostrils distended, eyes dilated, slaver dripping, hair bristling in helpless rage, arose the long wolf-howl. It came with a slurring rush upward, swelling to a great heartbreaking burst of sound and dying away in sadly cadenced woe—then the next rush upward, octave upon octave; the bursting heart; and the infinite sorrow and misery, fainting, fading, falling, and dying slowly away.

It was fit for hell. And Leclère, with fiendish ken, seemed to divine each particular nerve and heartstring and, with long wails and tremblings and sobbing minors, to make it yield up its last least shred of grief. It was frightful, and for twenty-four hours after, the dog was nervous and unstrung, starting at common sounds, tripping over his own shadow, but withal, vicious and masterful with his team-mates. Nor did he show signs of a breaking spirit. Rather did he grow more grim and taciturn, biding his time with an inscrutable patience which began to puzzle and weigh upon Leclère. The dog would lie in the firelight, motionless, for hours, gazing straight before him at Leclère and hating him with his bitter eyes.

Often the man felt that he had bucked up against the very essence of life—the unconquerable essence that swept the hawk down out of the sky like a feathered thunderbolt, that drove the great gray goose across the zones, that hurled the spawning salmon through two thousand miles of boiling Yukon flood. At such times he felt impelled to express his own unconquerable essence; and with strong drink, wild music and Diable, he indulged in vast orgies, wherein he pitted his puny strength in the face of things and challenged all that was, and had been, and was yet to be. "Dere is somet'ing dere," he affirmed, when the rhythmed vagaries of his mind touched the secret chords of the dog's being and brought forth the long, lugubrious howl. "Ah pool eet out wid bot' my han's so, an' so. Ha! Ha! Eet is fonee! Eet is ver' fonee! De mans swear, de leetle bird go peep-peep, Diable heem go yow-yow—an' eet is all de ver' same t'ing."

Father Gautier, a worthy priest, once reproved him with instances of concrete perdition. He never reproved him again.

"Eet may be so, *mon père*," he made answer. "An' Ah t'ink Ah go troo hell a-snappin', lak de hemlock troo de fire. Eh, *mon père?*"

But all bad things come to an end as well as good, and so with Black Leclère. On the summer low-water, in a poling-boat, he left McDougall for Sunrise. He left McDougall in company with Timothy Brown, and arrived at Sunrise by himself. Further, it was known that they had quarreled just previous to pulling out; for the *Lizzie*, a wheezy ten-ton sternwheeler, twenty-four hours behind, beat Leclère in by three days. And when he did get in, it was with a clean-drilled bullet-hole through his shoulder-muscle and a tale of ambush and murder.

A strike had been made at Sunrise, and things had changed considerably. With the infusion of several hundred gold-seekers, a deal of whisky, and half a dozen equipped gamblers, the missionary had seen the page of his years of labor with the Indians wiped clean. When the squaws became preoccupied with cooking beans and keeping the fire going for the wifeless miners, and the bucks with swapping their warm furs for black bottles and broken timepieces, he took to his bed, said "Bless me!" several times, and departed to his final accounting in a rough-hewn oblong box. Whereupon the gamblers moved their roulette and faro tables into the mission-house, and the click of chips and clink of glasses went up from dawn till dark and to dawn again.

Now Timothy Brown was well beloved among these adventurers of the north. The one thing against him was his quick temper and ready fist—a little thing, for which his kind heart and forgiving hand more than atoned. On the other hand, there was nothing to atone for Black Leclère. He was "black," as more than one remembered deed bore witness, while he was as well hated as the other was beloved. So the men of Sunrise put a dressing on his shoulder and hauled him before Judge Lynch.

It was a simple affair. He had quarreled with Timothy Brown at McDougall. With Timothy Brown he had left McDougall. Without Timothy Brown he had arrived at Sunrise. Considered in the light of his evilness, the unanimous conclusion was that he had killed Timothy Brown. On the other hand, Leclère acknowledged their facts, but challenged their conclusion and gave his own explanation. Twenty miles out of Sunrise he and Timothy Brown were poling the boat along the rocky shore. From that shore two rifle-shots rang out. Timothy Brown pitched out of the boat and went down bubbling red, and that was the last of Timothy Brown. He, Leclère, pitched into the bottom of the boat with a stinging shoulder. He lay very quietly, peeping at the shore. After a time two Indians stuck up their heads and came out to the water's edge, carrying between them a birch-bark canoe. As they launched it, Leclère let fly. He potted one, who went over the side after the manner of Timothy Brown. The other dropped into the bottom of the canoe, and then canoe and poling-boat went down the stream in a drifting battle. Only they hung up on a split current, and the canoe passed on one side of an island, the poling-boat on the other. That was the last of the canoe, and he came on into Sunrise. Yes, from the way the Indian in the canoe jumped, he was sure he had potted him. That was all.

This explanation was not deemed adequate. They gave him ten hours' grace while the *Lizzie* steamed down to investigate. Ten hours later she came wheezing back to Sunrise. There had been nothing found to back up his statements. They told him to make his will, for he possessed a fifty-thousand-dollar Sunrise claim and they were a law-abiding as well as a law-giving breed.

Leclère shrugged his shoulders. "Bot one t'ing," he said; "a leetle, w'at you call, favor—a leetle favor, dat is eet. I gif my feefty t'ousan' dollair to de church. I gif my husky-dog, Diable, to de devil. De leetle favor? Firs' you hang heem, an' den you hang me. Eet is good, eh?"

Good it was, they agreed, that Hell's Spawn should break trail for his master across the last divide, and the court was adjourned down to the river-bank, where a big spruce-tree stood by itself. Slackwater Charley put a hangman's knot in the end of a hauling line, and the noose was slipped over Leclère's head and pulled tight around his neck. His hands were tied behind his back, and he was assisted to the top of a cracker-box. Then the running end of the line was passed over an overhanging branch, drawn taut, and made fast. To kick the box out from under would leave him dancing on the air.

"Now for the dog," said Webster Shaw, sometime mining engineer. "You'll have to rope him, Slackwater."

Leclère grinned. Slackwater took a chew of tobacco, rove a running noose, and proceeded leisurely to coil a few turns in his hand. He paused once or twice to brush particularly offensive mosquitoes from off his face. Everybody was brushing mosquitoes, except Leclère, about whose head a small cloud was distinctly visible. Even Diable, lying full-stretched on the ground, with his fore paws rubbed the pests away from eyes and mouth.

But while Slackwater waited for Diable to lift his head, a faint call came down the quiet air and a man was seen waving his arms and running across the flat from Sunrise. It was the storekeeper.

"C-call 'er off, boys," he panted, as he came in among them. "Little Sandy and Bernadotte's jes' got in," he explained with returning breath. "Landed down below an' come up by the short cut. Got the Beaver with 'm. Picked 'm up in his canoe, stuck in a back channel, with a couple of bullet-holes in 'm. Other buck was Klok-Kutz, the one that knocked spots out of his squaw and dusted."

"Eh? W'at Ah say? Eh?" Leclère cried exultantly. "Dat de one fo' sure! Ah know. Ah spik true."

"The thing to do is to teach these damned Siwashes a little manners," spoke Webster Shaw. "They're getting fat and sassy, and we'll have to bring them down a peg. Round in all the bucks and string up the Beaver for an object-lesson. That's the program. Come on and let's see what he's got to say for himself."

"Heh, m'sieu!" Leclère called, as the crowd began to melt away through the twilight in the direction of Sunrise, "Ah lak ver' moch to see de fon."

"Oh, we'll turn you loose when we come back," Webster Shaw shouted over his shoulder. "In the mean time, meditate on your sins and the ways of Providence. It will do you good, so be grateful."

As is the way with men who are accustomed to great hazards, those nerves are healthy and trained to patience, so Leclère settled himself down to the long wait—which is to say that he reconciled his mind to it. There was no settling for the body, for the taut rope forced him to stand rigidly erect. The least relaxation of the leg-muscles pressed the rough fibered noose into his neck, while the upright position caused him much pain in his wounded shoulder. He projected his under lip and expelled his breath upward along his face to blow the mosquitoes away from his eyes. But the situation had its compensation. To be snatched from the maw of death was well worth a little bodily suffering, only it was unfortunate that he should miss the hanging of the Beaver.

And so he mused, till his eyes chanced to fall upon Diable, head between fore paws and stretched on the ground asleep. And then Leclère ceased to muse. He studied the animal closely, striving to sense if the sleep were real or feigned. The dog's sides were heaving regularly, but Leclère felt that the breath came and went a shade too quickly; also he felt there was a vigilance or an alertness to every hair which belied unshackling sleep. He would have given his Sunrise claim to be assured that the dog was not awake, and once, when one of his joints cracked, he looked quickly and guiltily at Diable to see if he roused.

He did not rouse then, but a few minutes later he got up slowly and lazily, stretched and looked carefully about him. *"Sacrédam!"* said Leclère under his breath.

Assured that no one was in sight or hearing, Diable sat down, curled his upper lip almost into a smile, looked up at Leclère, and licked his chops.

"Ah see my feenish," the man said, and laughed sardonically aloud.

Diable came nearer, the useless ear wobbling, the good ear cocked forward with devilish comprehension. He thrust his head on one side, quizzically, and advanced with mincing, playful steps. He rubbed his body gently against the box till it shook and shook again. Leclère teetered carefully to maintain his equilibrium.

"Diable," he said calmly, "look out. Ah keel you."

Diable snarled at the word and shook the box with greater force. Then he upreared and with his fore paws threw his weight against it higher up. Leclère kicked out with one foot, but the rope bit into his neck and checked so abruptly as nearly to overbalance him.

"Hi! Ya! Chook! Mush-on!" he screamed.

Diable retreated for twenty feet or so, with a fiendish levity in his bearing which Leclère could not mistake. He remembered the dog's often breaking the scum of ice on the water-hole by lifting up and throwing his weight upon it; and remembering, he understood what he now had in mind. Diable faced about and paused. He showed his white teeth in a grin, which Leclère answered; and then hurled his body through the air straight for the box.

FIFTEEN MINUTES LATER, Slackwater Charley and Webster Shaw, returning, caught a glimpse of a ghostly pendulum swinging back and forth in the dim light. As they hurriedly drew in closer, they made out the man's inert body, and a live thing that clung to it, and shook and worried, and gave to it the swaying motion.

"Hi! Ya! Chook! you Spawn of Hell!" yelled Webster Shaw.

Diable glared at him, and snarled threateningly, without loosing his jaws.

Slackwater Charley got out his revolver, but his hand was shaking as with a chill and he fumbled.

"Here, you take it," he said, passing the weapon over.

Webster Shaw laughted shortly, drew a sight between the gleaming eyes, and pressed the trigger. Diable's body twitched with the shock, thrashed the ground spasmodically a moment, and went suddenly limp. But his teeth still held fast-locked.

For the Love of a Man

WHEN JOHN THORNTON froze his feet in the previous December, his partners had made him comfortable and left him to get well, going on themselves up the river to get out a raft of saw-logs for Dawson. He was still limping slightly at the time he rescued Buck, but with the continued warm weather even the slight limp left him. And here, lying by the river bank through the long spring days, watching the running water, listening lazily to the songs of birds and the hum of nature, Buck slowly won back his strength.

A rest comes very good after one has traveled three thousand miles, and it must be confessed that Buck waxed lazy as his wounds healed, his muscles swelled out, and the flesh came back to cover his bones. For that matter, they were all loafing—Buck, John Thornton, and Skeet and Nig—waiting for the raft to come that was to carry them down to Dawson. Skeet was a little Irish setter who early made friends with Buck, who, in a dying condition, was unable to resent her first advances. She had the doctor trait which some dogs possess, and as a mother cat washes her kittens, so she washed and cleansed Buck's wounds. Regularly, each morning after he had finished his breakfast, she performed her self-appointed task, till he came to look for her ministrations as much as he did for Thornton's. Nig, equally friendly, though less demonstrative, was a huge black dog, half bloodhound and half deerhound, with eyes that laughed and a boundless good nature.

To Buck's surprise these dogs manifested no jealousy toward him. They seemed to share the kindliness and largeness of John

Thornton. As Buck grew stronger they enticed him into all sorts of ridiculous games, in which Thornton himself could not forbear to join, and in this fashion Buck romped through his convalescence and into a new existence. Love, genuine, passionate love, was his for the first time. This he had never experienced at Judge Miller's down in the sun-kissed Santa Clara Valley. With the Judge's sons, hunting and tramping, it had been a working partnership; with the Judge's grandsons, a sort of pompous guardianship; and with the Judge himself, a stately and dignified friendship. But love that was feverish and burning, that was adoration, that was madness, it had taken John Thornton to arouse.

This man had saved his life, which was something; but, further, he was the ideal master. Other men saw to the welfare of their dogs from a sense of duty and business expediency; he saw to the welfare of his as if they were his own children, because he could not help it. And he saw further. He never forgot a kindly greeting or a cheering word, and to sit down for a long talk with them ("gas" he called it) was as much his delight as theirs. He had a way of taking Buck's head roughly between his hands, and resting his own head upon Buck's, of shaking him back and forth, the while calling him ill names that to Buck were love names. Buck knew no greater joy than that rough embrace and the sound of murmured oaths, and at each jerk back and forth it seemed that his heart would be shaken out of his body so great was its ecstasy. And when, released, he sprang to his feet, his mouth laughing, his eyes eloquent, his throat vibrant with unuttered sound, and in that fashion remained without movement, John Thornton would reverently exclaim, "God! you can all but speak!"

Buck had a trick of love expression that was akin to hurt. He would often seize Thornton's hand in his mouth and close so fiercely that the flesh bore the impress of his teeth for some time afterward. And as Buck understood the oaths to be love words, so the man understood this feigned bite for a caress.

For the most part, however, Buck's love was expressed in adoration. While he went wild with happiness when Thornton touched him or spoke to him, he did not seek these tokens. Unlike Skeet, who was wont to shove her nose under Thornton's hand and nudge and nudge till petted, or Nig, who would stalk up and rest his great head on Thornton's knee, Buck was content to adore at a distance. He would lie by the hour, eager, alert, at Thornton's feet, looking up into his face, dwelling upon it, studying it, following with keenest interest each fleeting expression, every movement or change of feature. Or, as chance might have it, he would lie farther away, to the side or rear, watching the outlines of the man and the occasional movements of his body. And often, such was the communion in which they lived, the strength of Buck's gaze would draw John Thornton's head around, and he would return the gaze, without speech, his heart shining out of his eyes as Buck's heart shone out.

For a long time after his rescue, Buck did not like Thornton to get out of his sight. From the moment he left the tent to when he entered it again, Buck would follow at his heels. His transient masters since he had come into the Northland had bred in him a fear that no master could be permanent. He was afraid that Thornton would pass out of his life as Perrault and François and the Scotch half-breed had passed out. Even in the night, in his dreams, he was haunted by this fear. At such times he would shake off sleep and creep through the chill to the flap of the tent, where he would stand and listen to the sound of his master's breathing.

But in spite of this great love he bore John Thornton, which seemed to bespeak the soft civilizing influence, the strain of the primitive, which the Northland had aroused in him, remained alive and active. Faithfulness and devotion, things born of fire and roof, were his; yet he retained his wildness and wiliness. He was a thing of the wild, come in from the wild to sit by John Thornton's fire, rather than a dog of the soft Southland stamped with the marks of generations of civilization. Because of his very great love, he could not steal from this man but from any other man, in any other camp, he did not hesitate an instant; while the cunning with which he stole enabled him to escape detection.

His face and body were scored by the teeth of many dogs, and he fought as fiercely as ever and more shrewdly. Skeet and Nig were too good-natured for quarrelling—besides, they belonged to John Thornton; but the strange dog, no matter what the breed or valor, swiftly acknowledged Buck's supremacy or found himself struggling for life with a terrible antagonist. And Buck was merciless. He had learned well the law of club and fang, and he never forewent an advantage or drew back from a foe he had started on the way to Death. He had lessoned from Spitz, and from the chief fighting dogs of the police and mail, and knew there was no middle course. He must master or be mastered; while to show mercy was a weakness. Mercy did not exist in the primordial life. It was misunderstood for fear, and such misunderstandings made for death. Kill or be killed, eat or be eaten, was the law; and this mandate, down out of the depths of Time, he obeyed.

He was older than the days he had seen and the breaths he had drawn. He linked the past with the present, and the eternity behind him throbbed through him in a mighty rhythm to which he swayed as the tides and seasons swayed. He sat by John Thornton's fire, a broad-breasted dog, white-fanged and long-furred; but behind him were the shades of all manner of dogs, half-wolves and wild wolves, urgent and prompting, tasting the savor of the meat he ate, thirsting for the water he drank, scenting the wind with him, listening with him and telling him the sounds made by the wild life in the forest, dictating his moods, directing his actions, lying down to sleep with him when he lay down, and dreaming with him and beyond him and becoming themselves the stuff of his dreams.

So peremptorily did these shades beckon him, that each day mankind and the claims of mankind skipped farther from him. Deep in the forest a call was sounding, and as often as he heard this call, mysteriously thrilling and luring, he felt compelled to turn his back upon the fire and the beaten earth around it, and to plunge into the forest, and on and on, he knew not where or why; nor did he wonder where or why, the call sounding imperiously, deep in the forest. But as often as he gained the soft unbroken earth and the green shade, the love for John Thornton drew him back to the fire again.

Thornton alone held him. The rest of mankind was as nothing. Chance travelers might praise or pet him; but he was cold under it all, and from a too demonstrative man he would get up and walk away. When Thornton's partners, Hans and Pete, arrived on the long-expected raft, Buck refused to notice them till he learned they were close to Thornton; after that he tolerated them in a passive sort of way, accepting favors from them as though he favored them by accepting. They were of the same large type as Thornton, living close to the earth, thinking simply and seeing clearly; and ere they swung the raft into the big eddy by the saw-mill at Dawson, they understood Buck and his ways, and did not insist upon an intimacy such as obtained with Skeet and Nig.

For Thornton, however, his love seemed to grow and grow. He, alone among men, could put a pack upon Buck's back in the summer traveling. Nothing was too great for Buck to do, when Thornton commanded. One day (they had grub-staked themselves from the proceeds of the raft and left Dawson for the head-waters of the Tanana) the men and dogs were sitting on the crest of a cliff which fell away, straight down, to naked bed-rock three hundred feet below. John Thornton was sitting near the edge, Buck at his shoulder. A thoughtless whim seized Thornton, and he drew the attention of Hans and Pete to the experiment he had in mind. "Jump, Buck!" he commanded, sweeping his arm out and over the chasm. The next instant he was grappling with Buck on the extreme edge, while Hans and Pete were dragging them back into safety.

"It's uncanny," Pete said, after it was over and they had caught their speech.

Thornton shook his head. "No, it is splendid, and it is terrible, too. Do you know, it sometimes makes me afraid."

"I'm not hankering to be the man that lays hands on you while he's around," Pete announced conclusively, nodding his head toward Buck.

"Py Jingo!" was Hans's contribution. "Not mineself either."

It was at Circle City, ere the year was out, that Pete's apprehensions were realized. "Black" Burton, a man evil-tempered and malicious, had been picking a quarrel with a tenderfoot at the bar, when Thornton stepped good-naturedly between. Buck, as was his custom, was lying in a corner, head on paws, watching his master's every action. Burton struck out, without warning, straight from the shoulder. Thornton was sent spinning, and saved himself from falling only by clutching the rail of the bar.

Those who were looking on heard what was neither bark nor yelp, but a something which is best described as a roar, and they saw Buck's body rise up in the air as he left the floor for Burton's throat. The man saved his life by instinctively throwing out his arm, but was hurled backward to the floor with Buck on top of him. Buck loosed his teeth from the flesh of the arm and drove in again for the throat. This time the man succeeded only in partly blocking, and his throat was torn open. Then the crowd was upon Buck, and he was driven off; but while a surgeon checked the bleeding, he prowled up and down, growling furiously, attempting to rush in, and being forced back by an array of hostile clubs. A "miners' meeting," called on the spot, decided that the dog had sufficient provocation, and Buck was discharged. But his reputation was made, and from that day his name spread through every camp in Alaska.

Later on, in the fall of the year, he saved John Thornton's life in quite another fashion. The three partners were lining a long and narrow poling-boat down a bad stretch of rapids on the Forty-Mile Creek. Hans and Pete moved along the bank, snubbing with a thin Manila rope from tree to tree, while Thornton remained in the boat, helping its descent by means of a pole, and shouting directions to the shore. Buck, on the bank, worried and anxious, kept abreast of the boat, his eyes never off his master.

At a particularly bad spot, where a ledge of barely submerged rocks jutted out into the river, Hans cast off the rope, and, while Thornton poled the boat out into the stream, ran down the bank with the end in his hand to snub the boat when it had cleared the ledge. This it did, and was flying down-stream in a current as swift as a mill-race, when Hans checked it with the rope and checked too suddenly. The boat flirted over and snubbed in to the bank, bottom up, while Thornton, flung sheer out of it, was carried down-stream toward the worst part of the rapids, a stretch of wild water in which no swimmer could live.

Buck had sprung in on the instant, and at the end of three hundred yards, amid a mad swirl of water, he overhauled Thornton. When he felt him grasp his tail, Buck headed for the bank, swimming with all his splendid strength. But the progress shoreward was slow; the progress down-stream amazingly rapid. From below came the fatal roaring where the wild current went wilder and was rent in shreds and spray by the rocks which thrust through like the teeth of an enormous comb. The suck of the water as it took the beginning of the last steep pitch was frightful, and Thornton knew that the shore was impossible. He scraped furiously over a rock, bruised across a second, and struck a third with crushing force. He clutched its slippery top with both hands, releasing Buck, and above the roar of the churning water shouted: "Go, Buck! Go!"

Buck could not hold his own, and swept on downstream, struggling desperately, but unable to win back. When he heard

Thornton's command repeated, he partly reared out of the water, throwing his head high, as though for a last look, then turned obediently toward the bank. He swam powerfully and was dragged ashore by Pete and Hans at the very point where swimming ceased to be possible and destruction began.

They knew that the time a man could cling to a slippery rock in the face of that driving current was a matter of minutes, and they ran as fast as they could up the bank to a point far above where Thornton was hanging on. They attached the line with which they had been snubbing the boat to Buck's neck and shoulders, being careful that it should neither strangle him nor impede his swimming, and launched him into the stream. He struck out boldly, but not straight enough into the stream. He discovered the mistake too late, when Thornton was abreast of him and a bare half-dozen strokes away while he was being carried helplessly past.

Hans promptly snubbed with the rope, as though Buck were a boat. The rope thus tightening on him in the sweep of the current, he was jerked under the surface, and under the surface he remained till his body struck against the bank and he was hauled out. He was half drowned and Hans and Pete threw themselves upon him, pounding the breath into him and the water out of him. He staggered to his feet and fell down. The faint sound of Thornton's voice came to them, and though they could not make out the words of it, they knew that he was in his extremity. His master's voice acted on Buck like an electric shock. He sprang to his feet and ran up the bank ahead of the men to the point of his previous departure.

Again the rope was attached and he was launched, and again he struck out, but this time straight into the stream. He had miscalculated once, but he would not be guilty of it a second time. Hans paid out the rope, permitting no slack, while Pete kept it clear of coils. Buck held on till he was on a line straight above

Thornton; then he turned, and with the speed of an express train headed down upon him. Thornton saw him coming, and, as Buck struck him like a battering ram, with the whole force of the current behind him, he reached up and closed with both arms around the shaggy neck. Hans snubbed the rope around the tree, and Buck and Thornton were jerked under the water. Strangling, suffocating, sometimes one uppermost and sometimes the other, dragging over the jagged bottom, smashing against rocks and snags, they veered in to the bank.

Thornton came to, belly downward and being violently propelled back and forth across and drift log by Hans and Pete. His first glance was for Buck, over whose limp and apparently lifeless body Nig was setting up a howl, while Skeet was licking the wet face and closed eyes. Thornton was himself bruised and battered, and he went carefully over Buck's body, when he had been brought around, finding three broken ribs.

"That settles it," he announced. "We camp right here." And camp they did, till Buck's ribs knitted and he was able to travel.

That winter, at Dawson, Buck performed another exploit, not so heroic, perhaps, but one that put his name many notches higher on the totem-pole of Alaskan fame. This exploit was particularly gratifying to the three men; for they stood in need of the outfit which it furnished, and were enabled to make a long-desired trip into the virgin East, where miners had not yet appeared. It was brought about by a conversation in the Eldorado Saloon, in which men waxed boastful of their favorite dogs. Buck, because of his record, was the target for these men, and Thornton was driven stoutly to defend him. At the end of half an hour one man stated that his dog could start a sled with five hundred pounds and walk off with it; a second bragged six hundred for his dog; and a third seven hundred.

"Pooh! pooh!" said John Thornton. "Buck can start a thousand pounds."

"And break it out? and walk off with it for a hundred yards?" demanded Matthewson, a Bonanza King, he of the seven hundred vaunt.

"And break it out, and walk off with it for a hundred yards," John Thornton said coolly.

"Well," Matthewson said, slowly and deliberately, so that all could hear, "I've got a thousand dollars that says he can't. And there it is." So saying, he slammed a sack of gold dust of the size of a bologna sausage down upon the bar.

Nobody spoke. Thornton's bluff, if bluff it was, had been called. He could feel a flush of warm blood creeping up his face. His tongue had tricked him. He did not know whether Buck could start a thousand pounds. Half a ton! The enormousness of it appalled him. He had great faith in Buck's strength and had often thought him capable of starting such a load; but never, as now, had he faced the possibility of it, the eyes of a dozen men fixed upon him, silent and waiting. Further, he had no thousand dollars; nor had Hans or Pete.

"I've got a sled standing outside now, with twenty fifty-pound sacks of flour on it," Matthewson went on with brutal directness, "so don't let that hinder you."

Thornton did not reply. He did not know what to say. He glanced from face to face in the absent way of a man who has lost the power of thought and is seeking somewhere to find the thing that will start it going again. The face of Jim O'Brien, a Mastodon King and old-time comrade, caught his eyes. It was as a cue to him, seeming to rouse him to do what he would never have dreamed of doing.

"Can you lend me a thousand?" he asked, almost in a whisper.

"Sure," answered O'Brien, thumping down a plethoric sack by the side of Matthewson's. "Though it's little faith I'm having, John, that the beast can do the trick."

The Eldorado emptied its occupants into the street to see the test. The tables were deserted, and the dealers and gamekeepers came forth to see the outcome of the wager and to lay odds. Several hundred men, furred and mittened, banked around the sled within easy distance. Matthewson's sled, loading with a thousand pounds of flour, had been standing for a couple of hours, and in the intense cold (it was sixty below zero) the runners had frozen fast to the hard-packed snow. Men offered odds of two to one that Buck could not budge the sled. A quibble arose concerning the phrase "break out." O'Brien contended it was Thornton's privilege to knock the runners loose, leaving Buck to "break it out" from a dead standstill. Matthewson insisted that the phrase included breaking the runners from the frozen grip of the snow. A majority of the men who had witness the making of the bet decided in his favor, whereat the odds went up to three to one against Buck.

There were no takers. Not a man believed him capable of the feat. Thornton had been hurried into the wager, heavy with doubt; and now that he looked at the sled itself, the concrete fact, with the regular team of ten dogs curled up in the snow before it, the more impossible the task appeared. Matthewson waxed jubilant.

"Three to one!" he proclaimed. "I'll lay you another thousand at that figure, Thornton, What d'ye say?"

Thornton's doubt was strong in his face but his fighting spirit was aroused—the fighting spirit that soars above odds, fails to recognize the impossible, and is deaf to all save the clamor for battle. He called Hans and Pete to him. Their sacks were slim, and with his own the three partners could rake together only two hundred dollars. In the ebb of their fortunes, this sum was their total capital; yet they laid it unhesitatingly against Matthewson's six hundred.

The team of ten dogs was unhitched, and Buck, with his own harness, was put into the sled. He had caught the contagion of the excitement, and he felt that in some way he must do a great thing for John Thornton. Murmurs of admiration at his splendid appearance went up. He was in perfect condition, without an ounce of superfluous flesh, and the one hundred and fifty pounds that he weighed were so many pounds of grit and virility. His furry coat shone with the sheen of silk. Down the neck and across the shoulders, his mane, in repose as it was, half bristled and seemed to lift with every movement, as though excess of vigor made each particular hair alive and active. The great breast and heavy fore legs were no more than in proportion with the rest of the body, where the muscles showed in tight rolls underneath the skin. Men felt these muscles and proclaimed them hard as iron, and the odds went down to two to one.

"Gad, sir! Gad, sir!" stuttered a member of the latest dynasty, a king of the Skookum Benches. "I offer you eight hundred for him, sir, before the test, sir; eight hundred just as he stands.

Thornton shook his head and stepped to Buck's side.

"You must stand off from him," Matthewson protested. "Free play and plenty of room."

The crowd fell silent; only could be heard the voices of the gamblers vainly offering two to one. Everybody acknowledged Buck a magnificent animal, but twenty fifty-pound sacks of flour bulked too large in their eyes for them to loosen their pouch-strings.

The crowd was watching curiously. The affair was growing mysterious. It seemed like a conjuration. As Thornton got to his feet, Buck seized his mittened hand between his jaws, pressing in with his teeth and releasing slowly, half-reluctantly. It was the answer, in terms, not of speech, but of love. Thornton stepped well back.

"Now, Buck," he said.

Buck tightened the traces, then slacked them for a matter of several inches. It was the way he had learned.

"Gee!" Thornton's voice rang out, sharp in the tense silence.

Buck swung to the right, ending the movement in a plunge that took up the slack and with a sudden jerk arrested his one hundred and fifty pounds. The load quivered, and from under the runners arose a crisp crackling.

"Haw!" Thornton commanded.

Buck duplicated the manœuvre, this time to the left. The crackling turned into a snapping, the sled pivoting and the runners slipping and grating several inches to the side. The sled was broken out. Men were holding their breaths, intensely unconscious of the fact.

"Now, MUSH!"

Thornton's command cracked out like a pistol-shot. Buck threw himself forward, tightening the traces with a jarring lunge. His whole body was gathered compactly together in the tremendous effort, the muscles writhing and knotting like live things under the silky fur. His great chest was low to the ground, his head forward and down, while his feet were flying like mad, the claws scarring the hard-packed snow in parallel grooves. The sled swayed and trembled, half-started forward. One of his feet slipped, and one man groaned aloud. Then the sled lurched ahead in what appeared a rapid succession of jerks, though it never really came to a dead stop again...half an inch...an inch...two inches.... The jerks perceptibly diminished; as the sled gained momentum, he caught them up, till it was moving steadily along.

Men gasped and began to breathe again, unaware that for a moment they had ceased to breathe. Thornton was running behind, encouraging Buck with short cheery words. The distance had been measured off, and as he neared the pile of firewood which marked the end of the hundred yards, a cheer began to grow and grow, which burst into a roar as he passed the firewood and halted at command. Every man was tearing himself loose, even Matthewson. Hats and mittens were flying in the air. Men were shaking hands, it did not matter with whom, and bubbling over in a general incoherent babel.

But Thornton fell on his knees beside Buck. Head was against head, and he was shaking him back and forth. Those who hurried up heard him cursing Buck, and he cursed him long and fervently, and softly and lovingly.

"Gad, sir! Gad, sir!" spluttered the Skookum Bench king. "I'll give you a thousand for him, sir, a thousand, sir—twelve hundred, sir."

Thornton rose to his feet. His eyes were wet. The tears were streaming frankly down his cheeks. "Sir," he said to the Skookum Bench king. "no, sir. You can go to hell, sir. It's the best I can do for you, sir."

Buck seized Thornton's hand in his teeth. Thornton shook him back and forth. As though animated by a common impulse, the onlookers drew back to a respectful distance; nor were they again indiscreet enough to interrupt.